Sweet Home, Jamaica

Volume One

Claudette Beckford-Brady

Copyright © 2013 Claudsette Beckford-Brady

All rights reserved.

ISBN: **1490303014**
ISBN-13: **978-1490303017**

DEDICATION

For all the people who have encouraged and supported me throughout my life and especially on my writing journey. Too numerous to mention individually by name, but you all know who you are. Love you all to the max.

CONTENTS

1	A Shocking Discovery	1
2	A Secret Shared, and a Crumb of Information	22
3	A Letter to Mama, and Getting the best of Mr Critchlow	40
4	Caught!	56
5	Another Letter to Mama, and a New Understanding with Mavis	71
6	Silver Jubilee, a Thread of Hope, and the Pill	93
7	A Lover's Quarrel, and Infidelity Discovered	109
8	Close Encounters of the Sexual Kind	127
9	The Campbell Family	148
10	Dark Days	167
11	Meet the Keith Campbells	187
12	A Jamaican Vacation	205
13	I Find my Jamaican-ness	227
14	Down to Brass Tacks	246
15	Return to Gravel Hill	268

CHAPTER ONE

A Shocking Discovery

I was thirteen, going on fourteen, when I discovered that my mother was *not* my mother. That is to say, my father's wife, Mavis, whom I had taken for granted to be my mother, was in fact, not. It came as a great shock since up till then I'd had no reason to suppose otherwise.

I was the second of five children, one older brother and three younger sisters, two of whom were twins.

I had always been the odd one out for several reasons. First of all I was considered extremely bright at school while my siblings were, if not exactly dunce, at least of much lesser ability. Instead of being praised and encouraged, however, I was often made to feel as if I were doing something wrong.

Secondly, I was noticeably several shades darker of complexion than my brother and sisters which, up to the point of my discovery, had been a source of puzzlement to me, but which was now logically explained. Funnily enough it had just never occurred to me that I might be of different stock; why would it?

Thirdly, every child in the house was a favourite except me. My father's wife, Mavis, favoured her firstborn and only son, as well as her 'wash-belly,' which is a term used to describe a last and often un-expected child. As for my father, he made no attempt to hide the fact that he idolized his twin daughters who had been born on his birthday. He called them his birthday girls. *I* was nobody's favourite.

I held some resentment at what I considered such gross unfairness. After all, I was very intelligent and achieved great marks at school, invariably coming top of my class. I should have received some recognition for that, if for nothing else, but this was never forthcoming.

Whenever I reflected on the matter, I generally came to the conclusion that I was less loved because I was blacker than my siblings.

Far from having an inferiority complex though, I was strong minded and determined. My teachers described me as being wilful, headstrong and argumentative. I questioned everything and I was extremely vocal whenever my opinion differed from anyone else's. My teachers, in the main, thought this was good, but in my parents' opinion I was just simply "facety," or in plain English, rude or impertinent.

Well, the discovery came about as a result of my being "facety" to Mavis. The school had organized an outing to Stratford-upon-Avon for the English Literature class, to see *A Midsummer Night's Dream*. It was to be an afternoon performance which meant that we would not arrive back in London from Stratford till after dark.

My first mistake was in telling Mavis that I was going, instead of asking her if I could.

"Mum, I'm going to Stratford with my class to watch a

Sweet Home, Jamaica

Shakespeare play. Could you sign the consent form please?" I held out the letter from school with the tear-off consent slip to be signed by a parent. She ignored it.

"Ahoa! Yu turn big woman inside here? What yu mean yu *going* to Stratford wid yu class; who give yu permission, Mam?" Mavis was scathing in her sarcasm.

"That's why I'm giving you the consent slip, Mum," I said patiently, "so you can give your consent." My voice was reasonable, but I knew from past experience it could be read as insolent.

Mavis still ignored my outstretched hand. "But yu nuh need *my* consent. Yu tell mi seh yu-a guh a'ready!" She turned her back and started taking dishes out of the sideboard to set the table for dinner. I should have left it at that for the moment and approach her again when she was in a more amenable frame of mind; or perhaps I should have asked Daddy to sign the form. But I didn't.

"Look, Mum, there's no reason for me not to go," I persisted. "It won't cost you and Daddy anything; I have money to pay my fare."

Second mistake. I should have humbled my tone, apologised, and asked her nicely if I could go.

"I see! Yu is not only a big ooman who mek har own decision; yu have yu own-a money to'. Well, mek mi tell yu somet'ing, Michelle. As long as yu are a chile in *dis house* yu will ask permission when yu want anyt'ing, and don't inform mi of yu intention afta yu done mek di decision a'ready. Yu not goin'!"

"But Mummy, I *have* to go. This play is important for my English Lit. Exam."

Third mistake; don't be argumentative. Accept defeat for the moment and then when she has had time to calm down, approach her and ask her nicely. I would never learn!

I could see her starting to swell up like a bullfrog. I had

never seen a bullfrog swelling up, mind you, but I knew the saying well; she always used it on me when I dared to show my temper. *"Yes, gwaan swell up like bullfrog, I wi' know how to burst yu bubble!"*

Well now *she* was the one swelling up with temper and I don't mind admitting that I myself was beginning to get a trifle vexed. She responded to my last statement.

"Ahoa! Yu *have* to guh. I see! Well gwaan den nuh, if yu bad. Wi gwine to si which bull rule inside *dis* pen!"

Now I was getting reckless. My voice rose a decibel. "Why yu don't want me to do well in school? You and Daddy never give me any encouragement, nor any praise when I do well. Why oonu even bother to let me go to school at all?" And with that I flounced out of the room.

"Who yu t'ink yu talking to in dat tone of voice! Come back here to mi!" But I ignored her and ran upstairs into my room, slamming the door behind me.

Big, big mistake! The door flew open and I was grabbed by the front of my school blouse while slaps rained on my face. "Dyam wrenk and facety! *Nevah* yu talk to mi like dat again, or walk out when A talking to yu! And don't yu *evah, evah*, slam any door in dis house again! After all!"

I had definitely gone too far. She was in a roaring temper, such as I had not seen for many a day. She paused to catch a quick breath and then she was off again. "A don't know why yu faada bring yu come gi' mi. None-a mi own-a children dem evah dare to back-answer mi, but yu, smaddy else pickney, come-a wrenk wid mi; after mi raise yu from baby like one-a mi own. Yu is a ungrateful wretch, yu same pickney-gyal, yu!"

I had been trying to ward off her blows by raising my hands in front of my face, but at this astounding statement I went deadly still. I don't know if it was the fact that I had suddenly stopped moving, or whether she realized what she had just said, but she let me go rather abruptly and left the room.

I collapsed onto the bed in a stupefied daze. Phrases flashed in my head. "……yu faada bring yu come gi me." "……smaddy else pickney….." "…..mi own-a children dem……" "……raise yu from baby like mi own……"

I was roused by a knock on the open door and I looked up to see my brother standing hesitantly in the doorway. Even though Delroy was three years older than me and much bigger in body, I sometimes felt he was afraid of me. He stood there now looking apprehensive, as if he thought I might attack him. I stared silently at him and finally he spoke.

"Yu okay, Shell?"

Delroy and I had a very good relationship as brother-sister relationships went. I did not resent him for being our mother's favourite because he never took advantage of it or sought any special favours. And he was always ready to offer comfort or support whenever I needed it. Like now.

I didn't know how to answer his question. I didn't know if I was okay or not. I had just had a severe shock and was still trying to assimilate what I had learnt. My mother was *not* my mother! Who then, and where, was my mother? And how did I come to be raised by this woman, my father's wife?

My father was definitely my father, there was no doubting that. Not only did I resemble him, but she had, in effect, confirmed it by saying that my father had brought me to her.

I had a sudden thought. I ignored Delroy's question and posed one of my own. "Del, did *you* know?"

He shook his head. "I'm hearing it for the first time."

He obviously decided that it was now safe to proceed into the room and he came and sat beside me on the bed. We stared at each other in silence, neither one of us knowing what to say.

After a lengthy silence he said, almost fiercely, "It don't make no difference to me, Shellie. You're still my sister."

"Your *half* sister," I reminded him.

"No!" he said vehemently. "My *sister*; full stop." He tentatively put his arm round my shoulders, and suddenly the floodgates opened, and the torrent came.

Now, I prided myself on not being a crying sort of person; even when I was being beaten I would refuse to cry, which would infuriate Mavis no end, so no one was more surprised than myself when I started to blubber. It took Delroy completely by surprise because I don't believe he had seen me cry since we were very small children. On occasions when I felt I just *had* to cry I would go somewhere private and do so quietly and unobtrusively.

Poor Delroy was completely out of his depth; he just did not know what to do so he just held me. At one stage I was dimly aware that the twins had come to the door, but Delroy shooed them away. I cried for a very long time, and all through the crying I was thinking.

Why had I not been told that Mavis, my father's wife, was not my mother? If it had not slipped out in temper, would I *ever* have been told? Were they perhaps waiting until I was older, or did they have no intention of telling me at all, ever?

I'm not sure if I was crying from hurt or from temper but I do know that the more I cried, and the more I reflected, the angrier I became. How *dare* they keep such an important piece of information from me! I was going to be fourteen in two weeks; surely I was old enough to understand? Well I was going to make them pay. I wasn't sure how, but they would pay, both my father and his wife.

Not only would they pay for keeping that information from me, they would pay for not taking more interest in my academic achievements, and they would pay for making everybody a favourite except me. My resentment rose in my throat like bile and almost choked me.

Finally, and much to Delroy's relief, my crying subsided. The tears seemed to have had a cleansing effect on me. I felt very calm; angry, yes, but calm. I eased away from Delroy, embarrassed now by my display of emotion. I just wanted him gone.

"I'm okay now, Del."

"Yu sure?"

"I'm sure. Gwaan; I'll be fine."

He stood up and went to the door, but paused before exiting the room. "Look, Michelle, as far as I'm concerned, yu's still mi sister; I don't believe in this 'half' business. I'm not going to feel any differently about yu now because yu happen to have a different mother. We have a great relationship, mi and yu. Most brothers and sisters I know can barely stand each other. Mi an' yu different. Don't mek it change."

I stared at him in surprise. Delroy rarely made long statements, let alone philosophical ones. I felt a surge of affection for him and I gave him a watery smile. "Don't worry Del; nothing will change between me and you. I only hope you don't get caught in the crossfire when bullets start to fly."

He looked at me worriedly, knowing from experience that I could be very reckless when roused. "What yu planning to do, Shellie? Promise me you won't do anything stupid?" He was almost pleading.

I tried to reassure him. "Stupid? Oh, I won't do anything stupid. From now on I'm going to be so sensible and mature you won't even know me. I promise." He didn't seem convinced and I almost felt sorry for him as he slowly went out.

Delroy and I had been born in Jamaica while the twins, Rachel and Rebecca, and the baby, Samantha, were born in England. Delroy was seventeen, and although he was an avid reader he was not very academic. His literary fare consisted of Westerns, science fiction and electronics magazines. He loved tinkering with electrical things and was never so happy as when he was pulling radios to bits and putting them back together again. He had left school this past summer and was working in an electronics manufacturing company and attending college on Day Release.

He was tall, at five feet, eleven inches, with big bones, but no spare fat. He loved to play football and cricket and followed the progress of the West Indies Cricket team religiously, taking after our father in that respect.

He had never given our parents any trouble. He was thoughtful and soft spoken. Sometimes he would exasperate me with his patience and his kindness, and then I would call him a 'sissy' and tell him to act like a man and not a girl. Don't get me wrong; there was nothing effeminate about him, it is just that he was such a gentle person, and ever the peacemaker.

When he had left me alone I lay on my bed, and thought. Who was my mother? Where was she now; was she alive or dead? Was I with Mavis and my father because she was dead? If alive, was she still in Jamaica, or had she too emigrated in search of greener pastures?

Could she be here in England? It was not inconceivable. Or perhaps she had gone to Canada or the USA. *If* she was still alive.

How would I go about finding her; for find her I was determined to do if she were at all alive. Would my father be any help in my quest? I was currently harbouring great feelings of resentment against him, but I would need to get some information from him in order to start my search.

My thoughts were interrupted by the arrival of the twins at my room door. "Michelle, Mummy says if you want any dinner you better come downstairs now."

Sweet Home, Jamaica

The twins were nine years old and identical mirror image; one was right-handed, the other left-. We called them the Siamese twins because you rarely saw one without the other; they were almost inseparable. If you called one by name, they both came running. If you hit one, they both cried.

They often spoke in unison or finished each other's sentences. Even within the family it was difficult to tell them apart, so you can imagine how their poor teachers coped.

Their school had insisted that they wear different coloured hair ribbons; Rachel's were supposed to be red and Rebecca's green, but they regularly swapped them around. At one point the school had tried putting them in separate classes but this proved futile as they both went into a major sulk and refused to do any work. No amount of threats or promises could change their attitudes, and when they started swapping classes as well as hair ribbons, the school gave in and re-united them.

They and I got on fairly well in general, but from time to time we had stormy eruptions. They had learned from a very early age to take advantage of the fact that they were Daddy's favourites, and had landed me in hot water with him from time to time. But they were not spiteful or vindictive children, although they could sometimes be detestable.

This was one of those times. The smirks on their faces as they relayed their mother's message told me that they too had shared in my momentous discovery. I was actually very hungry, being one of those people whose appetites are rarely affected by trauma, but I informed them grumpily that I did not want any dinner. They withdrew, leaving me alone again with my thoughts.

As I continued to ponder my situation I had an idea. Perhaps I could find out something about my mother before going to my father for detailed information. If I could get hold of my birth certificate, it should show my mother's name and place of residence when I was born. That would be something to go on.

I knew that Mavis kept all our important papers in a biscuit tin in a suitcase on top of her wardrobe; I had seen her go in there to take out my passport for a school trip to France. I decided to get my birth certificate. I suddenly realised that I'd never even seen the document.

I couldn't get it tonight. I would have to wait until both Mavis and my father were out of the house. In the meantime I would have to decide how I was going to act with Mavis from now on. I no longer saw her as my mother and it would stick in my craw to have to call her Mum. I wouldn't do it; if they beat me to death I wasn't going to call her Mummy anymore.

I was nearly fourteen. In another four years I could leave home as an adult. In the meantime I would have to live under her roof and pay her the courtesy which that demanded. I couldn't call her by her given name; that would be insolent. I made up my mind that I was going to be icily polite to her in future.

It was early evening, not more than seven o'clock, but I decided to go to bed. I had a quick wash and got into my nightdress. I lay in bed wondering how my father would react when he found out that Mavis had let out the secret, for secret it must have been; otherwise I would have been told.

To my surprise I woke to find that the clock-radio had switched itself on which meant that it was time to get up. I couldn't believe it was morning already. I had expected to be unable to sleep, what with everything that was going around in my head, but not only had I slept, I felt extremely refreshed.

I got up and went into the bathroom to perform my

Sweet Home, Jamaica

morning ablutions, after which I went to the twins' room to wake them up. While they were in the bathroom I got myself dressed and then put my dressing-gown on over my school uniform to go downstairs and make breakfast.

Daddy and Delroy had already left for work and Mavis was bustling around trying to feed the baby her breakfast and pack up the bag for the nursery at the same time.

It was the same every morning; Mavis rushing so as not to be late for work, and as often as not, still being late. I wondered why she didn't just get up fifteen or twenty minutes earlier, in order to save the perpetual rush.

She looked up as I entered the dining room. I tried to read her expression but she returned her attention to the baby. "Good morning," I said politely.

"Maaning, Michelle. A need yu to pick up Samantha from di nursery fah mi dis evelin. A have to work late; wi short staff. An' start di dinner fah me till A come; di meat season up a'ready, just brown it an' put it on to cook. An' nuh badda full it up a water. Leave di rice till A come because yu always turn it into porridge."

My God, the woman was out-doing herself to act as if everything was as it had been before she dropped the bombshell! I was still trying to gauge her expression but she was giving the baby all her attention and refused to look at me. Well, I was not going to give her any satisfaction; I too could act as if nothing had changed; well, to some extent, anyway.

"Yes'm."

Did she notice that I had not said 'yes Mum,' but 'yes'm?' If she had she gave no indication of it. I went through to the kitchen and started breakfast for myself and the twins. A few minutes later Mavis called out that she was gone, and I mumbled an acknowledgement.

*

Claudette Beckford-Brady

The school day passed uneventfully. At lunch time I was tempted to tell my best friend, Joy, about the events of the previous evening, but decided to keep it to myself for the time being. I felt self-conscious though, as if people could tell that something about me had changed. Of course my common sense told me that this was only in my imagination, but it fed my anger against my father and Mavis.

During the day the English teacher asked for the return of the signed consent slips from all who would be going to Stratford. I had forgotten about it for the moment, but now I was more than determined to go. I spoke to the teacher privately, and told her that my parents were concerned that we would not return till after dark, and were worried about me coming home alone after the coach dropped us back at school.

Most of the parents would meet their children at the school gate, but I knew there was no chance of either Mavis or my father doing that for me, so I had to find a plausible explanation. I told the teacher that my father was on the late shift and that my mother – it galled me to call Mavis that – couldn't leave the younger children while she came to wait for me. I said that my brother would be willing but he was working and would also finish too late.

I put on a woe-begone face. "Miss, I want to go *so* badly; couldn't you give me a lift home in your car when we get back? My parents would be so grateful..." I smiled at her in my most servile manner.

"Well, yes; I think I could do that for my star pupil. I wouldn't want you to miss your first live performance of Shakespeare."

"Oh, *thank* you Miss!" But I wasn't finished with her yet.

"Um, Miss? I'm sorry to be such a nuisance, but could you write a letter to my parents telling them that you will bring me home, otherwise they might think I'm making it up because I want to go so badly."

"Of course Michelle. I'll get the Secretary to type it up and you can pick it up before you leave this afternoon."

"Oh, thank you so much, Miss Williams. You are the best teacher in the world!"

Now I was ready for them at home. I had thought about this carefully. The only reason they could have for refusing me permission was the one I had given the teacher. Money wasn't an issue; I saved the bulk of my pocket money in the Post Office each week. I could withdraw my fare and spending money.

This evening I would ask my father if I could go. If he said yes, fine. If he said no, I would present him with the letter from my teacher. If he still said no, I would go anyway, and suffer the consequences when I got home. My mind was made up.

I was the first one to get home that evening, even though I had had to detour to pick up Samantha from the nursery. Delroy didn't finish work till six, and no doubt the twins were idling their way home with their friends. This was indeed a stroke of luck; I could look for my birth certificate.

I didn't even stop to take off my coat or Samantha's. I just dumped her on the bed and hauled down the suitcase from on top of the wardrobe. I prayed fervently that it wasn't locked. It wasn't.

I would have to hurry; my life wouldn't be worth living if the twins came home and caught me rifling through Mavis' things. I quickly opened the biscuit tin and looked inside. There was a clear plastic folder with several passports and other documents inside. I ignored the passports and glanced hurriedly through the other papers; Dad and Mavis' marriage certificate, and a number of birth certificates. I found mine and slipped it into my skirt pocket.

I was about to examine the other documents when I heard the front door open and the twins laughing. I quickly put the plastic bag back into the tin, closed the lid and threw it into the suitcase. *Oh my God, they're coming up the stairs!*

I zipped up the suitcase but I wouldn't have time to heave it back on top of the wardrobe. I hurriedly shoved it into the corner behind the bed and leisurely started to remove the baby's coat.

"Hey Siamese," I called out, to make it look as if it was nothing for me to be in the parents' bedroom when they weren't there. "How comes you're just strolling in? I had to pick up Samantha and I *still* got home before you."

They came to the bedroom door and saw me removing the baby's coat. They did not question why I was doing it in the parents' room.

"We went..."

"...to the library."

One started the sentence and the other finished it. "Oh," I said. "Could you look after Samantha while I start dinner?"

Samantha did not need looking after. She was a very happy nine month old child, and you only had to put her down with something to amuse her and you could get on with doing whatever you were doing, but I felt the need to distract the twins.

"Okay," they said in unison and one of them, Rebecca I think, picked up Samantha and they went off to their room.

I hurriedly retrieved the suitcase and almost threw it on top of the wardrobe. I changed out of my uniform and went downstairs to start cooking.

Daddy came in before Mavis. He was in a good mood and he picked the rice and put it on to cook. "Yu gwine have to learn to cook rice yu know Shellie, or nuh man nuh

Sweet Home, Jamaica

gwine to married to yu," he joked.

He acted quite normally, so I assumed he had not yet discovered that the secret was out. Well I wasn't about to enlighten him - yet. If he didn't find out from Mavis or one of my siblings, I would bide my time and drop it on him when I was good and ready.

I was very angry with him but I wasn't ready to confront him yet. The trip to Stratford was too important to me, so I laughed at his joke.

After a few minutes of what I suppose might loosely be termed 'companionable silence,' I broached the subject.

"Daddy, my English class is going to Stratford-upon-Avon next week Friday to see a Shakespeare play. Could I go, please?"

"How much it gwine cost mi?"

"Nothing; I've been saving my pocket money and I can pay for it myself."

"Well, A don't si any reason why not. Talk to yu madda bout it when shi come."

"I asked her already, and she said I can't go."

He frowned. "Well if shi seh yu kyan't guh a'ready, why yu aaksing mi now?" He did not like to be put into a position of conflict with his wife.

"Because shi don't have no good reason for saying no, Daddy. It's very important for my English exam."

"Aah-right; when shi come A wi taak to har bout it."

"Thank you, Daddy."

I left the kitchen and told him I was going upstairs to do my homework. I did not want to be downstairs when Mavis came in from work, which would be any time now. I detoured into the twins' room to give them a bottle I had prepared for Samantha and to see if her bottom needed changing. It did, so I just decided to bathe her and ready her for bed. Then I went into my room to do my homework.

I was dying to look at the birth certificate, so I shut my door and removed it from my skirt pocket. I got out a volume of Shakespeare from my school satchel and opened it up, and then I put the certificate into the book. If anyone came in unexpectedly they would see me reading Shakespeare, and I could close the book, hiding the certificate inside.

My heart was pounding with excitement. I was about to discover the name of the woman who had given me life. Slowly, as if it were something to be savoured, I began to read the information on the certificate. It was not a full certificate, but one of those long narrow ones, stamped on the back as being a true copy of the original. I wondered where the original document was.

I started reading in the far left hand corner which was headed *Date and Place of Birth: Fourteenth December, 1960. Gravel Hill, St Catherine.* I moved on to the section headed *Name (if any).*

If any? How stupid. Of course there must be a name, otherwise why bother to register the birth? *Michelle Delise.* No surname. Next section headed *Sex: Female. Name and Surname, and Dwelling place of Father: George Hezekiah Freeman, Joe Ground, Clarendon: 23 years.*

Now I came to the crucial part. I read the heading; *Name and Surname and Maiden name of Mother.* I closed my eyes for a few seconds. This was the moment. I was about to find out the name of my mother.

Just as I opened my eyes to read the information, my room door burst open and the twins came in. I jumped guiltily and snapped the book shut. "How many times must I tell you to KNOCK before you come into my room?" I was furious.

"Hey, keep your hair on, we're not interrupting you and your boyfriend or anything, are we?" They giggled lewdly.

"Maybe not," I said, "but I need peace and quiet to do

my homework. Unlike you two, I take pride in my school work, because I intend to be somebody big one day, and education is the key. What oonu want, anyway?"

"Our mother says you're ..."

"...to come downstairs."

There it was. *"Our"* mother. I had been wondering when they would start alluding to the fact that we no longer shared a biological mother. Knowing the twins as I did, I had known it would not take them long. I decided that the best way to deal with them would be to ignore the allusion and act as if I hadn't noticed. I put down my book, pushed past them and started down the stairs, while they trailed along behind me.

The table was set for dinner and Mavis was in the kitchen, dishing up. I went to help bring the food to the table. She glanced briefly at me as I entered. "Evelin Michelle."

"Good evening Ma'am."

Either she didn't realize what I had said, or perhaps she mistook it for a shortened version of Mummy, or maybe she just chose to ignore it. Either way, she made no further comment.

When we were all seated at the table and Grace had been said, Daddy brought up the subject of the school trip. "Mavis, Michelle seh yu refuse har permission to guh pon a school trip. Why?"

Mavis looked daggers at me. I had been hoping that Daddy would approach her privately and not in front of the whole family at the dinner table, but he was not known for subtlety. Now she would swear that I was trying to cause dissension between her and Daddy, in front of the whole family.

"Dem not getting back till night. Yu want har walking di street after dark? Yu want man rape har, or skinhead attack har?"

Claudette Beckford-Brady

Daddy looked at me and shrugged his shoulders. He seemed prepared to leave it at that. I was having none of it. "The other children's parents are going to meet them when the coach drops them off. One of you could come and meet me too, or if you can't do that for me, Miss Williams says she will bring me home in her car."

I placed emphasis on the *'for me'* because I wanted them to feel guilty, but neither one of them showed any sign of having noticed. Mavis spoke; "A don't believe a word of it. Yu only saying dat because yu want to guh. Why would Miss Williams guh out-a har way to bring yu home? Yu too lie!"

It is well to know thine adversary, and how well I knew mine! I wanted to tell her that Miss Williams would go out of her way because I was her star pupil, and if my parents couldn't be proud of me, at least my teacher could. But I didn't.

"I have it in writing," I said. "The letter is upstairs in my bag." I made as if to get up but my father waved me down. "Sit down and finish yu dinner. Yu kyan show it to mi later."

Mavis' hostility was palpable. I could not wait for dinner to be over so I could get out of her presence.

I washed up the dinner things without protest. Usually I would complain that the twins never did any of the work; after all, they were nine years old and I had been washing dishes and doing housework since long before that age. I wiped down the stove and the counter tops and swept the kitchen floor. I couldn't wait to get back upstairs to my birth certificate.

The dining room was deserted; Daddy as usual had gone to the pub. The twins were in the living room watching television, and I guess Delroy was in his room tinkering with old radios. Mavis was probably in her room too. I turned off the light and went quietly up the stairs.

Sweet Home, Jamaica

I knocked at Delroy's door, and at his invitation I went in. He grinned at me. "Yu really know how to get Mum upset, don't you?"

"Yeah, and she knows how to get *me* upset. But in future I'm not going to let her get to me. I'm going to be quietly dignified, and the *very epitome* of maturity; you'll see."

Delroy sighed. "I really hope so, Shell; for your sake. How yu feeling otherwise?"

"Okay. Especially now that I'm going to Stratford." We grinned at each other.

I was tempted to tell him about the birth certificate, but he would probably be shocked that I had invaded Mavis' private space. Delroy was full of integrity.

"Anyway, Del, I'm off to do my homework. Good night."

"Night, Shell."

I went into my room and shut the door. I wished I could have locked it, but there was no lock on the door. I hoped there would be no more interruptions. I picked up the volume of Shakespeare and opened it to where the certificate was. I was not going to waste any more time. I went straight to the part headed *Name and Surname and Maiden Surname of Mother.* There it was in black and white. My mother's - my *real* mother's – name: *Delisia Campbell, Student, 17 years.*

Delisia. My middle name was Delise. I was named after my mother. That told me one of two things. Either my mother had named me herself, or my father had been fond enough of her to name me after her.

I carefully folded up the certificate and thought about where I could hide it. It was not going back into Mavis' biscuit tin; that was for sure. It was mine, and I was keeping it. She probably wouldn't miss it for years, and even if she did, I didn't care. She might suspect, but she couldn't prove, that I had taken it. But of course, if she asked me outright, I would not lie; I would have to own up.

I looked around my room. Where could I keep it where it would be safe from prying intruders? My eyes alighted on a small velvet covered jewellery box on my dressing table. My best friend, Joy, had given it to me on my last birthday. It had an upper and a lower compartment which could both be lifted out leaving the empty shell, but best of all, it had a lock and key.

I got an envelope from my stationery kit and sealed the certificate inside. Then I placed it in the base of the jewellery box and replaced the shelves. Finally I locked it. I'd have to find somewhere safe to hide the key.

In actual fact I probably had no need to go to such lengths to hide it. We were not a family who invaded each others' private things. My sojourn into Daddy and Mavis' sanctuary had been a deviation. The twins, although sometimes a right royal pain, always asked if they wanted to borrow any of my things.

I put the box inside my underwear drawer, but then on second thoughts I replaced it on the dressing table. It might look as if I was trying to hide it if it happened to be discovered in the drawer, and that might arouse suspicion or idle curiosity.

I quickly completed my homework exercise, then had my bath and got into bed. I had so much to think about. I now knew my mother's name. I had always known that I was born at Gravel Hill in the parish of St Catherine, but it was only a name to me. In reality I had no idea where it was, as I had been only three years old when I left Jamaica. Is that where my mother had lived? Did she still live there now?

I knew that Old Harbour was the nearest town to the country district of Joe Ground where my father came from. Was Gravel Hill in the same locality, I wondered?

Sweet Home, Jamaica

I decided I would have to get a proper map of Jamaica; the one in my school atlas showed only Kingston and Montego Bay. If I couldn't find one in the bookstores I would call the Jamaican High Commission and ask them to send me one.

I finally slept, and dreamed that I had found my mother, and that she was so pleased and surprised to see me that she hugged and kissed me half to death.

CHAPTER TWO

A Secret Shared, and a Crumb of Information

The next day, which was Friday, I handed in the signed consent form for the trip which was to take place the following Friday. I told Miss Williams that the money would be paid on Monday.

On Saturday morning, I went to the Post Office on Brixton Hill, and withdrew some money from my savings account. I made a point of saving at least half of my pocket money each week, so I had a tidy little sum put by.

After leaving the Post Office, I went to *W.H. Smiths*, the bookshop on Streatham High Road to see if I could find a map of Jamaica. I found several books about the West Indies in general, and Jamaica in particular, but none of them carried a good map which showed small towns and districts.

I found a telephone box that had not been vandalized, and looked up the number of the Jamaican High Commission. The phone rang for a long time and I was just about to hang up, having concluded that they did not open on Saturdays, when someone answered.

I explained what I wanted and the voice said they didn't have any, but suggested I try the Commonwealth Institute. I found the number in the phone book and called.

I was in luck. Yes, they said; they had a rather detailed map outlining all the parishes and showing not only the major towns but all the little districts in between. I could either come and collect it, or they would be pleased to mail it, if I sent a postal order to cover the cost of the map and the postage. I told them I'd be there within the hour.

I took a number 95 bus down to Brixton Underground station, which was within easy walking distance, but I was in a hurry and the bus was at the stop. I took a tube train to High Street, Kensington, where the Institute is located. A mere twenty minutes later, armed with my map, I was on my way back to Brixton. I had been out for several hours, but I didn't anticipate being questioned about my long absence as I had told them at home that I was going to the library to research a project.

Being Saturday, I had quite a lot of household chores to do, including washing all the school uniforms, dusting the furniture, and hoovering the house from top to bottom. I had gotten up very early to get them out of the way before I went out, so Mavis couldn't find anything to nag me about. Later in the evening I would have to put the peas to soak, and season up the chicken for Sunday dinner; but for now, the time was all my own.

I retired to my room to study my map. I used the index to find Old Harbour and marked it off. Then I looked for Joe Ground and Gravel Hill, but to my bitter disappointment there was no listing in the index for either one. I looked at the map very carefully. It was quite a detailed one; if I could not find those places on this map, I would be unlikely to find them on any other. Those places must indeed be very small country districts.

Just as I was about to fold the map and put it away I noticed a familiar name; Bellas Gate. My heart skipped. I *knew* that name. My father often mentioned it when talking about his life in Jamaica. It was very near to Joe Ground, (which Daddy pronounced 'Joe *Grung*') and that meant Gravel Hill was somewhere in the vicinity. I traced the road from Bellas Gate down to Old Harbour and was satisfied that I now had a general idea of where my birthplace was.

Finding it on the map would hardly help me, in any case. Even if I found it, what could I do? For the time being I had gone as far as I could go in obtaining information about my mother. If I wanted to find out more, I would have to ask my father. But I wasn't ready for that yet.

The following Friday I went to Stratford-upon-Avon with my English class. We visited Shakespeare's birthplace and Ann Hathaway's cottage. In the afternoon we watched *A Midsummer Night's Dream* being performed on stage. The roles of the fairies were played by naked children.

I had seen the film version, but watching it being enacted right in front of my face was most thrilling. I was glad I had been able to overcome the obstacles in my way and get to go.

The morning of my fourteenth birthday dawned bright and clear. It was a crispy cold morning; a frost had fallen overnight, but although it was mid December and winter, a pale sun was shining. I viewed this as a good omen for the coming year.

It was a Saturday morning and I got up very early to do my housework, as I planned to spend the day with Joy and some of my other friends. I was resenting more and more the fact that Rachel and Rebecca were not made to help with the housework. After all, they were big girls now. I resolved to speak very firmly to Daddy and Mavis about it.

Being fourteen made me feel very grown up, and I was confident that I could put forward a reasonable and logical argument. I had not had any conflicts with either parent during the past fortnight; in fact I had been most docile, but dignified, in my dealings with them; particularly with Mavis.

My relationship with her was distant, but polite. I rarely spoke to her unless she spoke to me first, except to give greetings or to relay messages. Since her revelation about my mother I had not called her 'Mum' again. Whenever she spoke to me I responded, "Yes Mam" or "No Mam," – a subtle difference, but if she noticed she had thus far given no sign of it.

On the morning of my birthday she called me into her bedroom and handed me a small gift-wrapped package. She always remembered our birthdays but I hadn't been looking for anything from her this year, given the cooling of our relationship.

She must have noticed my surprise because she said, "Yu t'ink A would ignore yu birt'day jus' because yu not speaking to mi, and yu stop call mi Mummy? A hope Am bigger dan dat, Michelle."

So, she *had* noticed. I felt guilty. To give her credit, she wasn't a bad parent, and she had never ill-treated me. A few cuffs and slaps from time to time when I was 'facety', and an occasional beating with the belt, but I wasn't the only one. The twins got a few slaps and the odd beating themselves, although never from Daddy. Delroy was never in trouble.

I felt that Mavis' favouritism of Delroy and Samantha was quite normal, as many parents favoured their firstborn and youngest. And her favouritism did not extend to physical differences in her treatment of us; more in the softer way she spoke and looked at them. And to be totally honest, Delroy deserved softer treatment because he was so gentle himself.

"Th..thank you..." I was embarrassed. I didn't want to say "Mum" but under the circumstances I didn't want to say "Mam" either. I added "...very much."

"Yu welcome Michelle. Happy birt'day."

I slunk out of the room.

"Damn!" I said to myself. *"Why did she have to go and buy me a present? To make me feel guilty I bet. Well you sure succeeded, Mave!"*

Back in my room I opened the present. It was a new camera. The twins had taken my previous camera on an outing to the sea-side and returned without it. I had been furious, and demanded that they buy it back. They hadn't, of course. I returned the camera to the box and placed it in a drawer. I wasn't sure yet how I felt about having it.

I had finished my work so I started getting ready to go out. I was meeting Joy and the others at the tube station, and we were going into the West End to window shop and maybe buy a few items of clothing. Daddy had given me £10 for my birthday, and his sister, my Aunt Violet, who lived in Leeds in the north of England, had also sent me five pounds in a birthday card.

I was almost ready to leave when the twins came into my room, without knocking as usual, all dressed up. I immediately knew what was coming.

"Mummy says..."

"...we can go..."

"...with you." As usual they shared the sentence between them.

"Oh no you don't!" I said angrily. "No way!"

"But Mummy says we can," they wailed in unison.

"And I'm telling you that you can't. This is *my* day out with *my* friends; I don't want two pissa-tail gyal trailing along behind me!"

Sweet Home, Jamaica

"We're telling Mummy!"

"Tell the Queen of England while you're at it!"

I started down the stairs and the twins brushed past me and ran to tell Mavis. Just as I opened the front door to go through, I was pulled up short by Mavis calling my name. I was tempted to pretend I hadn't heard, but I thought better of it. I shut the door and went into the dining room where she was.

"Yes Mam?" I felt no guilt in calling her 'Mam' now. I knew what she was going to say.

"Tek di twins dem wid yu nuh."

It wasn't a request. I took a deep breath. I wanted to scream at them. *Mature and dignified*, I reminded myself.

"Would you mind very much if I took them next Saturday instead? I'll take them in the evening so they can see the Christmas lights, but I'd just like to spend my birthday with my friends. Please," I added.

"Nex week is di last Satdeh before Chrissmus. It gwine to be too crowded."

But the twins had decided that they would rather wait till next week if it meant they could stay for the lights. "Oh, yes please, Mummy. We'll go next week."

I had gotten out of that quite nicely, but I was fuming that I'd had to compromise. I walked down Brixton Hill to the station and found that everyone was there except Stephanie.

"Hi-ya girls," I greeted them. "Likkle most we had the Terrible Two tagging along. I had to bribe them with Christmas lights next week to put them off."

Joy groaned but Yvonne said, "You could have brought them. I wouldn't mind."

"That's because you don't know them like we do," said Joy, which was true, because Joy spent a lot of time at our house and knew the twins well, while Yvonne I mostly saw only at school.

"Well they can't be that bad," insisted Yvonne, who had no siblings, and rather wished she had. Joy kissed her teeth. "I wish! By the way, where the hell is Stephanie? That girl ever late!"

"Speak of the devil," said Yvonne, as Stephanie alighted from a number 37 bus on the other side of the road. The rest of us all lived within walking distance of the station, but Stephanie lived in Clapham, a short bus-ride away.

We entered the station, purchased our tickets, and walked down to the platform where we caught a Victoria Line tube to Oxford Circus. Oxford Street was extremely crowded, as was to be expected eleven days before Christmas. We walked along slowly, going into all the boutiques and Department stores. We tried on everything that caught our eye, even when we had no intention of buying.

After a couple of hours of browsing, we went into a Wimpy bar for burgers and shakes. We had been having a grand time, giggling and generally being silly. When we sat down to eat, the spirit of camaraderie made me suddenly want to tell my friends about my recent discovery concerning my birth.

"If I tell oonu a secret oonu swear not to mention it to a soul?" They all answered together.

"What secret?"

"Of course."

"On my life and honour."

"Well..." I paused, wondering if maybe I should keep it to myself after all.

"Oh come on, Shell! You've got us all agog now. You've *got* to tell," insisted Stephanie. "We won't breathe a word, will we girls?"

"Absolutely not," said Yvonne, "cross my heart and hope to die."

"Shell, am I not your bestest friend?" This from Joy.

Sweet Home, Jamaica

"You *know* you can trust me."

I looked at them all with affection. We had practically been inseparable since we were four or five. We had met at Infant school; all of us newly arrived from Jamaica, and had naturally gravitated toward each other. We had stayed firm friends through Junior School and were ecstatic when we all passed our Eleven Plus exams and got selected for the same Grammar school, and although only Joy and I were in the same class now, we all remained close.

I decided to take the plunge. "Well," I said again, "Mavis is not my mother." There, I'd said it.

"Who's Mavis when she's at home?" asked Stephanie.

"My Mum, you silly ass," I said.

"But I thought you just said she *wasn't* your Mum. And there's no need to get insulting, Shell; I didn't know her name was Mavis."

"Sorry, Steph."

Joy was gaping at me as if I had grown two heads. "Not yu mother? Yu too lie!"

"Honest to God."

"But how comes?"

"Simple. She didn't give birth to me."

"So if she isn't your mother," Yvonne asked, "who is?"

"Well, I know her name," I said, "and that's about all."

"Gosh!" exclaimed Stephanie. "I think that's really exciting. How did you find out?"

I told them about the argument concerning the trip to Stratford and how I had infuriated Mavis into blurting out the information.

"What did your Dad have to say about it?" Joy asked.

"I haven't spoken to him about it yet. In fact I don't even know if he knows that I know.

"It's really strange," I continued, "because the twins ribbed me about it on one occasion, and that was it. Normally they would have kept on and on about it, but I suspect Mavis told them not to refer to it. She's probably apprehensive about Daddy finding out that she let it slip."

"But why keep it from you at all?" Yvonne was puzzled. "Surely you have a right to know about your parentage?"

"One would have thought so," I said.

"Maybe they were going to tell you on your eighteenth birthday," Joy soothed.

We speculated some more on why such an important piece of information should have been kept from me, but none of us could come up with a satisfactory answer. We finished eating and returned to our shopping.

I bought a blue mini skirt for one £1.99 and a yellow tank top for £1.49 in *Chelsea Girls* and Steph bought a pair of white hot pants. Yvonne and Joy bought denim skirts and we all bought platform shoes in *Curtis'*. I also bought myself some gold earrings.

Broke, but satisfied with our purchases, we headed back to South London. As we emerged from the underground station we saw my brother Delroy and two of his friends.

"Hey Shell; did you enjoy your shopping spree?" he asked.

"Yep. Where you lot coming from?"

"Football match at Clapham Common. We lost," he added ruefully.

"Commiserations," I consoled, "better luck next time."

We said goodbye to Stephanie who went off to catch her bus to Clapham and the rest of us started walking down Coldharbour Lane. Yvonne and Joy lived near each other on Somerleyton and Mayall Roads respectively, and although I lived on Josephine Avenue - the Brixton Hill end - I could go by way of Railton Road, so we all walked together, accompanied by Delroy and his two friends, Clive and Alwin.

My friends reached their corner and turned off, leaving

me with the boys. Delroy had told me that Clive fancied me, so I wasn't surprised when he came up beside me and asked if I would go to the Pictures with him tomorrow afternoon for the matinee performance. We both knew I wouldn't be allowed out for the evening showing.

Clive wasn't bad looking, and he had a nice athletic body. He was almost as tall as Delroy - about an inch separated them - and he had a small afro hairstyle. His eyes were very direct, boring into mine as if he wanted to see into my soul.

I really didn't have a lot of time for boys; I was more interested in my books, but all my friends either had boyfriends, or were desperately seeking. I decided that being fourteen now, it was time I took an interest, so I said I would go.

Of course I wouldn't be able to tell Mavis or Daddy that I was going out with a boy, I would have to say it was with Joy, and God help me if the twins insisted on coming. I couldn't shake them twice in two days. I would have to say that Joy and I were going to study together.

I stopped at the phone box on the corner of Tulse Hill and Brixton Water Lane and called Joy, who should be home by now. I set up my alibi with her, giggling as I told her I had a date. She was pleased but jealous, because she was one who didn't have a boyfriend yet.

It was after five when Delroy and I got in, and I put down my purchases and headed straight for the kitchen. I had to cut up the chicken and season it up for tomorrow's dinner. Mavis was just putting the finishing touches to the soup pot, soup being standard Saturday dinner.

"Did yu have a good time in di Wess Enn?" she asked.

"Yes, thank you."

"Yu buy anyt'ing nice?"

"A pair of shoes, a tank top and skirt, and some earrings."

Claudette Beckford-Brady

"Yu really splurge out, eeh? Set di table and bring di dish dem fi di soup."

*

The following afternoon I managed to get away with no hindrances. Generally speaking, the parents were quite easy-going about our going out, as long as it was daylight and we had done all our chores. I had arranged to meet Clive at the Brixton College bus stop and we were going to watch a film at Streatham Odeon.

I felt a bit self-conscious. This was my very first date, and I had no idea of how to proceed. However, Clive soon put me at ease. He was quite relaxed, and made intelligent conversation, asking me about my school work and my aspirations for the future. I was pleasantly surprised because I thought all teenaged boys were interested in only one thing.

It turned out that Clive was as academic as I was and had hopes of becoming a Barrister-at-Law. He was working towards a partial university scholarship, and to help his case he spent his school holidays working in a Solicitor's office and running errands for Barristers at the courthouse and Chambers.

I was surprised to discover that he was seventeen; I had thought him to be younger than Delroy, possibly because he was still going to school. He had already done O Levels and was in his final A Level year, after which he would go off to university.

We were early for the film, so we sat in a snack bar and chatted, and ended up not seeing the film at all. By the end of the afternoon I was hopelessly in love.

Christmas came and went, and 1975 started with mild, almost spring-like weather. School re-opened on the sixth of January and no one was gladder than I, because it meant I would be able to see more of Clive, whose school was almost next door to mine, on Tulse Hill. Since that first date we had seen each other at every available opportunity. I had had my first kiss on Christmas Eve, and was walking around in a perpetual state of bliss.

Clive too seemed to be on cloud nine, at least according to Delroy, who thought it a great joke. He had never seen Clive so smitten, he said, and he had seen him date a few other girls in the past. This gave me great encouragement as I had lain awake at night agonizing over the thought that he might not like me as much as I liked him.

At break time at school I bored my friends to tears about 'my boyfriend', and Yvonne and Stephanie, who had already changed boyfriends several times, told me that the novelty would soon wear off.

Joy was envious, and bemoaned the fact that the only guys who ever asked her out were either not good to look at, or they were 'lady-killers' with reputations of being only after one thing. I decided to try and set her up with Delroy, who I knew she liked, but who, although he was always pleasant, showed no special interest in her. He had dated a few girls but did not seem inclined to want to 'go steady' with any of them.

I had made several New Year's resolutions, including speaking to Mavis and Daddy about the twins and the housework, and more importantly, speaking to my father about my mother.

I decided to deal with the housework issue first. I waited until a Saturday morning after I had already done the chores. Daddy was in the living room watching cartoons, with Samantha as his excuse, although it was no secret how much he enjoyed them. Mavis was in the dining room unpacking the shopping which she had done that morning. I asked Daddy if he could come into the dining room as I wanted to talk to him and Mavis about something.

Of course I did not call his wife 'Mavis' to him; it almost

choked me to do so but I managed to get out the word 'Mummy'. He seemed rather surprised, but he put Samantha down on the floor and came straight away.

"Mavis, Michelle waan to talk to us about somet'ing."

I saw a quizzical look cross Mavis' face, and was that a flicker of apprehension? Did she think I was going to bring up the subject of my mother? They both looked at me expectantly, and I began.

"I think the twins are big enough now to help with the housework. When I was their age I was doing all the things I'm doing now; in fact even before I was their age. I don't think it's fair for me to do everything. They should help with washing the dishes and tidying up the kitchen, and I don't see any reason why they shouldn't wash their own school uniforms."

Was it my imagination, or did Mavis breathe a sigh of relief? I continued, "I think we should draw up a rota for the kitchen work and dusting the furniture. I'll carry on doing the hoovering myself."

I waited for their reaction. They looked at each other and Daddy shrugged his shoulders, putting the onus on Mavis. I hadn't ranted and raved, or spoken complainingly. I had simply stated my case calmly and matter-of-factly. There was no logical reason for them to disagree with me.

To my immense relief Mavis acquiesced immediately. "Yu right. Is high time fah dem to tek a interest in di house and learn how to do t'ings. A wi' talk to dem."

"Thank you."

I went to my room to get ready to go out. I had said I was meeting Joy and the girls to go over some school work, but in fact it was Clive I was meeting. We would go and change our library books and then go some place where we could talk.

Most of our time together was spent in deep conversations; we were both very serious about our school work, and had agreed that we would not jeopardize our futures by being foolish. It galled me that I had to lie in order to see him, when we were both so sensible and mature, but I knew there was no way I could tell the parents that I had a boyfriend, and especially one who was so much older than me; Clive would be eighteen in June.

He said he had wanted to ask me out for a long time, but Delroy kept telling him that I was too young. He said that for some reason he had thought I was older. When I turned fourteen Delroy gave him the okay, saying I was mature for my age, but warning him of dire consequences should he violate me.

I was both touched and annoyed at Delroy playing the role of my guardian and protector, but finally conceded that it was good to have some-one looking out for me. And he trusted Clive; otherwise he would not have given him the okay, and if Delroy trusted him, then I could too.

After we left the library we went to the Wimpy Bar on Brixton Road where we spent a couple of hours, making our burgers and shakes last a full two hours. If the weather had been warmer we would have gone to the park, but as it was we had to use whatever facilities were available.

I had told Clive about discovering that Mavis was not my mother, and how I was determined to find my real mother. He wondered if it wasn't better to let sleeping dogs lie, in case I was hurt and disappointed by what I eventually found out.

"After all," he said, "You don't know if she didn't give you away because she wanted nothing to do with you."

"Oh no," I said. "I'm sure it wasn't anything like that. She was only seventeen when I was born; I'm sure she was forced to give me up."

"See what I mean?" Clive said. "You've already convinced yourself that such was the case. Suppose you do find her and she's happily married, and her husband

and current family know nothing about you? Do you think she would be willing to jeopardize her position by welcoming you to her bosom?"

I was silent. That thought had just not occurred to me. Clive continued, "Delroy is older than you. That means that your father had an extra-marital affair and you were the result."

"No; he and Mavis didn't get married till *after* we all came to England."

"Well he was still in a relationship with Mavis, married or not, when you were born."

"You're right, and I hear what yu saying about being disappointed, but I still have to find out; for my own peace of mind."

"Well, I suppose if I were in your position I would want to find out too."

A short while later we left the Wimpy and started home. Clive lived on Brixton Water Lane which was the next street to mine but we went separately. It wouldn't do for me to be seen walking alone with a boy, and Delroy was off on his own pursuits.

After that conversation with Clive I found I was more anxious than ever to get more information about my mother, and I resolved to approach my father the moment I caught him alone in the house. I did not want anyone around when I brought up the subject, unless it was Delroy.

My opportunity came almost a week later. Mavis was working late again and I had picked up Samantha from the nursery on Effra Road and arrived home to find that Daddy was already home. The twins had Drama Club on a Friday evening so I knew they would not be home for a while. I didn't have to cook either, because we always had fish and chips on Fridays.

Daddy was in front of the TV as he usually was when at

home. "Daddy, can I ask you something?"

"What, Shellie?"

I was very nervous. I licked my lips and took a deep breath. "It's about my mother."

"Mavis? What about har?"

"No, not Mavis. My real mother."

On any other occasion his expression would have had me in fits of laughter. He was so flabbergasted that he didn't even notice that I had called his wife 'Mavis.' His eyes bulged, his mouth opened and closed like a fish out of water, and he actually gulped before he spoke.

"Who tell yu seh Mavis is not yu madda?"

"She did."

Now I'd dropped her in it. She would probably never forgive me.

"When shi tell yu dat?"

"Oh Daddy, what does that matter? The point is she accidentally let it slip, and I'm curious to know how I came to be with you and Mavis instead of with my own mother. Can't you tell me about her? Is she still alive? Why did she give me away, and why didn't you tell me about it yourself?"

He sighed and turned off the TV. My heart speeded up. He hadn't gotten mad. He was going to tell me!

"Wi nevah si di pint in telling yu,'cause Mavis have yu from yu-a four week old, and yu come een just like har own. Yu madda did suppose to guh to university afta she left school, and when she get pregnant wi agree dat I would tek di chile when it born. Mavis did vex at first, but afta shi get yu shi grow to love yu, just like yu was har own."

"So my mother had me for four weeks after I was born? How could she give me up? She didn't grow to love me in that time?" I asked plaintively.

"Michelle, it wassen as simple as dat. Shi was suppose

to give yu up straight a-weh as yu born, but shi refuse. It tek all kind a threat and promise fi mek shi give yu up, but har parents did spend nuff money pon har edication, and dem seh if shi don't give yu up, dem done wid har."

A lump formed in my throat and my eyes prickled. My mother *had* loved me; just as I had suggested to Clive, she had been forced to give me up.

"Do you know where she is now, Daddy? Didn't you make any arrangements to give her progress reports on me?"

"Michelle, everybaddy agree dat a complete break would be di best t'ing."

"Well *I* don't think so, and I bet my mother didn't think so either! Have you any idea where she is now, Daddy?"

"No, A don't, Michelle."

"Well tell me where she used to live and let me write to see if I can find her."

Daddy was beginning to get exasperated. "Michelle, fahget it! *Mavis* is yu madda now. Tell mi, shi treat yu any way different from di others? An' anyway, Delisia prably left Country and gone Town long time. A bright woman like dat not gwine stay a-country and teach school. Shi did waan to be a lawyer. Far all wi know shi might-a even left Jamaica."

"Well I could at least try."

"Done di argument child!"

He turned the television back on. There was no point in pressing him further, he would only get angry. But I was grateful for the few crumbs of information I had gleaned about my mother.

I picked up Samantha, who had been playing happily on the carpet, and went upstairs. I looked lovingly at her and she gurgled at me. I hugged her tightly and she squirmed to be put down. How could anyone give away their baby? I knew I never could.

Sweet Home, Jamaica

Despite what my father said, I resolved to write a letter and send it to Gravel Hill Post Office on the chance that my mother was still in the district. When my father wrote to his parents he addressed it to Bellas Gate P.O. and not to a specific address. I would try the same thing, substituting Gravel Hill for Bellas Gate.

Of one thing I was certain, I was going to try every avenue I could think of to try and locate my mother.

CHAPTER THREE

A Letter to Mama, and Getting the Best Of Mr. Critchlow

44, Josephine Avenue,
Brixton Hill,
London, SW2 2LA

Dear Miss Delisia,

I am writing this letter with the sincere hope that it might reach you.

I hope it does not come as too much of a shock for you to read what I am about to say, but in preparation I am asking you to sit down and make yourself quite comfortable before you continue to read.

Are you set? My name is Michelle Delise Freeman and I was born on the 14th of December, 1960 in the district of Gravel Hill. My father's name is George Freeman of Joe

Sweet Home, Jamaica

Ground District.

It has recently come to my knowledge that the woman I had believed to be my mother is not in fact my mother. On making further enquiries, I have discovered that you are my mother.

I hope you do not think I am out of order by writing to you. I found out about you by accident and when I tried to get more information from my father he told me to leave it alone. But I would so love to hear from you and hopefully be able to meet you one day. You would not even have to acknowledge the relationship if you don't want to, we could just be like pen-pals. I would love to tell you all about myself and how I am doing in school, but I will save that for another time, if I hear from you.

I hope you are well, and I look forward to hearing from you in the very near future.

Yours sincerely,

Michelle D Freeman.

The letter took me two days to write. It was extremely difficult to know what to say, and I did not know if I should address it to Miss Campbell or Miss Delisia, but eventually decided to use her Christian name. Finally I felt fairly satisfied, and marking it 'Private and Confidential' I sent it off.

I thought I would give it a month to get there and a month to receive a reply, and I lived on tenterhooks for the next eight weeks. I had told no-one except Clive that I had written the letter, not even my best friend, Joy.

After nine weeks had passed, then ten, then twelve, I began to feel discouraged. Clive did his best to cheer me up but I became moody and withdrawn. Delroy suspected that I was pregnant and was very relieved to have his suspicions allayed. Mavis asked me if I was sickening for something and the twins swore I was love-sick over some boy or other.

Daddy alone seemed not to notice my depression, but then he was hardly ever home anyway, and when he was, he was glued to the TV set. He had been extremely annoyed with Mavis for telling me about not being my mother, and Mavis had been very cool toward me for some time.

After three full months had passed I reluctantly concluded that either my mother was no longer in the district, or she wanted nothing to do with me. Secretly I felt it must be the latter, otherwise why had my letter not been returned when I had clearly marked it *'If not called for please return to sender'* with my name and address clearly written on the back of the envelope.

We were now in the full bloom of spring and the trees were once again clothed in glorious green. Fruit trees were in blossom, flowers were blooming and the April showers graced us by falling only at night.

Samantha had had her first birthday in March, and had taken her first tentative steps soon afterward. She was now stumbling around and pulling down tablecloths and anything else she could reach.

The twins, after some initial grumbling, had settled into the routine of helping with the housework. Delroy had helped Daddy to plant the vegetable garden and was otherwise fully occupied with his job, his football - which would soon be replaced by cricket - and tinkering with his electronics.

Clive no longer played football with Delroy because he was studying in earnest for final A Level exams. In fact we would all be involved in exams during May and June, but Clive's were more important because his entry to university depended on his results.

Sweet Home, Jamaica

Clive and I had celebrated our four month 'anniversary' and were still besotted with each other. Joy was disgruntled because I hardly saw her anymore except at school. Delroy had not shown any inclination to date her, despite my best efforts.

However, toward the end of June when exams were over and the school year was winding down toward the summer holidays, I persuaded him to take her to the Friday night disco in St Matthew's church hall. Clive was taking me, and Yvonne and Stephanie were both going with their respective boyfriends. Joy had stated emphatically that she would not be 'playing gooseberry' by going alone.

To my surprise, she and Delroy danced every dance together, and toward the end of the evening I noticed that they were nowhere to be seen. I wandered through the hall searching for them, as my watch told me it was almost time for the disco to end. Not seeing them anywhere, I went outside, and imagine my delight and utter amazement when I found them out there dancing the slow dance that was playing.

They were wrapped in each other's arms and Joy, who was facing outwards over Delroy's shoulder, had her eyes tightly closed. I went back inside and resolved not to say anything to them about what I had seen.

The disco ended and Stephanie and her boyfriend went their way and the rest of us – me, Joy and Yvonne and our respective escorts – started walking home. Delroy and Joy were deep in conversation and when we parted, to my further delight, he kissed her.

I was a bit puzzled that after all my previous efforts to get him to ask her out had proved futile, he should suddenly discover that he fancied her after all. However, I did not want to jinx them, so I decided to say nothing.

But Delroy himself brought up the subject. After Clive and I had spent five minutes kissing goodnight and he had gone up Brixton Water Lane, Delroy and I walked up Josephine Avenue. We walked in companionable silence for a while and then he said, "You can ask me about it if you want. I know you're dying to."

I feigned ignorance. "Ask you about what?"

"Come on Shell, this is me you're talking to."

"Oh, all right then. When did you discover you liked her after all?"

"Oh, I always knew I liked her. I just didn't think it wise to get involved with any of your friends, that's all."

"Why on earth not?" I asked.

"Because if there was ever a conflict between us you might suffer from divided loyalties," he replied.

"Rubbish," I said. "I'd examine both sides of the argument and take the side that was right."

"Or better still," responded Delroy, "stay out of it altogether." We linked arms and walked home happily.

The following Monday evening when Clive came to walk me home from school, Delroy, who had finished work early, came with him to walk Joy home. We made a jolly foursome as we laughed and talked and idled our way home. I didn't have to hurry home to cook, as it was Monday, and we always had 'Sunday-day left overs' on Mondays.

The last week of June Clive turned eighteen and we celebrated by going to an Indian restaurant for a meal. The evenings didn't get dark now till after nine, so the parents did not mind me being out, as long as I came in before nine. If I was out with my brother, I was allowed to stay till nine-thirty; but of course this only applied to weekends and not school nights.

Clive and I had arranged for Delroy to meet us on the corner of Brixton Hill and Brixton Water Lane at five past nine so that Delroy and I could go in together, and so make it look as if I had been with him all evening. After Clive and

Sweet Home, Jamaica

I left the restaurant, we had time to kill, so we walked up to Brockwell Park at Herne Hill.

There were still a lot of people in the park at that time of the evening, because as I said, it was still light. We found a quiet spot in the rose arbour near the duck pond, and settled down to some serious kissing.

We had been together for six months now, and had progressed to a little intimate touching, but we were both mindful of the fact that getting carried away could prove dangerous and costly in terms of our future aspirations.

I was planning to become a journalist, either in the print media or in television/radio. I had also decided that one day I would be a best-selling author. I loved the art of using words, and I read my dictionary the way most teenagers read *Mills & Boon* romance novels.

Clive was going to be a Barrister. We knew that a baby was definitely not a part of the equation.

We kissed, fondled, and conversed, and all too soon it was time to go and meet Delroy. We consoled ourselves that the summer holidays were coming soon and we would have more time to spend together, even though Clive would be working as a Solicitor's clerk, and there was also the possibility that I might get a summer job.

The exam results came out a few days before the end of term, and as usual I came top of my class in all subjects, with Joy and the others coming somewhere in the middle. And, as was to be expected, there was no lavish praise for my achievements at home, but Daddy did at least give me a cursory pat on the shoulder and a "Well done, Shell." Mavis, who I think still hadn't totally forgiven me for letting on to Daddy about my mother, said, "Yu soon get too big and important fi di likes a wi."

Delroy was the only family member who seemed really pleased that I did well in school, but I no longer cared what the rest of them thought. Clive was my focus now and if I could please him by doing extra well, it was as good as done. I wished I could let my mother know how well I was doing; that I had taken after her in intellect.

But of course, not having had any response to my letter, and not knowing her whereabouts, I could not let her know. I had not totally given up hopes of eventually finding her, but I had concluded that there was very little I could do for the present. But I had resolved that as soon as I possibly could, I was going to Gravel Hill, Jamaica, to start the process of finding my Mamma.

Obviously that could not happen until I had left school and gotten a job, but it was going to be a big priority in my life, the search for my mother.

The summer holidays came and I found ways of spending time with Clive despite the fact that we were both working. I had gotten myself a part-time job at *Boots*; the chemist on Brixton Road, but we were not working all the time, and we made the most of every bit of free time we had.

It was a blazing summer, that summer of 1975. The entire country was under a heat-wave. The sun threw out its heat with such ferocious intensity that one could have been forgiven for believing they were living in a tropical country. Flowers dried up and lawns were burnt brown; citizens were under threat of prosecution if they watered their gardens or washed their cars.

People slept with windows wide open at night, and by day the parks and beaches were packed with pale skinned White people, desperately trying to catch some colour while they could, knowing that this was a temporary phenomenon. The unlucky ones turned bright red like lobsters in boiling water, and their skin peeled. The lucky ones turned a nice golden brown. There were hundreds of cases of people suffering from sun-stroke.

Joy was scathing in her remarks after watching the

Sweet Home, Jamaica

skimpily clad sun-seekers on Brighton beach. "Watch di hypocrite dem; most of the time we're 'niggers' and 'black bastards' but as soon as they see a little sun, they can't wait to strip off to catch our colour."

Delroy had taken two weeks leave from work, and he and Joy had become a foursome together with Clive and me, and we took bus rides and went all over London. We visited London Zoo, Madame Tussaud's Wax Works museum, the Planetarium, and Buckingham Palace to see the changing of the Guards. We took a boat ride on the Surpentine in Hyde Park and another down the River Thames to Windsor, returning to London by train.

The twins often tried to accompany me when they saw me getting ready to go anywhere, but I had put my foot down firmly, and told them *and* the parents in no uncertain terms, that they should spar with their own age group. They sulked for a while but soon got over it.

On their tenth birthday in August, which was also Daddy's birthday, Delroy and I took pity on them and took them on the train to Brighton for the day. Joy came with us but I thought it best to leave Clive out of it as I didn't want to give the twins grist for their mill.

The summer went all too quickly and before we knew it September had arrived and we were back in school. My friends and I were entering the fourth year where we would have to choose our O Level subjects for the fifth form next year. The twins were beginning their last year at Junior School.

Delroy was enjoying his work as an apprentice electronics engineer; now he could pull radios and televisions to bits *and* get paid for it. As for Clive, he had decided to work for a year as a solicitor's clerk before going to university. I was extremely glad for this as it meant I would have him home for an extra year, and I suspected that our relationship was an equation in his decision to

Claudette Beckford-Brady

postpone university.

The Autumn Term got off to an interesting start as far as I was concerned. Our new Form teacher was Mr. Critchlow, whom we had not come in contact with before. He taught Advanced Mathematics, which we would be introduced to for the first time this year. Mr. Critchlow decided to seat us in the classroom in what he termed "Order of Intelligence."

Now, in the normal course of things, when you enter a new class at the start of a new school year, you are allowed to choose where you sit and who you sit next to. The only exceptions to this are the first year pupils, who are seated alphabetically until the teachers get to know their names, and then they can sit where they choose. Mr. Critchlow's 'Order of Intelligence' meant that we were seated according to our overall exam results, i.e. the highest placed students at the front of the class and the lower placed ones at the back.

Now all through our school life Joy and I had sat next to each other, and this new arrangement was not to our liking; indeed, it was not to the liking of the entire class, and we vociferously made our views known. Mr. Critchlow refused to change his stance so at break time we formed a class union.

I was elected President and a white girl named Annette was elected Secretary. We passed a resolution to sit where we wished in the class, and to take protest action if we were thwarted.

We did not return to our own Form room until after the lunch break as we all had different subject classes to go to. On our return for the afternoon registration we all chose our own desk. Mr. Critchlow, on discovering that we had blatantly disobeyed him, threw a tantrum and insisted we return to where he had placed us. As President and spokesperson I was pushed by the other girls to state our case. I stood up and began to address Mr. Critchlow.

"Sir, we do not see the need for us to be seated in any specific order since....."

"Be silent! Sit down! How dare you contradict me!" I was rudely interrupted. "Now everyone, please return to your places at once!"

No one moved. I tried again. "Sir, with all due respect....." Again I was interrupted.

"I said be quiet! Everyone to their places! NOW!"

As we had agreed at our meeting, if he did not allow us to sit where we chose, we would stage a peaceful protest; so everyone got up and we began to march in an orderly fashion from the classroom.

Mr. Critchlow's face was a study. He had obviously never before been so flagrantly disregarded, and he was almost jumping up and down in his anger. I was afraid he was going to have an apoplectic fit.

He was a small rotund man, no more than five feet two inches tall, with ginger hair and fat freckled cheeks. He was probably only in his mid fifties, but to us he was ancient. He flew to the door and tried to bar it but the force of girls gently pushed him to one side, and we exited into the school yard where we stood in four neat rows of eight and waited.

Sure enough, in a few minutes the headmistress, Mrs Walsh, arrived on the scene with Mr. Critchlow, almost purple with rage, dancing beside her.

"Girls, what is the meaning of this?"

I stepped forward. "Miss, our Form teacher is insisting that we be seated in class according to our level of intelligence, and we feel that this is both a form of discrimination and an infringement of our right to choose."

Mrs Walsh seemed nonplussed. She had obviously never had to deal with such a situation before. Mr. Critchlow interjected, "Such insolence!" and Mrs Walsh turned to him and said, "Please, Mr. Critchlow," in a tone of voice that silenced him.

She returned her attention to us. "Now girls; Mr. Critchlow has always seated his pupils this way and none have objected before."

"With all due respect Miss, just because a thing has always been done does not necessarily make it right. We spend most of our time in other classrooms according to our various subjects. This is our Home room, where we should have the freedom to have our desks next to our friends."

Mrs Walsh was silent for a moment while she considered. Then she said, "Some of you will be taking Advanced Mathematics with Mr. Critchlow. I think he has the right to seat you where he wishes for his own class."

"Perhaps so, Miss. We are willing to compromise. Not all of us will be doing Advanced Maths. Those of us who are would be willing to sit in whatever order Mr. Critchlow chooses for the duration of the maths lesson. Thereafter we will return to our places of choice."

I had taken it upon myself to say this without consulting my classmates, and I now looked to them for confirmation. They nodded their consent. Mrs Walsh looked at Mr. Critchlow. "Is this acceptable, Mr. Critchlow?"

Mr. Critchlow was fuming. "Really, Headmistress, we cannot allow ourselves to be dictated to by mere children. I insist they sit where I place them!"

"In which case," I said, "we will boycott your classroom altogether, including the maths class, we will keep our belongings in the cloakroom and attend our other classes from there."

Now Mrs Walsh was being forced to make a decision. She could order us to capitulate under threat of detention, or worse, suspension. I was quaking on the inside, but to all concerned I was calm and collected.

Sweet Home, Jamaica

"Okay, girls; please disperse to your various classes. I will consider the situation and inform you of my decision by the end of the afternoon." She left, and we went off to our classes, leaving Mr. Critchlow fuming in the schoolyard.

The English Literature class was already in progress when I got there, and I apologized to Miss Williams on behalf of myself and my classmates for being late. I didn't give her a reason and although she seemed curious she did not press me, merely bringing us up to date on what had transpired during our absence.

We did a double period of English Lit and then I had a single period of History. During the History class a Prefect came in with a message that the Headmistress wished to see me. I could sense the curiosity of the girls from other Forms that made up the history class, and the girls from my own Form gave me a 'thumbs up' sign for good luck.

I knocked on the Head's door and waited for permission to enter. Mrs Walsh opened the door herself and ushered me into her office. "Come in Michelle. Sit down."

"Thank you Miss."

She looked at me in silence for a moment or two and I wanted to squirm, but I kept up the pretence of being calm and collected.

"Well now," she finally said, "You are certainly articulate and have a fine command of the English language. May I ask what you intend to do when you leave school?"

I was taken by surprise. She spoke pleasantly and with no hint of displeasure. I stumbled out a response. "Aahm, I think I'd like to be a journalist of some sort."

"Yes; well, that seems like a good stepping stone into politics. Tell me, have you considered entering politics?"

What an idiotic question. I'm only fourteen, for heaven sake. "No Miss."

"Well I think you ought. Or perhaps the law. You certainly made a good case today."

I didn't know what to say, which belied her assumption that I would make a good lawyer or politician, so I humbly answered, "Thank you Miss."

"Well now," she said again, "regarding your dispute with your Form teacher; I have spoken with Mr. Critchlow and he has consented to you all sitting where you wish during registration. However, during any lessons taken in his classroom you will sit where he instructs you to. Is that clear?"

"Yes Miss. And thank you," I added as an afterthought.

"Now, in the future if you are not happy with any given situation, before you organize any further political protests, you will please consult with me. I believe any situation can be resolved through dialogue."

"Yes Miss."

She dismissed me.

I was riding high. My first incursion into political warfare and I had emerged victorious. Perhaps she was right. Maybe I should consider going into politics when I was older. I was feeling extremely heady with power. I couldn't wait till the end of the afternoon to inform the girls.

While I was in the Head's office I had missed the afternoon break and there were two periods to go before the afternoon was over. I thought the afternoon would never end, but finally it did and we all returned to our Home room.

The girls were all agog to find out the Head's decision, and feeling my power I made them wait while I sorted out my satchel and put what was not needed for my homework into my desk. The more astute of them noticed that my desk was not the one designated by Mr Critchlow and realized that we had won. They immediately went to their own choice of desks and so cheated me out of my announcement.

That evening when I told Clive about it, he said I was in danger of my head bursting, I was so swelled up. That deflated me somewhat, as I hated any form of criticism from him. I resolved to never again let power go to my head.

But I had made an enemy of Mr Critchlow. He seemed to think that I had instigated the whole thing on my own, and he decided to try and make my life a living hell by picking on me to solve the most difficult mathematical problems. However, luckily for me, maths proved no mystery to me and I excelled in this as I did in all other subjects. When he discovered this, it seemed to make him hate me all the more, and I fear the rest of the class suffered because he delighted in inundating us with homework.

We continued to have union meetings and other classes begged to become members. And, remembering that I wanted to be respected by Clive above anything else, I tried to deal with matters in a mature and intelligent manner. Without sounding conceited I must say that pupil-teacher relations improved greatly and I believe I came to be respected by teachers and pupils alike.

This was confirmed when the following September I was elected Deputy Head Girl of the school. This was indeed an unprecedented achievement, as both Head Girl and Deputy were always chosen from the Sixth or Upper Sixth, and here I was only a Fifth-former. I felt rather superior, and walked around with my head high, my chest pushed out, and an ego that was by far too large.

Clive brought me back to earth from Cloud Nine, and gave me perspective by telling me that, "Pride goes before a fall, y'know, Michelle. You can be proud of your achievement without being boastful and superior."

Clive was never shy to rebuke or chastise me, and I thought that surely if Daddy and Mavis knew him they would have no objections to my dating him, even though he was eighteen and technically an adult. But as things were, Clive and I would have to remain a secret for a while longer. After all, it was not only Daddy and Mavis that could keep secrets; I could too.

But unfortunately, secrets have a way of being revealed, as I was to discover to my cost before the end of the summer.

But for the moment, Clive and I continued to see each other in relative secret. His parents knew of, and were not against, the relationship, but they did say I should not keep secrets from my parents. They said it would look bad on them if my parents discovered that they had known about, and condoned their son having a relationship with Daddy and Mavis' under-age daughter.

I assured them that the relationship was strictly platonic, and pleaded with them not to tell. I went to great lengths to ensure that the twins got no hint of the relationship, for as sure as the grass is green, if they found out, then so would the parents.

Joy's relationship with Delroy was also a State Secret. Joy's parents were Pentecostal 'Born Again' Christians, and would have kittens if they knew their daughter had a boyfriend, and so Joy did not see as much of Delroy as she would have liked. But they created opportunities where they could, and their relationship began to take on a serious look.

Joy had been planning to do A Levels and go on to university, as were I and our other two friends, Yvonne and Stephanie. Now, however, she began to talk about getting a job as soon as she finished her O Levels next summer, and leaving home as soon as she was eighteen. She was making long term plans as far as leaving home was concerned; we would only be sixteen on our next birthdays, and although mine was just a few months away in December, she would not have hers till next May.

Clive and Delroy had both had their nineteenth birthdays this summer, a few weeks apart. Joy and I felt much superior to the girls at school who were going out with mere schoolboys. Both of our men had been shaving for a good while now, and they both hated it something rotten.

"Why do we have to grow hair on our bodies?" Delroy complained. "It's not fair; you girls should be inflicted with it too."

"And you men should be inflicted with monthly periods and childbearing," I had responded. But I think that secretly, Delroy was proud of his facial hair, and the fact that he had to shave.

So we spent another happy, sizzling summer, like the one last year, and I prepared to return to school, while Clive prepared to start his first term at university.

CHAPTER FOUR

Caught!

I was now almost sixteen years old, going into the Autumn Term of 1976. I was gearing up for mock O Levels in November/December, and the real thing in May and June of the following year. I was doing eleven subjects, and found that with my additional duties as Deputy Head Girl I no longer had time to deal effectively with student union matters, so I resigned as President and a new one was elected. I gave my full attention to my studies.

Clive had resigned his job and was about to start his first term at Durham University in the north of England. I helped him to pack and watched sadly as his luggage was stowed in the boot of his father's car, and he and his parents set off. I wished I could have gone with them, but of course that was totally unfeasible. It would be Christmas before I saw Clive again.

Needless to say, his parents were extremely proud of him. His father, Wilfred, who worked as a train driver on

Sweet Home, Jamaica

London Transport underground, said Clive was starting the process of lifting the family to higher heights, and his mother, who was a nurse, couldn't believe that her 'one-son' (Clive was an only child) had grown up already.

I wondered if when I started university my father and Mavis would at last be proud of me. To be truthful it no longer really mattered to me. Clive's parents had become surrogate parents to me and I called them Mum and Dad. They encouraged me in my school work and it was they I discussed important things with, and not my own parents.

I had told them about Mavis not being my mother, and my intention to search for my birth mother. Like Clive, they urged me to beware of rejection.

Meanwhile, the secret had somehow been revealed, and Mavis and Daddy had found out about Clive during the summer just ended, a few weeks before Clive had left for Durham. It had caused a major disruption in the house and driven Daddy to violence – a very unusual occurrence.

Clive and I had been together for some eighteen months and it was actually quite amazing that they had not found out sooner. To this day I do not know who told them, but one evening after I had been out with Clive, I came home to find them waiting for me.

I was half-way up the stairs to my room when I was pulled up short by a stern command.

"Jus' a minute, young lady."

Daddy never called me 'young lady' except when he was displeased. I had an ominous sinking feeling in the pit of my stomach. I could tell by the words, as well as the tone of voice, that I was in trouble, and knew immediately and intuitively that it had to do with Clive. I took a deep breath and went back down the stairs. He didn't waste any time but got straight to the point.

"A hear seh yu an' Myrkle bwoy a carry on indecent pan di road. Yu don't have nuh shame? An' who tell yu seh yu

Claudette Beckford-Brady

kyan keep bwoyfrien' by di way? Well, mek I tell yu dis; yu come een here wid pregnant-belly, yu wi' fine yuself right out pan di street, yu hear weh mi a-tell yu?"

I couldn't remember when I had ever seen him so angry. He was generally quite placid, and most of the disciplining was usually left to Mavis. She, on this occasion, however, just stood beside him looking at me and not saying anything.

I couldn't understand what he had to be so darned mad about; Clive and I had never done anything that could be remotely construed as being indecent. The most we had done in public was to kiss goodbye on a street corner, and that was generally under cover of night. I was about to tell Daddy this but he gave me no opportunity.

"Mi an' yu madda try to bring yu up as a decent smaddy, an' dis is how yu pay wi back; by shaming us in front a wi friends. Imagine, people have to come tell wi seh yu deh conduct yuself shamelessly pan de road!

"Well, yu hear what A saying, and hear mi good." He thrust his face down to mine. "Yu drop dat bwoy right now, and don't mek mi hear any more story bout yu and nuh bwoy, yu understan' me? Now gwaan to yu bed!"

This was too much. I was being unjustly accused without being given a chance to defend myself, and on top of that, I was being banished to bed like a naughty child. I was not having it! And him referring to Mavis as my mother further fuelled my anger. Well, first of all, I was most certainly *not* going to drop Clive, and secondly, I was going to have my say.

"Daddy, yu haven't even given me a chance to defend myself before you condemn me."

"Well ahright, guh ahead and defen' yuself. Mek I 'ear what kyan justify yu behaviour."

"Well, first of all I don't know what behaviour you are referring to. You accuse me of acting indecently; please be more specific and define the charge."

Daddy and Mavis hated it when I spoke in what they called my 'superior manner'. I think a lot of the time they didn't understand the words I used and it annoyed them. They mostly spoke the Jamaican patois while we kids mostly spoke Standard English, although at times we spoke patois too.

"Okay! It is *alleged* dat yu was seen kissing Myrkle an' Wilfred bwoy pan di corner-a Brixton Waata Lane. Di *eye-witness* is somebody who nuh have nuh reason to tell lie pon yu. Defend dat!"

Daddy was showing me that he too could use correct terminology. If I hadn't been so angry I would have saluted him. However, now I had to do what he said; defend myself.

"I don't deny I was kissing Clive, but it was dark and I didn't expect anybody to see us because we were under the trees away from the lamp-post. And in any case you can hardly call that acting indecent, people kiss in public all the time."

Whoops! I think I re-ignited his anger which had appeared to be cooling. He looked me directly in the eye and spoke slowly, as if to a three year old, *"Not…mem….bahs…of….my…fam…bi…ly!"*

I sighed audibly. "Well, I won't do it again if you feel that strongly about it."

"Dyam right yu won't! An' nuh more a-dis bwoyfrien business until yu leave school an' is out of dis house!"

"Daddy, be reasonable. You can't tell me not to have a boyfriend. I'm fifteen, going on sixteen. Every normal girl my age has a boyfriend. And I'm not stupid; of course I'm not going to get pregnant."

I would never learn. I should have acquiesced and let the situation cool down. After all, Clive would be leaving for college in a few weeks, and by the time he came home for Christmas I'm sure I would have convinced them that I was mature enough to have a boyfriend. But no, once again my recklessness had landed me in hot, dirty water. Daddy drew himself up to his full height of six foot, and glowered down at me.

"Wha' yu mean A kyan't tell yu nuh fi have bwoyfrien? A who a di parent, an' who di chile? Well, A seh yu not keeping nuh bwoyfrien'. Yu undastan' mi? Now gwaan a yu bed!"

Now I was getting angry too. I was not going to be treated like an unruly child when I was almost sixteen years old, and as mature as any eighteen or nineteen year old. I kept my voice calm and even, although I wanted to shout at him.

"Daddy, you are not being reasonable. My having a boyfriend does not impact on your life any at all, and it is not affecting my school work. Not that you and your wife would care, since you don't take any interest in my school work anyway, so I don't see what the big deal is. Furthermore, Clive will soon be off to university and I will hardly see him at all, so I don't see any reason to... *drop*...him."

There was an ominous silence. I looked at Mavis whom I had just referred to as *"your wife"*. In that moment I saw with defined clarity the meaning of "….swelling up like a bullfrog."

Suddenly, the boyfriend issue had been relegated to the back burner.

"Mi an' *my wife?*" Daddy's voice was soft and incredulous. "Mi an' my wife?" He repeated.

When the slap came it took me completely by surprise and the force of it turned my head halfway around on my neck. Now his voice was no longer soft.

"Yu dyam ungrateful wretch, yu! Bright and facety to'! How dare yu speak of yu madda in dat fashion? Dis

Sweet Home, Jamaica

woman *is* yu madda. Yu don't know any other. Shi raise yu from yu was four week old, an' shi nuh treat yu nuh way different from di pickney dem weh come out-a har owna belly! An' yu tek yu wrenking self come a disrespect har like dis. Apologise right now!"

I had never felt such overpowering anger in my life as I felt at that moment. This woman was not my mother and would probably never be accepted as such by me. For the first time in my fifteen years I felt hatred towards fellow human beings. My spine stiffened and I looked my father square in the eye, daring him to do his worst.

"I will not!"

"*Weh yu seh*?!" It was not so much a question as a statement of disbelief.

"I didn't disrespect her. I merely called her your wife, which is what she is. She is *not* my mother, and I will *never* call her Mummy again!"

My father started to remove his trouser belt without saying another word. I knew what was coming, but I would take it without shedding a tear, I resolved. I had not been beaten with a belt since I was about eleven when Mavis had last beaten me, and I had threatened to report her to Child Welfare. This was long before I even knew she was not my mother. There was no point in threatening my father with that; it would only infuriate him the more.

When Mavis was beating, she would make us hold out our hands and she would bring the belt down on our palms, but Daddy just hit wherever the whim took him. The belt landed across my back and I winced but did not cry out. It was mid summer and I was wearing only a thin blouse, so I felt the full sting of the blows. Other blows landed on my legs and across my arms as I held them up to protect my face. I knew that there would be heavy weals on my body when he was done.

He continued hitting me while I did my best to hold

back the tears; I would not give him the satisfaction. In the midst of my pain I was dimly aware of a shocked voice saying, "Daddy, stop it! Yu gwine kill har?" In his agitation Delroy had lapsed into patois.

The blows came to an abrupt stop. Through blurred eyes I could see Delroy holding on to Daddy's arm and a silent struggle taking place. Suddenly Daddy sagged and sat down on the settee, holding his head in his hands.

Delroy had grown as tall as Daddy and was of a bigger build. Since leaving school he had become more self-assured and confident, and he now demanded to know what was going on. I did not stay to hear the explanations but ran upstairs to my room, passing the twins all agog on the way, and shut the door. I found the strength to push the dressing table behind the door before collapsing onto my bed in tears.

A little later, I heard Delroy knocking on my door and asking if he could come in, but I ignored him. He tried the door, but finding resistance, he eventually went away. I cried until I finally fell asleep, still in my day clothes.

I woke up very early the next day and was out of the house before anyone else was stirring. It was not yet six o'clock and the only person I saw was the milkman, who looked at me very strangely. I suddenly realized that I must look a sight. I had put on a long sleeved blouse to hide the weals on my arms and a long maxi skirt to cover my legs. There was nothing I could do to hide the fact that my eyes were red and swollen and the backs of my hands were welted with the belt marks.

I walked briskly down Brixton Water Lane and rang Clive's doorbell. His mother opened the door in her nurse's uniform, obviously ready to go to work. When she saw me she gasped and pulled me inside.

"Fah heaven's sake, Michelle! What happen?"

"They found out about me and Clive and Daddy beat

me," I said, failing to mention the fact that the beating had more to do with my calling Mavis "..your wife" than to do with Clive. I took off the blouse and lifted the skirt to show her the weals on my back and legs.

"My God!" she ejaculated. "What in di worl' is wrong wid George Freeman? Him don't know seh dem wi' lock him up, and put you into foster care?"

She looked at her watch and seemed to come to a decision. She went to the phone and called the hospital, telling them that she had a family crisis and asked for the day off. Then she got out a jar of ointment and gently rubbed some on the welts, before making me breakfast, all the while grumbling about abusive parents.

I felt guilty, knowing that my parents were not abusive, and that I had driven Daddy over the edge of his temper with my facetiness. However, I refrained from sharing these thoughts with Miss Myrtle.

Clive came downstairs just as I was finishing my cup of tea and was most surprised to see me at his house so early in the morning. On seeing him I hugged him and burst into tears. I forgot for the moment that I was not a crying sort of person. His mother told him what I had told her and he held me tightly, not saying anything, but I could feel the angry tension in him.

Clive also declined to go to his job at the Solicitors' and I spent the entire day with them. When Clive's Dad came home from work in the afternoon he and his wife decided that they would go and see my parents when they came home from work.

I was very much against the idea, but Clive agreed with them and so, against my better judgement, we all went to my house. At first Daddy told them not to interfere in his domestic affairs, but Clive pushed his parents aside and got very high-handed and legal.

He put on his barrister voice and asked Daddy if he was

aware that he could be charged with child abuse and have me taken into care. Daddy got mad and asked him if he was aware that he could be charged with carnal abuse as I was an under-age child. That really set Clive off, and Daddy was no match for him. I could see that he was going to make a brilliant barrister and I swelled with pride, noting that his parents too were proud of his handling of the situation.

By the time he was finished Daddy was looking at him with what I swear was admiration and respect. Clive finished off by saying, "And finally sir, I beg to inform you that your daughter and I have been seeing each other for over eighteen months, and she is still chaste. She will remain so for the immediate future, and I must say that I resent in the strongest terms your implying that I am other than trustworthy where her chastity is concerned!"

Mavis and Daddy looked at each other in silence, and I? *I* wanted to shout with glee. I could see the pride in Miss Myrtle and Marse Wilfred's eyes and I was so proud I could have burst. Now they would see that they were dealing with a man, and not a boy. *My man.*

Daddy finally found his voice. "Well, A still t'ink she too young fi have bwoyfrien'," but now dat A si what kine of a young man yu is, an' A know seh yu parents is good decent people, A wi' turn a blind eye. But mek no mistake, young man, if yu breed har, she out-a-here just like dat," and he clicked his fingers.

"You need have no concerns on that score," Clive replied with dignity, getting in the last word, and he and I vacated the room, leaving the parents to talk some more.

After they had gone and I was in my room, my father came up and knocked on the door. I was surprised and apprehensive when I opened the door and found him standing there, but he soon put my fears to rest. He looked at me for a moment and then he said, "Yu young man seem like a mature an' intelligent chap, an' if yu get pregnant I know it will be because of yu and not because of him."

I bridled with resentment. I wanted to say to him that it usually took two, but I kept quiet. He went on, "Mavis is still yu madda an' yu wi' treat har wid di proper respect, yu undastan' mi?"

"Yes sir."

"An any time yu feel yu too big fi yu madda an' mi fi taak to, feel free fi guh live wid yu young man an' him people dem, y'hear?"

I didn't answer. He looked as if he wanted to say something else, but then he just turned round and went back downstairs. I had this strange feeling that he had wanted to apologise for beating me, but I had no way of knowing if this was so.

For the rest of the summer I had spent as little time at home as possible. I still had my summer job at *Boots,* and spent any spare time I had with my friends or at the library, until Clive and I could synchronize.

I was cordial to everyone at home but friendly only to Delroy and Samantha, who was now two years old. I kept even the twins at a distance although I had no grouse with them, but they either didn't notice or they didn't care. They had just discovered *Mills & Boon* romance novels and did not have a lot of time for anything else.

But now the summer was over, and Clive had gone off to university where I wouldn't be able to see him except during holidays. Although he was not at home I still spent much of my time at his parents' house, where he phoned me at least once a week. I had recently taken to calling his parents Mum and Dad and I think Miss Myrtle was glad to have someone who hero worshipped her son as much as she did.

Meantime, Joy and Delroy were still going out together,

and Yvonne and Mikey were 'going steady'. Stephanie had recently changed boyfriends and was now going out with a Rastafarian who seemed to be at least twenty-five, if not older. Her attendance at school became erratic and she sometimes turned up with bruises, citing silly excuses like falling downstairs or walking into a door.

Joy, Yvonne and I were not fooled; it was obvious to all but the very dim that she was being physically abused, and the only culprit, as far as we were concerned, had to be the new boyfriend. We tried talking to her about it but she refused to admit it and when we pressed her, she bluntly told us to mind our own business.

She did not return to school after the Christmas holidays and we learned with shock and dismay that she was pregnant. The girls and I went to visit her at home in Clapham, and tried to persuade her to give up the Rasta boyfriend and return to school to do her exams. She would have time to complete the exams because the baby wasn't due till the end of July.

She told us that she loved her boyfriend and was not going to give him up, and she refused point blank to even consider returning to school, saying that she was not prepared to come to school with "nuh big belly" to be ridiculed by everyone.

"But Steph," I pleaded, "we'll be there to give you moral support. You can't let all your years of hard work go down the drain."

"No," added Joy, "and think about after the baby is born, yu going to want a job and what kind of work could you get with no qualifications? Come on girl!"

But Yvonne was more concerned about the physical abuse than the exams. "Look here Steph," she said, "we're your friends, and you can't fool us. This Rasta bwoy - what's his name; Winston? - is beating you, and yu know seh once a man start put him hand pon yu, him nuh have no stop fi stop. If yu refuse to end this relationship, yu in for a long, painful ride."

She spoke passionately, lapsing into the patois in her earnestness. "And if you won't do it fi yuself, then do it fi yu baby. Girl, yu not stupid. Yu know where this whole thing could end. Do yuself and yu baby a favour and leave the bwoy; now!"

Yvonne was passionate about women's rights, and could not understand why women allowed themselves to be abused by men. She stated emphatically that it could never happen to her; she would kill first.

Joy and I also made our contribution to the boyfriend argument but Stephanie would not be swayed, and we finally gave up and let her alone. But we continued to be friends with her, and although she no longer came to school, we all still met from time to time.

Joy, Yvonne, and I now gave our full attention to our studies. We would be doing O Levels this school year to take us into our A Levels next year. After my A Levels I was planning to attend Goldsmiths College at the University of London to do my degree in Media and Mass Communication. Yvonne had decided to go into teaching and was also planning to attend London University to do her Batchelor of Education degree.

Joy, meantime, was still vacillating between going on to further education and just getting a job when she left school. It wasn't that she didn't want to go to uni but she was anxious to start earning so she could leave home as soon as possible. Her parents were Pentecostal Church of God Christians who demanded her constant attendance at church, and attempted to restrict her from any activity which did not revolve around the church.

Whenever Joy wanted to go to the Pictures or anywhere else with either Delroy, or me and her other friends, she had to make up some story to tell her parents.

Claudette Beckford-Brady

She hated lying to them but she had made up her mind that she wanted to live *her* life and not theirs.

Joy was not as bold and assertive as I was. She tended to retreat from confrontations, preferring to give up her rights rather than cause dissension. She and Delroy suited each other perfectly and I was happy to have my best friend as my prospective sister-in-law.

Yvonne on the other hand, was boisterous and aggressive. She took offence easily and always suspected people's motives. Daddy would say "shi si duppy round every corner;" meaning that she was always suspicious and expecting the worse. But she was not timid; she was a physically powerful girl, tall as well as big, and she was quick to throw punches.

One day at school, in an argument with a white girl, I was told to "go back to your jungle and swing in the trees with your monkey relatives." I decided to treat the remark and its maker with the contempt they deserved, and ignore them. Yvonne took umbrage at this, and when she realised with horror that I was not going to chastise the girl, she took it upon herself to do so, and punched her, knocking out two of her teeth.

During our school life she had had quite a few fights, and most people knew not to rile her. She even had fights with her boyfriends; they usually came off worse, and her relationships did not generally last very long. At least up till now. She had been with Mikey now for over two years and they were 'going steady.'

Mikey was a year older than us, and had already left school. He was working as an apprentice carpenter at one of the London Boroughs. He was good looking, and knew it, and I felt he was a trifle conceited. I noticed that he ogled every female in his immediate eye-range, but he seemed to have a genuine liking for Yvonne, and I knew she could take care of herself.

Sweet Home, Jamaica

Indeed, she had had at least two fights already, defending her turf (Mikey) from other female predators. I tried to tell her that Mikey was the one she should blame, as the girls could not force him to take an interest in them, but she said that he was "...only a man, after all, and you know how weak they are, Shell. If somebody offers them something on a plate, they're not going to refuse. We are the ones who have to keep the predators at bay."

I didn't agree, but couldn't be bothered to argue the point. I only knew that I was not going to compete with any woman for any man. My man must respect me enough to be faithful, and if he wasn't, then it was "bye-bye." I would not compromise.

But luckily for me, I did not have that worry; at least, if Clive was two-timing me, it was a well kept secret. I wasn't worried about him being a couple of hundred miles away, and out of my sight; I trusted him implicitly. If I was being naïve – well, at least ignorance is bliss.

Clive was about to finish his first term at Durham University, and I was looking forward to the end of term when he would be home for Christmas. Since our relationship was out of the closet now I could openly visit him at his house, as well as be seen in public with him.

Daddy and Mavis had started to treat me with rather more respect, speaking to me on equal terms and asking my opinion on things. I silently acknowledged their efforts, and adjusted my own attitude accordingly.

Clive had been instrumental in easing some of the tension between Mavis and I. Whenever he came to my house he would insist that we spend some time talking to Mavis before we followed our own pursuits. Clive was a bit of a comedian, and could change his voice and impersonate people. He often had us in fits of laughter, and little by little the atmosphere between Mavis and I eased.

My sixteenth birthday came and went, and Clive came home for Christmas. Marse Wilfred invited us over to their house for cake and drinks, and the invitation was returned. Our two families were drawing closer, and often Mavis and Miss Myrtle would visit each other for a chat, while Daddy and Marse Wilfred would go to the pub together.

So Christmas came and went, and we entered the year 1977 with peace and accord at home, and my love for Clive sustaining me during his absence at university.

CHAPTER FIVE

Another Letter to Mama, and a New Understanding with Mavis

It was now the Spring Term of 1977. I was sixteen years old and in the Fifth Form, gearing up for my O Level exams in another few months. I was studying extremely hard, and spent almost no time at home, being either at the public or school libraries, or otherwise at Clive's parents house.

Mavis had complained that I only came home to sleep, but since I did all my chores when they were due, she couldn't really do anything, except complain. I had insisted that the twins now take their turn with the hoovering and cooking, citing my impending exams and their increasing age as just cause. They were eleven years old; it was time they learned to prepare simple meals.

Daddy and Mavis were showing a lot more interest in my school work now, and I appreciated the effort. I was not so angry with them anymore; I concluded that I'd had a very good life with them, and had never really been ill-treated. Mavis was in fact a very good mother, and if she hadn't been provoked I need never have known that I was not her biological child.

Mavis was petite, shapely, and very pretty. She was shorter than both Delroy and me and in a year or so the twins would also be taller than her. Daddy looked like a giant beside her, but they were very compatible and very happy. She had a light complexion and her hair was not black like ours, but a kind of light brown with flashes of red. She was the prettiest person I knew.

The Easter holidays came and Clive came home from Durham. I had not seen him since Christmas because he had not come home at half-term. I met him at the station and we kissed ardently, not caring if anyone wanted to report to my father that I was acting 'indecent' in public.

Our feelings for each other had not diminished over the two years and four months of our relationship, if anything they had grown stronger and I fantasized regularly about making love with him. But we had discussed it, and agreed, reluctantly, that we would wait till I was at least seventeen.

It was a rainy Easter and we stayed indoors much of the time. In any case we both had exams coming up shortly and we spent a lot of time testing each other on our respective subjects. One rainy afternoon when we were in Clive's bedroom studying, we paused for a kiss and cuddle session, and our feelings almost overwhelmed us.

Clive was almost twenty, and had had a few sexual encounters before he and I got together. He had told me about them, without naming names, and said that since he and I started going out he had not even looked at another girl. I believed him, and I knew it must be much harder for him to abstain than it was for me.

On this particular afternoon we had been fondling each

other through our clothing. Whether it was the stormy weather outside setting the mood, or the fact that we were alone in the house - both his parents were at work- whatever the reason, the intensity of our feelings almost carried us away.

Always the reckless one, I was ready to throw caution to the winds, make love to my man, and hang the consequences. I could feel how much he wanted me as he pressed himself against me and ground his hips. He stroked and suckled my breast through my blouse and suddenly I removed the blouse altogether.

I was not wearing a bra and he sighed deeply when I bared my breasts to him for the very first time. He reached out and reverently touched each one and his breathing became sharp and irregular. Seeing the effect my naked breasts had on him excited me further and I pulled his head down to replace his hands.

As his lips closed around my nipple I gasped and pressed harder against him. I took his hand and placed it on my other breast and he squeezed one nipple while suckling the other. I could hardly contain myself. I had never felt such intense, excruciating pleasure and I writhed in the agony of my ecstasy.

We fell onto the bed and I managed to get my hand between our bodies and undo the front of his pants. By blind luck, or instinct, I found my way into his briefs and for the first time in my life felt the tumescence of naked manhood against my flesh. My hand seemed to know exactly what to do and Clive moaned as I squeezed and stroked him.

He slipped his hands beneath my skirt and into my panties. I wanted more. "Take off your pants," I whispered as I writhed desperately against his fingers which were sending almost unbearable thrills through my body.

"Oohh God!" he groaned. "Shell, we've got to stop."
"Nooo, please!"
"Yes. Yes, we do."

He removed his hands from my panties and rolled away from me. I felt totally bereft. I was almost in tears. "I want you so much, Clive."

"I know. I want you too, but we can't, not yet. We have to be in control, Shell, and anyway I don't have a Durex.

I suddenly remembered what Daddy had said to me last summer. *"Yu young man seem like a sensible and intelligent chap, and if yu get pregnant it will be because of you and not because of him."*

I had resented his statement at the time but now I recognized that there might be some truth to it. If Clive hadn't put on the brakes I would have gone full speed ahead. I took some deep breaths and tried to calm myself. Clive got up and went out of the room and I could hear water running in the bathroom. I put on my blouse and straightened the rest of my clothing. When he returned he smiled at me and said lightly, "That was a close call."

I had never loved him so much as I did at that moment. I can't imagine any other nineteen year old boy who would have the presence of mind, let alone the inclination, to call a halt at such a crucial time, or to be so considerate of another person. I returned his smile and we hugged.

The rain had stopped and I decided that it was as good a time as any to go home. Clive agreed and he walked me home. Mavis and Daddy had gotten to know him slightly better and I could tell that Daddy really liked him. When they spoke he did not speak to Clive as man to boy but as man to man, and Clive responded in kind.

Daddy was home when we got there, and he invited Clive in and offered him a beer. Clive declined the beer but accepted a lemonade shandy, and Daddy asked how he was getting on at university.

Daddy took more interest in Clive's education than he did in mine but I didn't resent it. I was very proud of Clive and wanted everyone to know how brilliant he was. I even overheard Daddy proudly telling one of his friends that, "Mi daughter young man going university y'know. Him going to be a barrister."

I left them to their conversation and went into the kitchen to see if Mavis wanted any help. We had declared a truce and she had even told me that I could call her Mavis since I didn't want to call her Mum. I told her that I couldn't do that because I would feel as if I was being impertinent, and she had just shrugged her shoulders and left it. I continued to call her 'Mam.' But we had made sufficient progress in our relationship to have casual conversation when we were in the kitchen together.

It was the Thursday before Good Friday, and she was scaling and cleaning fish. There were a lot of fish as she had invited Clive and his parents to spend Good Friday with us. I took a bowl and a knife and started to help her without being asked. She gave me a brief smile and asked me how the studying was going.

"Not bad," I said. "I think I should manage to pass most subjects with fairly good grades."

"Yu too modest. A bet yu will pass everyt'ing wid distinction."

I looked at her in surprise. I had no idea she even knew such a word as distinction, and she spoke simply and with assurance, and her statement came over as being entirely genuine. I smiled at her and we worked on in companionable silence.

After a while I said, "By the way, where is everybody? It's awfully quiet."

"Di twins an' Samant'a deh next door playing with Colleen dem."

Claudette Beckford-Brady

The family next door, the Brennans, had recently arrived from Ireland. They were a large family; six boys and three girls. One of the daughters, Colleen, was in the same class as the twins, and there was a baby girl just a few months younger than Samantha. They had all become fast friends and spent a lot of time in each other's homes.

Mrs Brennan did not work, and had offered to mind Samantha when Mavis was at work. Mavis gladly accepted the offer; it was much easier leaving Sammie next door than having to take her to the nursery. Samantha had taken to the Brennans, all eleven of them including the father, and they in turn accepted her as an addition to their family, and sometimes it was a major problem to get her to come home.

Mavis and I finished cleaning and seasoning the fish and then I helped her with the dinner. She asked Clive to stay and eat with us and he accepted. I fetched the twins and Sammie from next door, with Sammie screaming a loud protest.

By this time Delroy had come in from work, and he and Clive shook hands warmly. "Wotcha, Clive; what's happening man?"

"Everything nice, my brother. How's the work?" Clive replied.

"It's great, man. I love it," said Delroy. "Money a little small, but I'm gaining skill and experience. I can now totally dismantle a television set and put it back together again," he added proudly.

"That's great, Del. I'm gaining skill and experience too. I can now totally say, *"what's the use of learning Latin,'* in Latin."

We all laughed and Daddy asked, "Dem still teaching dat thing?"

"I'm afraid so," Clive said mournfully.

After we had finished eating Clive helped me to tidy up

the kitchen, as it was my turn. I was glad that it was my turn because it meant that tomorrow it would be one of the twins, and there would be a lot more dishes to wash, what with Clive and his parents coming to spend the day.

The next morning, Good Friday, I got up early and cooked ackee and saltfish and made fried dumplings and chocolate tea. It was a spontaneous action; a spur of the moment idea, and Mavis was so pleased she actually hugged me. Clive had suggested that I make more of an effort to be amenable, and since I would do anything to please him, I tried. And I must admit, it made for a much more pleasant life for me too.

Clive and his parents arrived shortly after ten and the men immediately set up a domino table, with Clive and his Dad playing pardy against Daddy and Delroy.

"Well, Wilfred, A ready to dish out some six-love," boasted Daddy to Clive's Dad.

"Yu willing to put yu money weh yu mouth is?" Marse Wilfred challenged.

Miss Myrtle broke in, "No gambling on Good Friday," and her husband quickly reassured her, "Don't worry, Mummy, we only playing for nuts," and he held up the tin of Cashew nuts.

"And please try to play quietly," Miss Myrtle added.

"Don't be silly, Mummy. People can't play domino *quietly*. We have to *slap!* di dominoes down pon di table; like *suh!*" replied Marse Wilfred, and he slammed down a double six and grinned up at his wife. She sucked her teeth and went out of the room.

It had started raining again and so the twins and Samantha couldn't go outdoors. Delroy had brought home a second-hand TV from work, and they asked him if they could go into his room to watch it as they couldn't hear the one in the living room because of the domino game. He said they could, and they too left, taking Sammie with them.

I was at a loose end. I didn't want to watch television with the twins, I couldn't play domino with the guys, and I felt that if I joined Mavis and Miss Myrtle they - or Mavis at least - might feel that I was being presumptuous in wanting to join 'big people' conversation. Not knowing what else to do I retreated to my room.

I was still at a loose end. Joy would be coming over but I wasn't expecting her till later, because she had to go to Easter Service at church. I didn't feel like reading and there was nothing else to do. I turned on the radio and lay on the bed day dreaming.

My mind returned, as it often did, to the problem of locating my real mother, whom I was still determined to find. It was just over two years since I had written that letter which had never received a reply, or been returned. I wondered for the umpteenth time, had my mother received it and decided not to get involved, or perhaps it was still sitting in the post office at Gravel Hill uncalled for, and nobody had bothered to return it to me. It might even have been lost somewhere in the postal system.

I sat bolt upright. I ran that thought again. *It might even have been lost somewhere in the postal system!* Why hadn't I thought of that before? Was I grasping at straws? Well, no matter if I was; nothing tried, nothing done. I decided to write another letter. This one might reach her.

I got out my writing pad and took a pen from my school bag. I chewed the end of the pen and stared thoughtfully at the paper. How to begin? What to say? The first letter had taken me two days to write. I made an attempt.

8th, April, 1977

Dear Miss Campbell,

Sweet Home, Jamaica

I wrote to you in January of 1975 but got no response to my letter. I do not know if this is because you did not receive it or whether perhaps you decided to let sleeping dogs lie. In the event that you did not receive it I have decided to write to you again. If, however, you did receive it and decided not to respond, I am begging you to reconsider.

If you have not received the original letter, what I am about to say may come as a shock, so I would request that you take a deep breath and make yourself comfortable.

My name is Michelle Delise Freeman and I was born on the 14th of December, 1960 in Gravel Hill. My father's name is George Freeman from Joe Ground District.

It was brought to my attention that my father's wife, whom I had always assumed to be my mother, was not the person who had given birth to me. I believe I need say no more on that score.

What I would like to say is this. I do not wish to disrupt your life or cause you any problems or embarrassment, but I would love to hear from you, even if it is just to acknowledge receipt of this letter. Not knowing is the hardest thing of all, so even if you feel dis-inclined to correspond with me, at least please acknowledge receipt.

I would like you to know a little about me in the hope that it might encourage you to correspond with me. I am doing extremely well in school, coming top of my class in all subjects. I particularly like English, both Language and Literature, and I have hopes of taking up journalism as a career. I also read, write, and speak French extremely well.

I am currently preparing to sit my O Level exams (eleven subjects) which I will follow up with A Levels next year. After that I hope to do the University of London's Media Studies and Mass Communications Degree course, at the end of which I intend to become a journalist.

I am a voracious reader and hope to be a writer some

day. I love words and how they can be used to paint a picture like an artist uses paint. My Father says that I talk like I eat a dictionary for breakfast every morning.

My physical attributes are as follows: I am five feet eight inches tall, and weigh ten stone. My complexion is dark chocolate and my hair is long and thick. My personality I think is fairly pleasant, although I am often accused of being facety because of my outspoken-ness. And some people think I am a show-off because I use big words and do well in school.

Whoops! I didn't mean to ramble on like that or blow my own horn. Well I will leave it at that and see if I hear from you. If you do receive this, please, please write me back.

I do hope you and your family are well and I look forward to hearing from you very soon.

Yours sincerely

Michelle D Freeman.

I read the letter over and decided to send it exactly as it was written, although I thought perhaps I had gone overboard a bit. But what the heck, if she didn't get it, it wouldn't matter, and if she did at least she would know a little about her daughter.

I sealed the letter into an airmail envelope from my stationery kit and addressed it. Again I marked it to be returned if not called for, and put my name and address on the back. I would not be able to post it till Tuesday, after the Easter weekend was over, so I put it carefully between the pages of my French Literature book and then placed the book into my satchel.

Downstairs the men were still playing domino; you could hear their loud laughter and the slamming of the dominoes onto the table. Daddy had also put some records on the radiogram and a Derrick Morgan ska rhythm added to the jollification.

I went into the dining room where Mavis and Miss Myrtle were having their own little party. I asked Mavis if there was anything I could do, and she said I should slice up some bun and cheese and take it in to the men. I did so.

They were in high mood and several beer cans and shandy bottles littered the floor. Daddy looked up as I entered and said, "Bring some more beer, Shell."

I placed the bun and cheese on a side table and picked up the empty cans and bottles from the floor. I brought a shandy for Clive who wouldn't drink anything stronger, and beer for the others and then I sat and watched them play.

Marse Wilfred looked at the dominoes in his hand and asked Daddy, "Huh-much piece yu have, George?"

"T'ree piece," Daddy replied.

"Delroy?"

Delroy placed four fingers on the table. Marse Wilfred grinned at Clive and said, "We have dem, pardy, we have dem!"

I gathered from their conversation that Daddy and Delroy were about to get another six-love. Marse Wilfred stood up and brought down his winning dominoes onto the table with a series of resounding crashes. "Tek dat! An' dat, an' dat! Si deh Freeman, dat's how man play domino!"

"Bwoy, yu lucky todeh, Wilfred, just lucky," Daddy said ruefully.

"Lucky yu mumma frock tail!" Marse Wilfred ejaculated, then he seemed to remember that I was there. "Whoops, sorry Shell."

I grinned. "Oh, don't mind me."

They took a break from their game to eat the bun and

cheese and then went right back to it. Marse Wilfred shuffled the dominoes and they each pulled their pieces. They studied their hands and Daddy said, "Pose," and they were off again.

Clive looked at me and shrugged his shoulders. I could tell he had had enough but if he stopped playing his Dad wouldn't have a partner. I gave him a sympathetic smile and picked up the phone to call Joy.

She picked up on the first ring. "Hello?"

"Hiya Joy, what yu up to?"

"Shell! Great minds think alike; I was just about to pick up the phone to call you. What's going down?"

"There's a house full of people and I'm all alone. I thought Delroy said you were coming over?"

"I am, but I had to go to church this morning and then help my Mum do some things. I'm coming now, though."

"Thank God. Hurry, will you?"

"I'm on my way." She hung up.

Ten minutes later she rang the doorbell. I got some bun and cheese and some pop, and we retreated to my room and settled down for some serious girl-talk.

"I saw Steph yesterday in Marks and Spencer's," Joy said. "Her stomach's enormous, like she's having twins or something." She sat on my bed and tucked her legs under her, making herself comfortable.

"She's about six months gone, aint she?" I asked.

"Yeh. And she had bruises. They were fading but I could still see them. I feel really sorry for her."

"So do I," I said, "but what can we do? We've talked to her; we can't force her to leave him." I sat down beside her on the bed.

"Actually, I think she does want to leave him, but she's scared of him. At least that' the impression I got."

"So why the hell doesn't she go to the police or somebody?" I said angrily.

Sweet Home, Jamaica

"Come on Shell, you know the deal. Police don't intimidate guys like Winston. She would probably only end up with a worse beating. I see him on the 'Front Line' all the time selling weed. And I'm sure he's got some girls on the street hustling for him."

The 'Front Line' was the section of Mayall and Railton Roads where there were a lot of empty and dilapidated houses. These had been taken over or 'squatted' by some of South London's young black men who lived either outside the law, or on the fringes of it. Many of these men had 'stables' of girls, who were sent out to 'work' the streets as prostitutes, while the men collected the money. In short, they were pimps.

I did not doubt that Joy was right about Winston having girls on the streets. These men were predominantly dreadlocked Rastafarians who sported big hats called 'Beavers' and large gold chains, and drove expensive cars. We just couldn't understand how an intelligent girl like Stephanie could have gotten herself involved with a guy like that.

"Well," I said, "Steph has made her bed and unfortunately she's got to lie in it. I wish there was something I could do for her, though."

Joy sighed. "Me too."

We were silent for a while each with our own thoughts. Then Joy said, "Can I ask you something, Shell?"

"Of course. What?"

"You won't think I'm out of line, will you? After all, we are best friends."

I felt slightly exasperated with her. "Joy, how will I know what I think until I know what the question is?" I stared at her in curiosity, wondering what was coming next. She got up and closed my bedroom door after looking out to see if anyone was nearby. She had my curiosity well aroused now.

"Shell, have you ever.... Aahm, I mean have you and Clive...?"

I burst out laughing. "God, Joy, I've never known you to be so hesitant. Just spit it out, will you?"

I knew what she wanted to ask me, and I wanted to know about her and Delroy too. She was right to have shut the door. Some serious girl talk was about to go down.

Amazingly enough, although we were best friends, we had never discussed in intimate details the relationships with our respective boyfriends. I guess we either thought it was sacred territory or else we were afraid of jinxing ourselves. But now things seemed to have taken a different turn.

Joy looked sheepish. "I'm not sure I'm brave enough to ask you right out, Shell."

I decided to have some fun with her. "Outright, Joy, outright."

"What?" She was bemused.

"The word is *outright,* not *right out.* Ask me *outright.*"

Joy kissed her teeth and gave me a push. "Oh, give over, Shellie Freeman! Nuh romp with mi. Help mi nuh?"

The intensity of the situation made Joy fall into the use of patois. I took pity on her "You want to know if Clive and I have had sex, is that it?"

"You don't mind me asking, do you? I know we're best friends and all that, but if mi too fast, just seh so."

I grinned at her. "Fair exchange is no robbery. I'll tell you mine if you tell me yours. Deal?"

"Deal."

She was watching me eagerly, waiting for me to begin. "We *almost* did. Yesterday, in fact, but Clive put the brakes on."

"Were you disappointed?" Joy asked breathlessly.

"Devastated," I replied. "Now you."

She looked away from me and said, almost in a

whisper, "Yes."

I was fascinated and jealous. I drew closer to her. "All the way? When? What was it like? And where? Not at your house, surely?"

She shook her head emphatically. "Oh no! We… Delroy… booked a room at a guest house in Balham."

"So it was planned, then?"

She nodded. "Hmm hm." Then she burst out, "Oh Shell, I've been dying to tell you. It was the most wonderful experience of my life!"

I stared at her in amazed fascination. "Well, you don't look any different," I said inanely.

Now it was her turn to laugh at me. "Well of course I don't, you silly goose! I *feel* different, though. All warm and glowy inside."

I was too fascinated to tell her that there was no such word as 'glowy.'

She continued, "God, Shell, it's the most amazing feeling; I never knew there was such intensity of feeling ever in this world!" Then her voice became worried. "But suppose he finishes with me? I'm scared to death."

"Why on earth would he do that?" I was puzzled. "Wasn't it good for him too?"

"He says it was. But he might think I was too easy. Men are like that, you know. They all want sex with their girlfriends, but they all want to marry virgins."

"Not my brother," I said adamantly. "Delroy has integrity. I hope you used a Durex?"

She nodded. "Of course. Tell me about you and Clive. Why did he stop?"

"Well, I guess because we had discussed it and decided that we should wait till I was at least seventeen, but I think that if he had had a Durex we would have gone all the way."

Joy was amazed. "Seventeen? That's eight months

away. You'll never last out that long."

"I know I won't. That's why I'm going to talk to Mavis about going on the Pill."

Joy stared at me in what I would consider a mixture of stupefaction and admiration. "You never are! She'll go spare!" she gasped.

"Maybe not. I think she would prefer that to my getting pregnant. After all, she ought to appreciate the fact that we've been together for nearly two and a half years and never crossed the line. That ought to show her how mature I am."

Then, as if to belie my alleged maturity, I added, "Anyway, she must expect me to want a *little bit*. I'm a normal teenage girl full of hormones. But after all!" and we giggled like two naughty children.

Actually, it had never occurred to me to speak to Mavis about going on the Pill; it was just something that popped into my head as Joy and I were talking. But the more I thought about it, the more sensible it seemed. Sooner or later – probably sooner – Clive and I were going to get carried away with our feelings, and next time we might not have the will-power to stop in time.

I was under age so it was no use asking our family doctor to prescribe the Pill without my parents' consent, and the same applied to the Family Planning clinic.

As I pumped Joy some more about the intimate details of her first sexual experience, there was a knock on the door, and the twins came in with Samantha in tow. I could never get them to wait for an invitation to enter, but at least they knocked now, instead of just barging in without warning as they used to do.

"Shell, can you take Sammie now; she's playing up and we can't control her." As usual they shared the sentence between them.

"Why don't you take her downstairs?" I asked.

Sweet Home, Jamaica

"We did. Mummy says to bring her to you."

I sighed. "Okay. Come here Sam-Sam." I held out my arms and she came to me. The twins went out.

"You being a naughty girl, Sam-Sam?" I asked her. She swung her head from side to side in denial. "Tham-Tham not naughty. Tham-Tham good girl," she lisped. Wachel, Becca naughty."

I looked around for something she could play with and not seeing anything immediately at hand, I gave her my big teddy bear that Clive had bought me last Valentine's Day. The bear was bigger than she was and she loved it. I was going to have trouble trying to get it back from her.

Joy and I resumed our conversation and then started a game of Scrabble. Samantha was quite content playing with my teddy bear so she didn't interfere with our game. However, before we had gotten very far, Mavis called us downstairs to eat.

There were ten of us plus Samantha, so it was a good thing we had one of those tables that could be extended. The extension had been pulled out to accommodate our guests.

The table was laden with a veritable feast. There was no meat as traditionally we did not eat meat on Good Friday, but there was plenty of fish, both steamed and fried, with vinegar onions and peppers. There was yam, green bananas and dumplings as well as white rice, and a lettuce, cucumber and tomato salad. We washed it all down with a carrot and beetroot juice cocktail.

We had a jolly time around the dining table, eating, drinking, and as they say, making merry. Daddy, who had been imbibing beer for the better part of the day, kept telling what he thought were funny jokes, and laughing hilariously, not realizing that, for the most part, he was the only one laughing. Clive did perfect imitations of the British 'upper class' accent, and parodied his eccentric

Claudette Beckford-Brady

professors at his university.

After we had all stuffed ourselves to bursting, Joy and I took pity on Rachel, whose turn it was to wash up the dishes, and did them for her, after I had made it clear that she would have to take my next turn.

When we had finished tidying up the kitchen we joined everyone in the living room where a dance was in progress. Ska music was belting out from the radio-gram and even Samantha was dancing. Daddy and Marse Wilfred had us laughing fit to burst at their demonstration of the 'funky chicken' and the 'crush potato' dances.

When we had all danced off the dinner, Mavis served up apple pie and custard, which we ate in the living room while we watched *The Sound of Music* on TV. Samantha had exhausted herself and had been put to bed. The twins were watching Delroy's TV in his room, leaving just us older ones downstairs.

As I sat beside Clive and we held hands I thought to myself how amazing it was that at the age of sixteen I could sit holding hands with my boyfriend in front of our parents, and it was okay. I looked over at Joy who was sitting on the carpet leaning back against Delroy's legs.

She caught my glance and smiled, and I had the strange feeling that she was thinking along the same lines. This definitely could not take place in front of her own parents, who were very strict. She was terrified that they would find out that she was seeing Delroy; much less that she was having sex with him.

Joy was what we referred to as a 'Sunday-day Christian.' She had no choice but to go to church with her parents on Sundays and several other evenings during the week, and she had gotten baptized and was a member of the choir. However, the rest of the time she was just one of us, an ordinary teenager.

Finally the evening was over. Delroy left to walk Joy

home, and Clive and his parents started making moves to leave also. Hugs and kisses and slaps on the back were exchanged and thanks and goodbyes said, and suddenly, the house seemed empty. I said goodnight to Daddy and Mavis and went up to my room.

The following morning Mavis and I were in the kitchen and she was in an upbeat mood.

"Yesterday went well, don't it Shell?" She didn't wait for an answer but went on, "A nevah realize what fun Myrtle could be; she mek mi feel quite young again."

"But after yu not old," I said.

"Well sometime mi feel it. Anyway, it was nice having dem here. An' yu young man is very sensible and mature fah him age."

I could have burst with pride. I loved it when people remarked on either Clive's or my own maturity. It had been a long time since I had seen Mavis in so light a mood, and I suddenly thought that if I was ever going to broach the subject of my going on the Pill, now was the opportune time. She had just admitted that Clive was very mature; that was a positive sign.

Despite the confidence I had displayed to Joy, I was doubtful about her going along with the idea. It might even spoil her good mood. I glanced sideways at her. She was humming as she worked. It might be a long time before I caught her in as good a mood again. *Oh, what the heck, she can't beat me for asking*! I decided to chance it.

"Aahm, Mam?"

"Yes Shell?"

"I want to ask you something that might shock you a bit, but I don't want you to get all uptight about it, right? If you disagree, just say so, and we'll leave it at that, okay?"

She didn't say anything, just wiped her hands on a dish cloth and looked at me expectantly. My skin pringled and I felt the sweat start under my armpits. I was more nervous than I thought I would be. Mavis was still waiting.

"Aahm... Well, you know Clive and I have been together for nearly two and a half years now?" I paused, but she didn't say anything. This was going to be much harder than I had expected. I stumbled on. "Well, aahm, I thought, aahm... I mean.......I was wondering.....d'you suppose I could.... gonthepill?" I blurted out this last part at top speed, making the last few words sound like just one.

There was absolute silence in the kitchen. I was afraid to look at her, but when after a few seconds she had still not made a response, I sneaked a glance at her. She was looking at me as if she thought I'd lost my mind. When she spoke it was in a wondering, amazed voice.

"But anybody evah si mi trial? Yu nuh easy! Is mad yu mad?!"

Thinking I'd gotten my answer I spoke quickly. "Okay; forget I ever mentioned it. And Mam?"

"What?"

"Don't mention this conversation to Daddy, *please?*"

But she wasn't finished. "Fah heaven's sake, Michelle, yu only sixteen. Why yu t'ink A would-a let you start tekking di Pill at such a young age. When yu old enough fi mek yu own decision is when yu can start tekking it."

She didn't sound angry and I was thankful for that at least. And I suppose her response was no more than I had expected anyway. I shrugged my shoulders. "I guess you're right, Mam. Can we pretend this conversation never took place?"

"Well no, Michelle. A t'ink it could bear some more discussion. Yu having sex?"

To my surprise I found I was not embarrassed to talk to her about it. "No, but we nearly got carried away the other day. I just thought it better to be safe than sorry."

She was thoughtful for a while and then she said, "Well, Clive going back to school in a couple-a week, suh di problem wi' guh weh fi a few mont's. Yu just have to mek sure seh nutting don't happen between now an' when Clive guh weh. In di meantime, A have to t'ink bout it some more, far as God is mah witness, A don't know weh fi seh."

She went on, "A know what A *should* seh; after all, yu only sixteen, but A swear seh sometime yu mek mi feel like yu eighteen or more. Yes, A really have to seh yu very mature and responsible fi a girl your age. A have to give yu credit fi dat. Let mi t'ink bout it some more, Michelle."

You could have knocked me down with a feather! No harsh angry words. No threats to tell my father. Compliments, even, on my maturity and responsibility. And calm reasonable discussion. I looked at Mavis with new respect, and, I might add, affection. I went up to her and kissed her cheek.

"Thank you for not blowing your top. I was presumptuous, I suppose, to come to you with such a question. You are, and have always been a very good mother, and although I haven't really shown you, I do love and respect you. Even if I don't get the answer I want, that won't change." I added, as an afterthought, "Mum." It was a subtle change from "Mam" but it registered with her.

As I spoke I realized that it was the truth. I did love her, although it had never occurred to me before; I guess I had just taken it for granted that one automatically loved one's parents. And she was a parent in every sense of the word despite the fact that she had not given birth to me.

She was touched by my statement and perhaps more so by my calling her "Mum." Her eyes were moist as she hugged me. "Thanks Shellie. Yu know I love you too."

I hadn't thought of it before but I realized that she did love me. "I know you do, Mum; even when I don't deserve it."

She smiled. "Everybaddy deserve to be loved, Shellie."

From that moment on our relationship changed. I was still determined to find my biological mother, but now I unconditionally accepted Mavis as my mother, and no longer as just my father's wife. We drew closer together and I believe the rest of the family noticed it, although only Delroy remarked on it.

"So, Shell, what's the story with you and Mum?"

"What story?" I played ignorant.

"This new woman to woman closeness I notice between you two."

"Oh that." I pretended to shrug it off nonchalantly. "Mum just realized that I'm not such a little girl anymore and I realized that she's a great Mum, that's all."

Delroy hugged me. "That's great news. I'm glad."

Clive was very pleased as well when I told him that Mum and I had reached a new understanding. "I'm really glad, Shell. You need a mother to talk certain things over with; friends are no substitute. What brought on the change?"

I didn't want to tell him about asking to go on the Pill. If and when it happened I wanted to surprise him. "Oh, we had a woman to woman chat and I suddenly realized that Mum is a very reasonable person." We smiled at each other.

CHAPTER SIX

Silver Jubilee, a Thread of Hope, and the Pill

After Easter I posted the new letter that I had written to my birth mother and, in the hustle and bustle of O Level exams, promptly forgot all about it. Exams came and went, and the summer term drew to a close.

The Queen was celebrating her Silver Jubilee this year and the whole of London was full of excitement. Scores of foreign tourists descended on the city, as did the British populace from far and wide. Every hotel, every guest house, every bed & breakfast rooming house was booked solid.

Security was at a premium, primarily due to the constant threat from the Irish Republican Army (IRA) who had bombed sections of London on several occasions. They were fighting to get the English out of Northern Ireland and govern their country themselves. The English were not budging and the war in Northern Ireland had spread to the English mainland in the form of bombings of the London underground and other prominent London locations.

I wanted to go to Central London to watch the Jubilee procession but everyone except the twins were against it. Daddy said the closest I would get to the procession was the TV screen, because he didn't want to have to identify little pieces of my body after the IRA had blown me up.

Clive and Delroy were absolutely certain that the IRA would not let such a golden – or should I say, silver – opportunity go by without incident. I argued that with the massive security sweep and the thousands of police and soldiers in the city, the IRA didn't have a chance. They all scoffed at me.

Anyway, Daddy was adamant that we were to venture nowhere near the celebrations and so we all sat and watched it on TV. As I had predicted, it all went off without any IRA participation and I was most vexed that I had missed the excitement of the live celebrations for nothing.

Later in the evening there were firework displays all over London, and we were allowed to go to Clapham Common, where there was also a circus. The entire family went, as did Joy, and Clive and his parents. Samantha, who was now three years old, was enthralled with the circus performers and screamed with delight at the fireworks.

We bought fish and chips on the way home, and when Miss Myrtle saw how much salt and vinegar I put on mine she was aghast.

"Goodness gracious Michelle! Yu want to rotten yu bones an' send up yu blood pressure? Yu musn't use suh much salt; it not good fah yu."

"I tell her all the time Mum," said Clive, "but yu know Shellie – enjoy it now, suffer the consequences later."

I looked daggers at Clive. I knew he was making fun of me because in the heat of my passion I always professed not to care if I got pregnant or not. He returned my gaze

Sweet Home, Jamaica

blandly and I poked my tongue out at him. Mavis saw me and said, "Dat's a bit childish for a mature sixteen year old, don't yu t'ink?" and the twins giggled.

When the exam results came out I had passed all subjects with distinction. It was more than I had hoped for, because despite my confidence in my own abilities, eleven subjects took a lot of doing. This time the parents seemed genuinely delighted at my achievements and they bought me a portable typewriter as a reward.

During the summer holidays Clive worked at the solicitors' office full time and I worked three days a week at Boots Chemist, and volunteered two days at the library. I was torn between working five days, and earning more money, and working at the library, which would help me tremendously in my quest to increase my knowledge; the library won out.

I had been anticipating the summer holidays with great excitement, hoping that Mavis would take me to the family planning clinic to be prescribed the Pill. When a whole week of the holidays had gone by and she showed no sign of doing so, I decided to broach the subject.

Clive and I found time to spend together during the evenings and at weekends, and we found that more and more we wanted to venture further in our lovemaking. I had not told him about the earlier conversation with Mavis, and he still expected that we would wait till I was seventeen, which was still some four months away.

As usual he was the one to put on the brakes whenever we were in danger of crossing the line; sometimes the intensity of my feelings were so overwhelming that I didn't care if I became pregnant or not. But dear Clive was not taking any chances. He was one in a million.

I planned to approach Mavis one Sunday afternoon when the rest of the family were off on their own pursuits. Daddy was down at the pub with his cronies, Delroy was playing cricket at Brockwell Park and the twins and Samantha were next door at the Brennans.

Mavis had offered to straighten my hair for me because Joy had gone off to some church convention in Birmingham with her parents. I had tidied up the kitchen after dinner, and then washed my hair. I got out the little paraffin stove that we used to heat the hot-comb, and lit it. I thought it prudent not to approach the subject of the Pill until after Mavis had finished using the hot-comb.

After she had straightened my hair she asked me if I wanted her to put in the setters for me. I could do it quite well myself, but I told her yes, please. Mavis sat on the settee and I sat on the carpet leaning back against her.

We were very comfortable with each other now, and chatted more like sisters a lot of the time. However, I was careful to maintain the proper respect, and not to allow familiarity to breed contempt.

"How yu want yu hair style, Shell? Fine curls, or yu just want di ends curl under?" She went on before I could reply. "Yu know seh yu shouldn't use hot comb in yu hair? Yu have good hair; yu get dat from yu madda. She have Indian eena har."

My heart almost stood still. Mavis had volunteered some information about my mother. I turned my head and looked up at her. She looked normal; not like she regretted what she had said. She went on in a normal voice, "Yu still intend to try and fine har, Shell?"

I was caught completely off guard. I hadn't even realized that Mavis knew that I had been trying to locate my mother. I didn't know what to say. We were getting on so well now, I didn't want anything to spoil it. I thought carefully before I replied.

"Well, I would like to know her some day, but for now I'm going to concentrate on my education and my career. I have a great Mum already; if I find my biological mother it will only be a bonus."

I had obviously said the right thing. Mavis bent down and kissed my cheek. "Thanks, Shell. But di reason A aaks, mi an' yu faada planning a trip home around Christmas, and A was t'inking A could aaks around and si if A kyan fine out anyt'ing about har whereabout."

I stood up and looked hard at Mavis. She looked candidly back at me. "You would do that, Mum?"

"A would if yu want mi to."

"What do you think Daddy will say?"

She patted the settee beside her. "Sit down, Shell." I sat down beside her and she continued. "Well, to tell yu di truth, yu faada t'ink wi should leave well alone, but A told him dat yu have a right; at least to try, if yu want to."

"You've discussed this with Daddy already?" I asked in surprise.

She nodded. "Yu have to si wid Daddy. Is a part of him life dat him not proud of. Him feel responsible fah di break-up between Delisia and har fambly. Di only good t'ing dat come out-a di situation, was yu."

I wanted to know more. I had completely forgotten that I was supposed to be asking her about my going on the Pill. This was far more important.

"What situation, Mum? Can't you tell me about the circumstances surrounding my conception and birth?"

My, my, Michelle. Di *circumstances surrounding yu conception and birt'?* Well, A wasn't at yu *conception* of course..."

She paused, and I thought I saw a flicker of something cross her face. Bitterness, perhaps? A painful memory? Probably both. Daddy had been unfaithful to her.

She looked at me in silence for a moment. Then she seemed to come to a decision. She suddenly sat up straight and looked me directly in the eye.

"Look, Shell. Don't tek dis personal, but A really didn't

like yu madda. Shi did know dat A was along wid George an' dat wi have a chile, but shi nevah care. Shi did just waant George."

I had a deflated feeling. Mavis didn't like my mother. But then, I asked myself, would I like any woman who tried to take Clive away from me? *Not bloody likely*! I'd commit murder to prevent it!

"That's understandable Mum. But what was she like, differently? Did you know her well?"

"Not really. Wi wasn't from di same district. I come from Ginger Ridge and shi come from Gravel Hill. Shi did live nearer to yu faada dan I did. Har parents did have nuff land, an' sen' har guh private school. A hear seh shi was a very bright girl. Dat must be where yu get yu brains from."

We were both silent for a while. I was thinking that I now knew the reason why Daddy and Mavis had not shown much interest in my academic achievements; it reminded them of my mother.

"Sit down here, Shell. Mek mi finish yu hair."

I sat down on the carpet and leaned back against her. She started to put the rollers into my hair. But my curiosity was not yet satisfied.

"After Daddy brought me to you, did my mother ever try to see me?" I asked. Mavis shook her head.

"Not to my knowledge. But wi nevah stay a-Country long; yu faada buy piece a land in Old Harbour and wi move guh dung dere, and from desso we come a England."

"So Mum, if you don't like her, why would you want to help me find her?" I asked. Mavis used her hand to turn my head to the side so she could better put in the setters.

"A didn't seh A *don't* like har, A said A *didn't,* but it was all a very long time ago, an' wi was all very young. Everybaddy mek mistake an' A don't hold nuh grudge gainst har. Matter a fack, A'm di winner two time over, because A get both George an' yu."

Sweet Home, Jamaica

She smiled down at me and I smiled back, although a little feeling of unease had suddenly crept upon me. I didn't realize where the feeling of unease came from until later when I was telling Clive about the conversation.

Mavis finished putting in the setters and I donned a headscarf and walked round to Clive's. I told him about the conversation I had just had with Mavis and he said, "So, you're still planning to find her, and now you're getting help. And from such an unlikely source, I might add."

He didn't sound pleased. He had never been totally convinced that looking for my mother was the right thing to do, but I thought that since Mavis had now come on board he might not be so against the idea. I hated it when he was not pleased with me, and on any other matter I probably would have conceded, but not on this most important matter. I tried to pacify him.

"But Clive, don't you remember you said it was only natural to want to know one's parent, and that if you were in my shoes you'd probably want to find her too? Don't you remember saying that?" I pleaded.

"Yes, I do; but I'm still doubtful. This could potentially open up a can of worms."

"How?" I asked.

"Okay," he said, "there are a couple of scenarios here. One; you find her, she rejects you outright, or she has a husband and other children who know nothing about you. Think of the turmoil you could cause in their lives.

"Secondly, your finding her could inadvertently throw her and your father back onto each others' horizons. Suppose there is still some spark there and they start up something again? What would that do to your Mum...to Mavis?"

Again I felt that little flicker of unease I had felt when Mavis told me that she had won. Looking back on it I think

Claudette Beckford-Brady

I detected an adversarial tone to her voice, as if to say she was ready to fight for her man again, if necessary. But I pushed it aside as being in my imagination. I said as much to Clive.

"I think that's being overly pessimistic. Dramatic even. Daddy and Mavis are a solid institution; no-one's going to break them up. Anyway, I have a scenario of my own. How about this; I find her and she's delighted to see me, and welcomes me to her bosom. How's that!" I spoke peevishly.

Clive had burst my bubble of excitement over my newly acquired information, but I was not to be put off. Mavis had volunteered to help, and any information she could come up with would be gratefully received. At least it was a thread of hope.

I had completely forgotten to ask Mavis about going on the Pill, but now I found that it was no longer urgent. The time that was normally spent fantasizing about making love with Clive was now spent weaving scenarios around the finding of my Mamma, and our re-union. We still petted heavily but I was more able to contain myself.

However, a week after our conversation regarding my mother, Mavis called me and asked me, "How are things going with Clive?"

"Okay," I replied.

"Just okay? Do I sense a cooling off on your part?"

I was quick to deny it. "Oh no. Everything's great. Really," I assured her.

To tell the truth I was still slightly resentful of Clive for the stance he had taken over the search for my mother, but that did not change the way I felt about him. I still loved him to death.

"Hmm. How long yu an' Clive been going out now?"

"It will be three years on my birthday," I said proudly.

"Since yu was fourteen. An' we nevah fine out till yu

was nearly sixteen. Bwoy, oonu good nowadays."

She paused for a moment, as if considering her next question, and then she asked, "Yu still a virgin?"

"Yes, Mum."

I became quietly excited. I was sure she was going to bring up the subject of the Pill.

Sure enough, she went on, "Well A have to give oonu credit, both yu an' Clive." She paused again, as if not quite sure how to go on. Then she said, "Yu know, yu madda have yu when she was just seventeen. A was nineteen when Delroy born. Both of us was too young.

"Yu have a good chance fi mek somet'ing of yu life. A wouldn't want yu to have a accident an' en' up wid a baby too soon, suh A gwine tek yu to di doctor on Tuesday fi get di Pill."

Just like that. I didn't know what to say. Finally she said, "Well, waapen, di puss have yu tongue?"

All I could think of was "wait till I tell Joy." Clive didn't even enter my mind for the moment. I couldn't believe it, and Joy never would. She would be so jealous!

Mavis was still waiting patiently for me to say something. I managed to stammer out, "Th...th...thank you, Mum," before slinking off to my room where I could digest this new situation. Halfway up the stairs I stopped and called down, "Mum?"

"Yes Shellie?"

"Don't tell Dad, right?"

"A guess is a private matter. A won't tell him."

"Thanks, Mum."

I was embarrassed at the thought of my father knowing that I was, or rather would be, having sex. Mavis was really a great Mum. I resolved to do something special for her. Her next birthday would not be till next February, so I would have to create an occasion.

Up in my room, I pinched myself to see if I was

dreaming. No, I definitely wasn't. This was real. I was going on the Pill. I was going to make love with Clive. I wouldn't mention a word to him about it until the appointed time. He would be so surprised! But I had to tell somebody.

I'd not seen a lot of Joy in recent weeks. Since the Silver Jubilee celebrations back in June we had seen each other only a few times. We both had holiday jobs and when we weren't working we were with our respective boyfriends.

In addition to this, Joy's parents were pressuring her about her reluctance to attend church. They accused her of 'backsliding,' and got the Pastor and all the church people to come to their house to pray for her. She was forced to go to church, sometimes three or four times a week.

So we hadn't seen each other for a couple of weeks, although we had spoken on the phone quite a few times. I wanted to phone her, but there was no phone in my room. There was one in the parents' room, with an extension downstairs in the living room. Everyone was out again except Mavis and me. I wondered where Mavis was. I didn't want her to hear me phoning Joy.

I tiptoed to the top of the stairs and listened. Sunday afternoons were always quiet in our house as everybody was off on their individual pursuits. I heard only silence. I wish I knew whether Mavis was in the living room or the dining room. Then I heard her outside calling Kitty to come for her dinner, and I ran lightly down the stairs and hurriedly dialled Joy's number. Her mother answered the phone. Drat, this would slow things down.

"Hello, Sister McKenzie. Can I talk to Joy, please?"

"Who is this? Michelle? I'm sorry Michelle, Joy is doing har Bible Study right now, and then we will all be going to evening service. What is this about?"

Sweet Home, Jamaica

"Oh, it's nothing important, Sister McKenzie, it's just that I haven't seen her for a while and I'm just checking to see if everything is okay." *Liar!*

"Everything is fine, Michelle. Joy is finding har way back to the Fold, bless the Name of Jesus. Why yu don't come to church with us Michelle, and surrender your life to the Lord Jesus Christ?"

"Aahm, I will, sometime. Anyway could you tell Joy that I phoned please?" I was anxious to get off the phone since I couldn't speak with Joy.

"Alright, Michelle. Goodbye and God bless you."

"Bye."

I hung up and went back upstairs. *'Joy is finding her way back to the Fold...'* That's what you think, Sister McKenzie; she only killing time till she can run far from the Fold.

I was tense with excitement. What to do? I would normally be at Clive's this time on a Sunday afternoon, but he and his parents had gone to Coventry in the West Midlands to visit relatives who were over from Jamaica. I decided to go visit Stephanie who had had her baby a few days ago and was still in the hospital.

I could hear voices downstairs in the back yard and I went to the window and looked out. Mavis was standing talking over the fence to Mrs Brennan, who, despite having nine kids already, was pregnant again. I called down to them.

Excuse me, please."

They both looked up. "Hi Mrs Brennan, how are you?" I called. She replied in her deep Irish brogue, "An' a pleasant afternoon t'you m'dear."

I spoke to Mavis. "Mum, I'm gonna run over to St. Thomas' to visit Steph. She had her baby a couple days ago."

"Okay, Shell. Look pon mi bedside table yu si some

money. Tek five pounds an' tell har to buy somet'ing fi di baby."

"Oh Mum, thanks! That's really kind of you; I know she'll appreciate it."

I suspect that Steph being pregnant was probably part of the reason Mavis had acquiesced to my going on the Pill. Anyway, whatever the reason, I was glad. Now Clive and I wouldn't have to worry about accidents.

I stood at the bus stop for at least a half hour before the right bus came. There were plenty of 159s and 109 Blackfriars, but the 109 Westminster that I wanted was nowhere in sight. I had just decided to take a 159 and come off at Whitehall and walk back across Westminster Bridge, when I saw the 109 Westminster pull up behind.

It deposited me right outside St. Thomas' Hospital on the south side of Westminster Bridge, and I went to the gift shop to buy some fruit and flowers for Steph before taking the lift up to the Maternity ward. When I found Stephanie's bed I discovered that Yvonne was also there.

"Wotcha girls," I greeted them. "How are you, Steph, and the baby?"

"Wotcha Shell," they both replied, and then Steph said, "We're both fine, thanks, but this little blighter refuses to sleep nights. I'm knackered."

I went to the cot beside her bed and looked down at the little bundle of joy. He was a beautiful baby. He had a full head of thick curly hair and his little hands were curled tightly into fists. He was adorable.

Oh Steph, he's beautiful! Look at all that hair. Can I hold him?"

"Sure. I wish he'd wake up. He sleeps all day and keeps me awake all night."

I bent down and picked up the baby. A feeling of great love surged through me. If I could feel this way over someone else's baby, then imagine how I would feel over my own. I imagined the anguish my own mother must have felt when she was forced to give me up. I cuddled the baby close to my heart.

Then I had a thought. Stephanie had started to follow in her boyfriend's footsteps and had begun to grow dreadlocks. "You're not going to locks him, are you, Steph?"

Stephanie scowled. "Don't start on me, Shellie; I've already had the lecture from Yvonne here."

I quickly changed the subject. "Okay, sorry. Have you named him yet?"

"I thought I might call him Nkrumah Neziah."

Yvonne and I looked at each other. It did not surprise me that Stephanie had opted to give her son African names. Since she had started going out with Winston her whole ideology had changed. She was now living in 'Babylon' and white people were now the enemy; they had enslaved us and even now we were still living under 'Babylonian captivity.'

The only way to free ourselves from this captivity was to go back to Africa, to a place named Shashamane, which had been given to the descendants of African slaves by Emperor Haile Selassie, who was the Rasta God.

Stephanie had taken to wearing long African garments and head wraps and also had taken up smoking marijuana, or weed as it was generally known. Yvonne, Joy and I had risked Stephanie's ire by trying to reason her back to sanity. We had tried in vain. Stephanie said we were confused by our 'brainwashed education' and should start learning about our African history and heritage.

"*Nkrumah Neziah*? Steph, have a heart." I had to say something, even at the risk of angering Steph. "The poor child will be ridiculed with a name like that." I pleaded with her.

"What yu mean ridiculed? Him is African; him should

have a African name. I an' I parents sell out I an' I birthrights by accepting the slave names that they were given. It's up to I an' I generation to put things right by embracing I an' I African culture with the ultimate aim of finally returning home to the Motherland."

I gave up. Winston had her totally brainwashed. I despaired for the child, but there was nothing I could do. It was Steph's life - her child. I just prayed that things would work out for her.

I decided to tread safer waters and changed the subject. "My mum's taking me to the Doctor's on Tuesday to be prescribed the Pill," I informed them self-importantly.

"Yu too lie!" said Yvonne. "I don't believe a word of it!"

"Honest to God. Cross my heart and hope to die." I made the standard oath that said *'this is the absolute truth.'* Stephanie said sardonically, "An extremely wise idea."

Yvonne gazed at me with the same kind of awe that Joy had displayed when I told her of my intention to ask Mavis. "I do believe she's telling the truth, Steph. Bloody hell, Shell, however did that come about?"

"Oh, me and Clive nearly crossed the line last Easter, and so I told my mum that it was better to be safe than sorry, and she agreed."

It obviously had not been as simple as that, of course, but they were not to know that.

"Wow," said Yvonne, "I can just see me going to my mum with something like that. I would get one box cross mi face!"

"So, are you and Mikey relying solely on Durex?" I asked her. She nodded. "Unfortunately so. Maybe I could share your Pills?" she added hopefully.

"Don't be silly Eve. You have to give them your medical history and they prescribe the one that's appropriate for you. What's right for me might not necessarily be right for you. And in any case, they only give enough for one person; if I shared them with you, I'd have to renew the prescription twice as fast."

"My, my! Haven't we done our homework!" Stephanie quipped. I cut my eye at her.

On Tuesday Mavis took me to our family doctor to be prescribed the Pill. I wished that she had taken me to the Family Planning clinic instead; it would have been more anonymous – my family doctor had known me practically all my life and it was kind of embarrassing to have him know that I was going to be having sex. But he was in walking distance and we would have had to take a bus to the clinic, and Mavis just thought I was being silly.

As it turned out, it was pretty okay. Dr Perry was quite on board with the idea and said he wished more parents were as fore-sighted as Mavis.

"Teenage girls *will* have intercourse," he said. "You can't stop them, so the sensible thing to do is to protect them."

I left the Doctor's surgery floating on air. I could now legitimately have sex. I wouldn't have to sneak around and hide, or hold down my feelings any more. Clive and I deserved this; after all, we had been discipline itself over the two and a half years of our relationship.

Clive and his parents had returned from the West Midlands late on Monday evening, and I had not seen him yet. He had gone to work at the Solicitors office and so I would not see him till evening. Joy was at her summer job and I was going in late to mine. I would have to contain my excitement all day.

Mavis sensed my pent up excitement and said, "Don't mek it guh to yu head, Shell. Yu been pretty sensible up to now, and member seh di Pill won't start working straight away, suh if yu decide not to wait, use a Durex."

"Yes Mum."

She put her arm around me and said, "Imagine, mi little girl grow up," and I swear I saw a glint of a tear in her eye. I hugged her back and said, "I won't let you down, Mum."

She smiled and whispered, "Don't let yuself down, Shell; dat's di most important t'ing."

We parted company at the bus stop. Mavis was going to take a bus to work, but my job was within walking distance and I felt like walking. In fact I felt like running, and jumping, and shouting, but of course that was out of the question.

The day just would not end. And every customer I served was either stupid, or crotchety or just plain rude, but of course the customer is always right, so I bore it all with fortitude.

And of course, eventually, the work day did end.

CHAPTER SEVEN

A Lover's Quarrel, and Infidelity Discovered

I rushed home from work and cooked the dinner. It wasn't hard; the meat and the peas had been cooked from early this morning; I only had to make the dumplings and peel the food and season the pot. Soup was standard fare on Tuesdays in our house, as it was in many Jamaican households.

After we had all eaten (not that I could manage much in my excitement) I rushed upstairs to get ready to go to Clive's. I bathed in my favourite bubble bath and put on what I considered my sexiest outfit. I knew that the Pill was not going to give me any protection immediately, but since I had permission to have sex, I saw no reason to wait. The doctor had included condoms on the prescription, which I had filled at the chemist where I worked.

As I was going downstairs on my way out, I ran into the twins. They were going to be twelve in a few weeks and were pestering the parents to let them have a birthday party. Dad was on board with the idea but Mum said it was all right for him; he wouldn't be the one doing all the work, and had told them to wait till next year when they could have a 'coming of teen-age' party.

That was not to the twins liking; they wanted a party this year. They had been trying to solicit my help with persuading her, and were bending over backwards to be nice to me.

"Oooh, Shell, you look ..."

"...really nice."

As usual they shared the sentence between them, with one starting it and the other finishing it. It never failed to amaze me how they did that. Of course they also had independent conversation but invariably they would seek confirmation from each other. For instance, if Rachel alone had told me that I looked 'really nice' she would have ended with, "...doesn't she, Becca?" and Rebecca would have replied, "...really nice."

"Thanks, Siamese," I said.

"Did you ask Mum..."

"....about the party?" The preliminaries out of the way, they got straight to the point.

"Not yet. I'm waiting to catch her in a really good mood," I replied.

"But our birthday..."

"...is only..."

"...three weeks away." They finished in unison.

"That's plenty of time," I assured them. "I promise, I'll talk to her."

"'Kay then, have a..."

"...nice time."

"Thanks," I said again.

I went downstairs and told Mavis I was off to Clive's. She looked markedly at my outfit and for the first time I felt a little self-conscious and slightly embarrassed.

"Yu know, yu don't have to rush into anyt'ing right away, Shell. Yu wait suh long a'ready, yu nuh can wait a likkle longer?"

"But why, Mum? I've got some Durex like you told me to. Dr. Perry put some on the prescription with the pills."

She shrugged her shoulders. "Well, still be careful." She became emotional again and hugged me. "I love yu."

I hugged her tightly. I couldn't understand why she was being so emotional about the whole thing, but I loved her for it. "I love you too Mum. And don't *worry*, all right?"

"Ahright. Gwaan now, and don't stay out too late."

I stopped at the phone box on the corner of Brixton Water Lane to phone Joy. I had not seen or spoken to her for over a week, and she still was not aware that I had been given permission to go on the Pill.

I was lucky this time. Joy herself answered the phone. "Girl, where you been?" I demanded. "I've been calling you since last week Sunday!"

"Sorry, Shell. I got your messages, but I'm under 'heavy, heavy manners.'" Joy sounded rueful. "I can't make a move without the parents interrogating me as to when, where, why and with whom. I swear I had more freedom when I was ten."

"Of course you did. At ten you were not thinking 'boys and sex.' Are you alone, can you talk?"

Hmm hm. Everyone's out."

"Good. Your mum said you were finding your way back to the Fold."

"She wish! They're trying to *force* me into the Fold, but I'm just biding my time."

"*I* know that. But why don't you just tell them outright that you don't want to be a Christian? They can't force you to be one."

Joy sighed. "It's not that I don't *want* to be a Christian. But why does it have to be so bloody hard! Thou shalt not do this; thou shalt not do that... Christ, Shell, I want to have *some* fun."

"Hush, never mind." I tried to console her. "Time is the master. We'll be officially adults next year; then you can please yourself."

"Only if I leave home first. Anyway, what's up?"

I had been dying to tell her my news, but now I felt bad for her. She and Delroy still had to sneak around and snatch moments together when they could. When Joy was not at her summer job, she had to be at home or at church. She would have a little more freedom when school resumed in September but until then, as she said, she was under heavy manners.

I decided not to tell her that I now had the freedom to have sex, with my mother's blessing. That would be like pouring salt in her wound.

"Oh, nothing much. I'm at the phone box on Clive's corner. I'm on my way to see him."

"Lucky you! Your parents are the greatest." Joy sighed again. "I wouldn't be surprised if you told me that your mum was letting you go on the Pill. It would be just your good luck. I wish I had your parents and your luck."

I almost confirmed her statement but decided against it. I would tell her when she was feeling better; right now she was feeling sorry for herself and I didn't want to make it worse.

"Yeah, they are great parents; most of the time anyway. Well, I'm off. When will I see you?"

"Can't say, Shell. You know the score; any time I can steal for myself has to be spent with Delroy. I don't see nearly enough of him."

We hung up and I walked slowly down to Clive's house. I really felt bad for Joy. Her parents had put her in a terrible position by trying to jam religion down her throat. Now she sometimes lied to them regarding her whereabouts and she felt guilty about it.

Marse Wilfred opened the door. "Waapen, Shellie girl? Chile, yu look good enough to eat, A wish A was Clive age; A would-a gi' him a run fi him money."

I laughed. "Don't be silly, Daddy Wilf. If you were Clive's age, then Clive would not exist. Where is he, anyway?"

"Him upstairs."

"Mum not home yet?" I referred to Clive's parents as Mum and Dad.

"A guess she soon come. Yu want some dinner?"

"Oh, no thanks, I just had mine not too long," I replied.

"Well, A gwine finish mine an' leave. Mi deh pon a split shift, have to work till eleven tonight."

I went up the stairs to Clive's room. He was lying on his stomach on his bed reading one of those great big legal books that one always sees in solicitors' offices.

"Hey Clivey."

"Shell! Hi, I didn't hear the doorbell." He sat up and put the book to one side.

"Just as well Dad was here then, ain't it?" I said. "Whenever you have your head stuck in a book you can hardly hear anything." The same was often said about me.

I went and sat next to him on the bed and we kissed. Then he stood up, pulling me up with him. He held me at arms length while he checked out my outfit.

I was wearing a very brief pair of white hot-pants which hugged my hips provocatively, and a white tank top with no bra. My feet were clad in white strappy sandals with three inch platforms. I had been afraid that Mavis would make me change, but she hadn't. I knew I looked good. I had a shapely body; small waist, nice legs, a round backside and good firm breasts.

"Hmm, sexeee! You shouldn't be allowed to walk the streets alone, looking like that. Some-one might steal you." He held me up close against him, wrapped his arms around me and nuzzled my ear. "Did you miss me?" he asked.

"Nope, not at all," I lied.

"Just as well, I didn't miss you either."

Our actions belied our words. While we were talking we were kissing and nuzzling at each other. It was Tuesday evening and we had not seen each other since Thursday night, because they had left early Friday morning to go to Coventry, and had not returned till late Monday night. It had been the longest five days of my life, but now the waiting was over; I hoped in more ways than one.

Since Mavis had told me on Sunday that she was taking me to get the Pill on Tuesday, I had been fantasizing about how I was going to surprise Clive with the news, and how it would be when we finally made love. I was tense with pent up excitement and, although I was expert at hiding my inner feelings, Clive was usually able to read me. Now he drew back and looked keenly at me.

"Okay, spit it out. I know you're dying to tell me."

"Tell you what, Sweetheart?" I feigned ignorance.

"I don't know. But whatever it is, it's got you all in a tizzy."

"*Me* in a tizzy? That'll be the day. I'll have you know I'm the Queen of Cool, Calm, and Collected, thank you very much."

Clive put his two hands on my shoulders and playfully shook me. "Quit stalling, child, or else I'll have to spank you."

"Ooh, yes please, Daddy."

Clive pretended to lose interest. "Okay, suit yourself. I guess you'll tell me in your own good time. How are Joy and Delroy, and the rest of the family?"

Joy, Delroy, and the rest of the family were the last things on my mind. Clive knew that showing dis-interest would goad me into telling; it had never failed to work. But this time I would confound him.

"Everyone's fine. The twins are pestering the parents to let them have a birthday party next month, and Joy is under heavy manners at home." I spoke in what I considered to be a normal conversational tone.

He looked at me in silence for a long moment, and then he said, "Michelle Freeman, I don't know who you think you are talking to, but this is me, the person who knows you best in the entire world.

"Now, I know that you have some momentous news that you are dying to share, but you are obviously enjoying the anticipation, so I won't rush you. I will venture a guess, though, and say it is something to do with finding your biological mother."

Clive never referred to Delisia as my 'real' mother; he considered that to be Mavis. I ignored his attempt to draw me out. Instead I put my arms around his neck and started kissing him amorously. He resisted for a brief second and then he was kissing me back passionately.

He fell backwards onto the bed and I fell on top of him. I pressed kisses all over his face, neck, and chest. I heard his breathing change and knew he was getting aroused. I ground my hips against him and felt his erection against my leg. It never failed to thrill me that I could make him want me so much.

He groaned and rolled over with me so that he was now on top. He pressed hard against me and ground his hips, while one hand squeezed a breast. I was thrusting my hips wildly against him and getting giddy with desire, when we heard the front door slam and Miss Myrtle calling up the stairs.

"I'm home. Is anybody here?"

We jumped guiltily apart, and Clive tried to get his breathing and his voice under control before calling down,

"Evening, Mum. Me and Shellie are here. Dad's gone back to work."

We could hear Miss Myrtle coming up the stairs and we went out to the landing to meet her.

"Evening Shell, how yu do?"

"Hi Mum. I'm doing great, thanks. Did you enjoy your trip to Coventry?"

"Very much. Clive get to meet summah him Jamaican cousin dem an' I si mi brother an' sistah-in-law fi di first time in ovah fifteen 'ears. It was wonderful. Oonu eat a'ready?"

I told her I had eaten at home and Clive said he would eat later. She went back downstairs. I was ready to pick up where Clive and I had left off, but he seemed disinclined. I started to kiss and fondle him and his response was rather less than ardent; in fact I would go so far as to say it was only luke-warm.

"Come on," I whispered. "What's wrong?"

Clive pushed me away. I felt a sense of rejection, although I knew what was wrong. He sat on the bed and put his head in his hands. I sat on the chair in front of his study table and took a packet of Durex condoms from my bag. I placed it on the table. I glanced at Clive. His head was still in his hands. I went over to the bed and knelt in front of him, placing my hands on his knees.

"Clive?" He looked up. "Could you please make love to me?"

He got up abruptly, brushing my hands away. "Dammit, Michelle, this is agonizing enough without you making it worse!" He spoke angrily. "Look at you. Yu come in here dressed in that tight little thing, and throw yuself all over me, and expect me to have self-control! Yu t'ink mi mek out-a stone or something?"

Clive rarely spoke patois. It spoke to the intensity of his feelings. I replied gently. "Of course you're not made out of stone, and I don't expect you to have self-control. I just asked you to make love to me." I looked directly at him as I said this.

He stared at me with incredulity. "I don't believe you, Michelle Freeman! Have you heard anything I just said?" He grabbed my arm and pushed me towards the door. "I think you should go home, otherwise I won't be responsible for my actions."

He grabbed my bag off the table and thrust it towards me. That is, he started to thrust it toward me, but in mid-thrust he spied the Durex on the table. His expression, and his attempt to abort the thrust, was comical to see, but I dared not laugh. I turned away slightly to conceal a smile.

His voice, when he finally found it, was even more incredulous than before. He picked up the Durex and thrust it under my nose. "What, in the name of God, is this?"

"Don't be obtuse, Clive. It's a packet of three condoms. I want to make love to you and I'm bloody tired of waiting!"

It was not going at all the way I had fantasized and planned it. In my fantasy Clive was overcome with desire for me and was on the verge of throwing caution to the winds and make love to me without giving a damn for the consequences. I would then whisper softly in his ear that Mavis had given us permission to go ahead, and produce the Durex. He would be delighted and kiss me passionately and then we would make slow, sensuous love.

Instead, he was angry and I was beginning to get a trifle mad myself. When he saw the Durex he should have shut his door and started to make mad, passionate love to me, instead of waving it under my nose like a cheesy sock.

When he spoke again it was in the slow patient voice one used when speaking to some-one of limited intelligence. "I thought it was understood that we would wait till you are seventeen. It's a matter of maturity, Michelle, and being *absolutely certain,* before taking an irreversible step.

"I could have bought condoms at *any* time in our relationship, but I love and respect you too much to rush you into something you might not be quite ready for."

I hated it when he was patient and reasonable, which was nearly all the time. But I *was* mature enough, and I was *absolutely certain* that I would not regret giving my virginity to the man I loved more than anything or anyone. And damn it all, he was only twenty years old; he had no business being restrained and reasonable. He should be the one pressuring me for sex, not the other way round. I told him as much.

"Bloody hell, Clive Richards, you've just turned twenty; not a hundred! You should be bloody well all over me; Christ, I'm giving it to you on a plate! Why are you making me beg you for it?" I was really angry and my voice had risen. "Is there something wrong with you or is it that you are already getting it somewhere else?"

I had not meant to say that. I trusted him implicitly. Before he could make a response his mother appeared in the doorway. "What on earth is di matter? A can hear yu all the way downstairs, Michelle."

I was embarrassed. How much had she heard? Was she aware that I was pressuring her son for sex? I cringed mentally, but outwardly I recovered quickly. "Sorry, Mum. I guess I'm a little over-excited. Everything's fine, honest."

She looked quizzically at Clive, who nodded. She did not seem inclined to leave. "Is argue oonu deh argue? Mi nevah know seh oonu was like normal couples. A don't believe A evah hear oonu a argue before." She smiled at us.

"Is a good sign. Not'ing in dis life is perfect, an' relationship between man an' ooman is di leas' perfect an'di most complicated. Oonu have nuff more argument fi guh true in oonu relationship, but di secret is how oonu hangle dem." She smiled at us again. "Fix yu face, Clive. A gwine leave oonu mek oonu sort it out, whatever it is."

She went out and closed the door behind her. Clive was scowling darkly. The minute the door closed behind his mother he turned on me.

"Getting it from somewhere else? *You* are the one who is crazy for sex, not me! And why yu so anxious for it, anyway? Yu taste it a'ready? Is that why yu so hot for it?"

I stared at him in anger and disbelief. He *knew* how much I loved him. He *knew* I was a virgin and that I was saving myself for only him. How could he even *think* that I could give myself to anyone but him? It didn't occur to me, or even matter, that I had just accused him of the very same thing.

I felt tears prickle the back of my eyes. Inanely, it occurred to me that each time I had cried over the last two years had had to do with Clive. I had cried when the parents found out about us and Daddy had beaten me, and now I, who was not a crying person, was about to cry again. But dammit, I would not!

I forced back the tears and drew myself up to my full height. I stared haughtily at him and said, in a fairly steady voice, or so I thought, "Well, Clive Richards, if that is what you think of me, there is no more to be said. Thank you for a pleasant interlude; it was nice while it lasted."

I grabbed my bag, threw the door open and flew down the stairs and out of the front door before he could gather his wits. As I ran up Water Lane I could hear him calling my name but I ignored him. The tears that I had held back now came flooding out, blurring my vision, and making it difficult to see.

I didn't want to go home. I would have to make explanations. Joy was probably at Bible Study or something, and no doubt Yvonne was out with Mikey. As I turned the corner onto Brixton Hill I saw a number 95 bus at the traffic lights. The light was green on my side, so I dashed across the road and ran down to the bus stop. I got there just in time to put my hand out and stop the bus as the lights changed.

As I climbed into the bus I looked out the window and saw Clive running down the road, but he was on the wrong side and the traffic was still fairly heavy, although it was after seven o'clock. The bus drove off and I fumbled in my bag for some silver. It was a pay-as-you-enter bus and I had to pay before I could go sit down.

The bus was fairly empty at this time of the evening. The ones going in the other direction towards Streatham, Tooting and Croydon were fuller with people still commuting home from the City and West End.

I climbed upstairs and sat in the very front row of seats. No-one else was on the upper deck. I was glad, and gave vent to my tears.

This was not how it was supposed to be. Right about now I should be in the throes of passion, or lying in Clive's arms, sexually sated. Instead I was on a London bus crying my heart out.

I had not realized that the bus had reached the end of its route until I head the driver shout, "All out."

I descended the stairs and alighted from the bus. I was at Elephant and Castle. Obviously the bus was not completing its route to Cannon Street, but was turning around here.

I looked around. Being mid-summer it was still full daylight at eight o'clock in the evening and a lot of people were on the streets. There were lots of restaurants and a couple of cinemas located in the vicinity, not to mention several public houses.

I went into a Wimpy bar and ordered a strawberry milk

shake. I didn't really want anything but I couldn't sit in there and not buy anything, so I nursed the shake while I ruminated.

How could Clive treat me so callously? All I wanted to do was show him how much I loved him by giving him my most prized possession. It was quite obvious that he did not want me. I'd been throwing myself at him for over two years and not once had he taken advantage of it.

It wasn't natural. *He* wasn't natural. There was something wrong with him. No red blooded young man with raging hormones could be so reluctant to have sex.

So what was he doing with me then? If he didn't want me, why did he pretend to love me? In my anger and frustration I lost all logical reasoning. I convinced myself that Clive was a homosexual who only wanted a girlfriend as a cover to throw people off the scent. I conveniently forgot how often I had felt his erection against my body and how agonized he became when we had to stop short.

I sat for nearly an hour, crying quietly into my shake. If anyone saw me, I neither knew nor cared. Finally I realized that it was beginning to dusk up outside, and I knew I had to get home before full dark.

I didn't have to wait long at the bus stop. From here I had a multiple choice of buses to Brixton. Numbers 95, 109 or 133 would deposit me on Brixton Hill, but if I saw a 35 or 37, I could run down to their stop and take one of them. They would leave me at convenient points for an easy walk home.

A number 133 came and I got on. As usual I went upstairs. The upper deck was quite full tonight and I could not find a vacant double seat, so I had to sit beside someone. As I sat down I thought I glimpsed a familiar figure two rows in front on the opposite side. I took a closer look. It was Mikey, Yvonne's boyfriend.

The seat next to him was occupied but one just behind

was vacant. I was about to move to the seat behind him when I noticed something. There was a white girl in the seat beside him and something about their body language arrested me. I stayed where I was and quietly observed them.

They were sitting very close together and as I watched, Mikey put his arm around her. She leaned her head on his shoulder and said something and they both laughed.

I was in shock. I felt as if my world had just crumbled some more. Yvonne was madly in love with Mikey; they were going steady and she was talking about getting engaged as soon as she was eighteen. Now here he was canoodling with a white girl on a public London bus.

I got up and went back downstairs. I didn't want to see them. It put me in a position of conflict with myself. Yvonne was one of my best friends. Was it my place to apprise her of the situation, or should I mind my own business and leave well alone?

When the bus reached my stop I had still not made a decision. But I had big problems of my own. I decided to put Yvonne and Mikey on the back burner.

It was now just after ten o'clock and pretty dark. I practiced what I was going to say when I got in. Daddy wouldn't be in from the pub till at least ten-thirty, so he wouldn't require any explanations, but Mavis – well...

Clive always, without exception, walked me home whenever I had spent the evening at his house, and usually spent some time talking with Mavis, and Daddy if he was home. When I turned up on my own, Mavis would smell a rat, especially because she knew this was supposed to be a special evening for me.

I tried several different explanations in my mind. Clive wasn't feeling well so I told him I could see myself home. Or Clive had walked me to the door, but decided not to come in. I didn't like either of them. If I said Clive wasn't well, Mavis would probably call his mum to see how he was feeling, or ask him next time she saw him. I might just get away with the second explanation.

As I turned the corner into Josephine Avenue, a figure separated itself from the shadows and came toward me. It was quite dark; the street lights were spaced quite a ways apart and there were a lot of trees and shrubs in the front gardens of the houses, which contributed to the shadows. I felt apprehensive as the figure drew closer. I held my head down and increased my pace.

I began to feel conscious of my sexy white outfit and wished I were wearing something more concealing. I had been getting plenty of wolf whistles and leers since leaving Clive's house, which I had pointedly ignored, but I knew I was dressed provocatively. Now I was on a dark street, alone, at night, and I was scared. The figure was getting closer.

I decided to cross to the other side of the road, despite being on the right side for my house. As I crossed the road, the figure too started to cross. I hesitated, considered briefly turning back, but then decided against it.

"Don't show fear," I told myself. I decided that if he tried anything I would kick him in his groin, scream at the top of my voice, and run into the nearest gate.

As the figure drew closer to me my subconscious mind registered something familiar in his profile and movement. My head was lowered and I was watching him surreptitiously as we drew level. I went to step past him, and he held onto my arm.

I drew breath and opened my mouth to scream, forgetting to kick him in his groin, but before I could get the scream out, the person said, "Take it easy, Shellie, it's only me."

I almost fainted in relief, but anger came to my rescue. "What the bloody hell yu think yu doing, frightening people like that! And why are you accosting me on the street, anyway. Leggo mi han'!"

I pulled away from him and started to cross the road back to my side of the street. We were only about half a dozen doors away from my house. I felt totally stupid. How could I not have realized that it was Clive, the man I knew so well? But I had not allowed myself to take a look at the figure; I had watched it only from my peripheral vision.

He grabbed my arm and prevented me from leaving. "Calm down, Michelle. Don't create a scene and attract attention. We need to talk."

"I don't have *anything* to say to you, and it's late. I have to go in." I wanted to hug him and tell him I was sorry, but some stubborn streak in me made me lash out at him. "I never want to see you again!"

I tried to free myself from his grasp but he held me fast. "Be quiet and stop acting like a five year old! Yu know how long I've been standing around on the street waiting for you to come home? Yu know how worried I've been?"

I could hear the anger in his voice but his tone was low. "Well no one asked you to!" I snapped.

He was beginning to lose patience with me. "Are you going to stop acting like a spoilt child and hear me out, or do you want to go home alone and have to make explanations."

I stopped trying to pull away from him. I did not want to have to make explanations, which I would have to do if I went home alone, especially at this time of night. The situation was not beyond salvaging. Mavis was expecting me to lose my virginity tonight, so she probably was expecting me to be out later than usual. I could take the time to hear what he had to say.

"That's better. Now, do we discuss this misunderstanding like two fairly mature people, or do we call it a day and go our separate ways?"

My heart lurched. I couldn't live without him. He was the kindest, gentlest, most considerate person I knew. His angry outburst earlier on had been nothing more than pent up frustration. Deep inside I knew this, but his words had cut like a knife. I thought of his statement earlier. *It's a matter of maturity, and being absolutely certain, before taking an irretrievable step.*

And then I remembered seeing Mikey and the white girl on the bus and thought how Yvonne had given him her virginity, or her 'cherry' as she had referred to it. She could never get it back, and she was going to be heartbroken if and when she discovered his infidelity.

It suddenly came home to me how much Clive must care about me, to deny himself in the face of so much temptation, and I might say, generosity on my part; to be prepared to wait until he felt I was absolutely ready. He knew that once I made the commitment I could not take it back.

For the second time in one day, I started to cry. I cried quietly, making no sound, but the tears rolled down my cheeks and my shoulders shook. Clive held me against him and said, "Hush. Hush, it's alright. It'll be okay."

After a while he said, "Look, we can't stay here. Let's go inside; we can talk in your room."

"NO!" I found my voice to give vehement denial. "No," I said again, more quietly. There was no way I could get past Mavis without her seeing that all was not as it should be. The twins would probably be in bed; it was past ten o'clock, and although it was the holidays they were not allowed to watch TV after nine-thirty. I had no idea where Delroy was, but Daddy would probably be sauntering home from the pub any time now. No, it had to be somewhere other than my house.

"Okay," Clive said. "We'll go to my house. Come on."

It was only a few minutes walk. As soon as we got inside Clive went to the phone and called my house. He told Mavis not to worry, that I would be home in a while.

His house was quiet; only the hall light was on. His Dad was working till eleven, and his mum was on the early shift so she had gone to bed already. We went quietly up the stairs and into Clive's room.

CHAPTER EIGHT

Close Encounters of the Sexual Kind

Once in the room, Clive sat me down on the bed and went out, saying he would "soon come." I noticed that the Durex was still on the table. I wondered if I should take it up or just leave it. I decided to leave it.

When Clive returned a few minutes later he had a tray with two cups of Ovaltine and some chocolate digestive biscuits. He also had a wet flannel with which he commenced to wipe my face. I grabbed the flannel from him.

"I can wipe my face myself. I'm not a baby."

"Yes you are; you're *my* baby." He grinned disarmingly at me, and I wanted to smile back, but that stubborn streak made me contrary.

"I am *not* your baby. If I were, you would love me, but you obviously don't."

Now why did I go and say that, when I had already

agreed with myself that it was because he loved me that he wouldn't rush me into sex. I glanced sideways at him to see how he had taken my outburst. He looked at me, rolled his eyes heavenward and shook his head.

"Michelle Freeman, what am I going to do with you?" he asked gently. You already know that you are the light of my life. Do you have any idea how hard it is *not* to make love to you? Especially when you are forever throwing yourself at me? And wearing those skimpy little outfits? God, woman, have a heart!"

I felt terrible. Clive was right. I had been thinking only of my own gratification, and never really stopped to think how this whole thing was affecting him. He had already had sexual experience, so I assumed it was much harder for him to abstain than it was for me.

I wanted to make it up to him. I had been a total idiot, and spoilt what could otherwise have been a very special evening. Why couldn't I have just told him that I had been given permission to have sex, and been prescribed the Pill. Perhaps he would have been more inclined to forget the '*when you are seventeen*' business if he knew that I had my Mum's open approval.

"I know. I'm sorry," I said humbly. He came and took my face in his hands and kissed my lips and said, "You are too volatile, Miss Freeman. You need to learn restraint."

"Yes Sir. I'm sorry Sir. I promise I'll learn restraint. Is there a reward for learning restraint?" I smiled coquettishly up at him.

He put a mock-severe frown on his face and said, in a caricaturistical impersonation of one of his professors, "*Learning* the lesson is its *own* reward, young lady."

His expression and his tone of voice were so comical that despite myself, I burst out laughing. Clive did great impersonations when he was in the mood. He could do his parents and everybody in my family, as well as certain prominent people such as Prince Charles and the Duke of Edinburgh.

We drank our hot chocolate and ate our biscuits. I wanted to get straight into our talk so that things could be straightened out and get back to normal. Despite the light-hearted banter and my laughter I was still not really feeling any better. I wanted Clive to be completely pleased and happy with me again.

But he seemed in no hurry to start talking seriously, so I decided to open the subject myself.

"Clive, can we talk about what happened earlier?"

He drained his cup and placed it on the table beside the packet of Durex condoms. I wish I had removed it from the table after all. He picked it up and said, "We'll start with this."

I didn't want to start with that. I wanted to tell him the whole story from the beginning; how I had approached Mavis on the question of the Pill, and how she had eventually taken me to the doctor, where I had been given the Pill and the condoms. I tried to interpret his tone of voice to see if I should interrupt or wait for him to continue. I decided to wait.

He was silent for a few moments. I waited patiently, or perhaps I should say, impatiently, but I pretended to be patient. He twirled the pack of Durex around in his fingers, all the time looking hard at me. I wanted to squirm; I felt like a naughty child brought up before the school headmaster, but I maintained a calm exterior.

After a prolonged silence, just as I was about to lose my pretended patience and pre-empt him, he finally continued. "First of all," he began, "you cannot make unilateral decisions regarding this relationship. You cannot decide *on your own* that it is time to make love, go out and purchase condoms, and confront me with the done deal. We should have discussed it first, and if condoms were to be bought, I should be the one doing the buying."

I hated it when he put on his courtroom voice. And he wasn't even a qualified lawyer yet. I was certain that when he finally got into a courtroom to practice his profession he would be a force to be reckoned with.

"Secondly," he continued, "it was my understanding that the subject had already been discussed, and that we had agreed to wait until you were seventeen."

"You agreed," I interjected. He looked at me with his courtroom face and said, "I was under the impression that we had arrived at the decision together."

"I've been ready to make love to you forever and a day, Clive. It was *you* who insisted on waiting till I was *mature enough,* while in my own opinion I've been *mature enough* for a long time. Anyway," I rushed on before he could say anything, "my Mum put me on the Pill. I think that means I can have sex with parental consent."

I had never before, in our two and a half year relationship, seen Clive at a loss for words. His mouth opened and closed without a word coming out. His expression was one of shocked disbelief.

However, he recovered in an instant, as befitted his professional calling. "Shellie Freeman, do I understand you correctly? Your mother has put you on the Contraceptive Pill?"

"Yes." His tone of voice made me want to add "Sir."

I did not like his tone of voice. He should be overjoyed, sweep me up in his arms and make passionate love to me. Instead, he almost sounded angry.

"And I was not important enough to be included in the decision making process, because of course it does not involve me in any way." His voice dripped cold sarcasm.

I was perplexed. Whatever was the matter with him? He was a twenty year old man, for Christ sake. He ought to be ecstatic that we had the freedom to do what many of our friends had to do clandestinely.

I was beginning to feel unwanted and insecure again. "Clive, don't you *want* me?"

"Don't pretend to be dense, Michelle. You *know* I want you. That is hardly the point. You - and your mother - made a decision which impacts directly on me, without giving me the opportunity to have an input. *That* is my present contention."

"Yes, but it impacts *pleasantly* on you," I replied. What would your input have been? Would you have vetoed the whole thing?"

I injected a self-pitying tone to my voice and continued, "Well I'm really sorry. I was under the mistaken impression that you wanted me as much as I wanted you. I thought I would surprise you with my news, and that you would be pleased. I was obviously wrong on all counts." I got up and picked up my bag as a prelude to leaving.

"Sit down. You can drop the self-pitying tone. It won't work with me. Yu seh yu mature; well act like it." He spoke quietly, but it was an order.

I sat down. I hated him, but I loved him. He came and sat on the bed next to me. "Look here, Michelle, it's nearly eleven fifteen. I need to get you home. We'll finish this discussion tomorrow, but I just want to say one thing."

He took my two hands in his and brought them up to his lips, kissing each one. "I love you. I want to make love to you, but when I do, it must be at the right time and for the right reason. It cannot be just to gratify your baser desires."

"Clive! *Baser desires*? How could you say a thing like that to me? I want to make love to you because I love you! If I wanted to 'gratify my baser desires' as you put it I know plenty of guys who would willingly accommodate me."

It was true. I was always being propositioned, sometimes by total strangers and often by older men. If my head was easily turned, or if I hadn't been so in love with Clive, maybe I would have fallen already.

"Okay. You're right. I'm sorry." He kissed my hands again and got up. "But it's really late and I need to get you home. Tomorrow evening after work we'll finish thrashing this out, okay?"

I had no choice but to concur. "Okay," I said reluctantly.

Everyone was in bed when I got in. Mavis had left the key under a flower pot outside the front door, and the stair light on. I tried to be quiet going up the stairs but she was obviously listening out for me, because she came out of her room.

"Everything okay, Shell?" She obviously wanted to know how the evening had progressed. I was always a little surprised at my lack of embarrassment when talking to her about personal matters. I guess that spoke to how close we had become and how much I considered her my real mother, despite my longing to find my biological mother.

"I guess so, Mum, but..." I dropped my voice to a whisper, "...I'm still a virgin."

"Oh? An' yu stay out suh late? How come? A guess yu disappointed, eeh? Yu want to talk 'bout it?"

"Now? Don't you have to be up early in the morning?"

Dat don't matter if yu want to talk. Yu more important dan a bunch of geriatric white people."

"Mum! That's not nice." Sometimes Mavis got very frustrated with the elderly and often senile residents at the old peoples home where she worked in Balham. This week had started out to be a very trying one for her, and she had threatened to take the rest of the week as 'sick leave.'

"Yu right, Shellie, but sometime dem is too much. Nuh-body kyan't tell mi seh dem nuh doodu up demself fi purpose just so I.have to clean it up. Anyway, like A said, yu more important. Let's guh mek some tea an' have 'girl talk.'"

I smiled. I loved it when Mavis and I had 'girl talk.' It made me feel very grown up. She had told me all about how she and Daddy had met and how they had gotten together. She had told me how hurt she had been, and how they nearly broke up when she had found out about Delisia, my mother. She told me how Daddy had finally persuaded her not only to take him back, but to take me as well.

We made tea and sat around the dining table talking, comfortable with each other. I was wondering what she had told Daddy about me being out so late. I asked her and she said, "Yu nuh worry yuself 'bout dat."

I had not intended to relate to her the entire events of the evening; I had intended to edit out the part about my running off in tears and ending up at Elephant and Castle, but I found myself telling her everything, including my seeing Yvonne's boyfriend on the bus with a white girl.

"Why do men have to do that, Mum? Don't they know how painful it is for the other person? I'd die if I found out that Clive was cheating on me."

"Well yu certainly wouldn't die. A can vouch for dat. But don't yu believe dat only men cheat. Woman do it to', an' A don't t'ink is any less painful fi di man."

I hadn't thought of that, but I supposed she was right. But she wasn't really interested in that particular subject just at the moment. She wanted to know why Clive was not pleased at the steps we had taken.

"I suppose because he still thinks I'm not mature enough, but mainly, I think, because he wasn't a part of the decision making process."

Mavis ignored the second reason and pounced on the first one. "Not mature enough? Really?" She was surprised. "Why him would t'ink that? Yu seem pretty mature to mi."

"Thanks." I smiled at her. "But Clive only wants to make sure that I am, in his own words, *'absolutely certain, before taking an irreversible step.'*

Mavis smiled. "Di more A hear of dat bwoy, di more A like him. An' him quite right; him should-a involve inna di decision. A wi' apologize to him tomorrow."

We sipped our tea in companionable silence for a while, and then Mavis said, "Well, mi bed calling mi. Let's go up."

I quickly rinsed out the cups and we went up to bed.

I was very tired on Wednesday morning after my late night, but I dragged myself out of bed and went in to work. It was one of the longest days I had ever known, but eventually evening came. I rushed home from work and did my few chores. I did not have to cook because Mavis had come home early. Despite her threat to take the rest of the week as sick leave, she had gone to work as usual.

At dinner the twins kept kicking me under the table and rolling their eyes in Mavis' direction. I guiltily remembered that I had promised to ask her about their birthday party. Every one was at the table, including Delroy of whom I had not seen much in recent days. I decided to bring up the subject; if Mavis was still dead set against it, we could gang up on her and overwhelm her.

"Mum, have you decided about the twins' party yet?" I opened the subject. The twins looked at Mum in eager anticipation. Her reply put a scowl on their faces.

"A tell di twins a'ready to wait till next year. A can't tek on nuh extra work now, t'ings too stressful at work."

I decided to put in a big effort on the twins' behalf. "If it's just a matter of the work I would help and I could get either Joy or Yvonne to give a hand. In fact you wouldn't have to do anything; I'm pretty sure we could arrange the whole thing ourselves, as long as we get the money to buy the necessary things."

I looked at Daddy as I said this. He was not averse to the twins having a party and had already said he would finance it. He nodded his head. "No problem, but only if yu madda agree."

Everyone looked at Mavis expectantly. She couldn't really come up with any more objections. Daddy would pay, we would do the work; she was effectively out-maneuvered. She shrugged her shoulders. "Okay, oonu win. Guh ahead an' plan oonu party."

The twins were ecstatic. "Thanks Mum..."

"...and Dad and..."

"Shell." They finished together.

It was my turn to tidy up the kitchen after dinner, but fair exchange being no robbery I got the twins to take my turn. I hurriedly bathed and left to go to Clive's.

He opened the door himself. Marse Wilfred and Miss Myrtle were both at work. "Wotcha Shell, come on in." He closed the front door behind me and then we kissed. Things were back to normal between us, there was no residual tension from last night.

"Your Mum phoned me a while ago," Clive said.

"She did? What did she say?"

"She apologized for not involving me in the decision to put you on the Pill. She said that she was impressed by our forbearance and felt that we were both mature enough to ascend to the next level in our relationship."

I looked at him sceptically. "G'weh! Yu too damn lie, Clive Richards. My Mum probably never heard the words 'forbearance' and 'ascend' never mind use them in a sentence."

"Yu too damn patronizing, Michelle Freeman," Clive retorted. "You make it sound like your mother is illiterate. She is a much brighter woman than you give her credit for, and although she may not have used those exact words, her meaning was quite clear."

Clive was always championing Mavis. He said that I put her down all the time, and not only Mavis but everyone I perceived not to be as intelligent as me. He said I was too full of my own importance, and that if people didn't use big words, I looked down on them, which I vehemently denied. Still, I felt a little guilty at belittling Mavis' vocabulary and I also wanted Clive to be absolutely pleased and happy with me again, so I placated him.

"You're right. I'm sorry." I do tend to under-estimate other people's abilities. I'll try to do better."

We were downstairs in Clive's living room. I was impatient for him to say, "Let's go upstairs," but he seemed content to just sit there and chat. I had thought that since he had spoken to Mavis he would be as anxious as me to 'ascend to the next level' of our relationship.

So what on earth was the matter with him? Why hadn't he taken me straight upstairs and made love to me? I dared not bring up the subject to him because I didn't want him to think I was sex mad, but I wanted him so badly that it was all I could do to act casually normal.

`I was not fooling Clive. He read me like a book and after a few more minutes of general chit chat, when it became apparent to him that my mind was elsewhere, he said, "Come here," and I went and sat next to him on the sofa. He took my face in his hands and said, "I know what's on your mind, but all in good time." He kissed me and stood up. "Let's go upstairs."

At last! My excitement knew no bounds. I stood up and he took my hand and we went upstairs to his room. When he opened his room door, I gasped in pleased surprise. Although it was still daylight outside, his window curtains were closed and there was an Avon perfumed candle burning on the table. The table itself was spread with a white cloth, and a bottle of grape juice was cooling in an ice bucket. There was a dish with a selection of nuts and fruit, and, the crowning glory of the table, in the centre, was a vase of red and white roses.

"Oh Clive! It's beautiful! When did you do all this?" I buried my face in the roses. The scent was heavenly.

Clive smiled without answering. I could see that he was pleased that I was pleased. "Sit down, Shell." He put an Al Green cassette into his tape deck and opened the grape juice. He poured two glasses and handed one to me.

"A toast," he said, holding up his glass. I felt very womanly. Here I was, about to become a woman in the full sense of the word, drinking grape juice with my soon to be lover. I held up my glass and smiled into my man's eyes. He smiled back into mine, and said softly, "To good loving."

I was weak with excitement and anticipation. Clive held his glass to my lips and I followed his cue and did the same to him and we fed each other grape juice. Then he kissed me and, saying he would return shortly, he went out of the room.

I sipped my juice and nibbled a peanut. I knew that Clive was bathing as I could hear the water splashing. He must have run his bath earlier when he made the other preparations. I waited impatiently for him to return, all the time speculating on how it would be to make love for the first time. I suddenly thought of his parents. How soon would they be home from work? I wasn't particularly eager for them to know that I was in bed with their son.

Clive came out of the bathroom in a terry robe, smelling of Imperial Leather. He shut the door behind him as he came into the room, and locked it. Locking it was totally unnecessary; his parents would never dream of entering his room without knocking and waiting for an invitation.

I thought how ironic it was that Clive did not need a lock on his door, and yet he had one, while I who really needed it, had none.

Still, I was afraid that his parents would come home while we were in the throes of passion, and realize what we were doing. It would be okay for them to know *after* we had done it, but I would be mortified if they caught us at it. I voiced my concerns to Clive.

"Relax. They won't be home for hours."

"They won't? How comes?"

"I told them I wanted some quality time alone with my best girl."

I was aghast. "Clive! You might as well have come right out and told them we were going to have sex!"

Clive took a sip of his grape juice and popped a nut into his mouth. He grinned at me. "Shell, they weren't born yesterday. Anyway, what's the big deal; you have the thickest skin I know. Don't tell me you're starting to get sensitive?"

I glared at him. "I'll have you know I am *extremely* sensitive, Clive Richards!" He sat on the bed beside me. "Shut up and kiss me," he commanded.

I didn't need telling twice. I put my arms around his neck and glued my lips to his. He kissed me back passionately and we fell back on the bed. I had made sure to wear something that would not be difficult to get out of, and Clive had already found his way beyond the buttons, to my breasts.

I gasped as he lightly ran his finger around a nipple. Then he rolled it between his finger and thumb and I could have died and gone to heaven, right there and then. I somehow managed to drag the blouse right off and bared my entire bosom to him. He kissed both breasts and then closed his mouth around a nipple and suckled hard, while fondling the other breast.

I couldn't stand it! The pleasure was too intense. "Ooh, Clive," I moaned, all the while trying to get him out

Sweet Home, Jamaica

of his robe. I struggled with the robe but it just refused to come off. I groaned in frustration and Clive, ever sensitive to my needs, left my breasts long enough to slide the robe over his shoulders and down his arms.

Now I could feel his skin. But it wasn't enough. I needed us both naked. I pulled away from Clive and quickly slipped out of my skirt and panties. He took the opportunity to completely discard his robe. For the first time we were both completely naked in front of each other.

There was no hint of embarrassment or inhibition from me. I didn't feel self-conscious in any way; it felt absolutely right to be here with Clive like this. He held me at arms length and looked at me in the dim light of the single candle. His eyes roamed my body from head to toe and he sighed deeply and whispered, "You're beautiful, Shell, every inch of you," before he pulled me into his arms.

I too had been examining his body. I had never seen a naked man before. My friends and I had sniggered over magazines with pictures of naked men and women, but in the flesh, this was my first experience. On previous occasions I had felt the evidence of Clive's manhood, but I had never actually seen it. Now the full glory of it was standing erect in front of me.

Clive was kissing me, but I was ready to proceed further. Never the patient one - and seeing quite clearly that foreplay could be dispensed with; after all, Clive was more than ready, the evidence was there pressing against me – I pulled him down on top of me and thrust my hips hard against him.

He groaned and maneuvered himself into position, and without preliminaries we joined and became one.

I had watched a movie once where the female star was asked by her leading man, after they had made love, *"Did the earth move for you, darling?"* At the time I had thought it to be a stupid question, but now I could understand it absolutely.

Not only did the earth move, but I was swept up and up, away into the nether regions of space, and whirled around in a vortex of exquisitely agonizing sensations, which expanded and expanded until they exploded into zillions and zillions of pin-pricks of pure and absolute ecstatic pleasure.

When I finally floated back to earth and was able to open my eyes and look at Clive, I could see that he too had been whirling through space; not that I had had any doubts, I had felt him spinning through the vortex with me. We held each other tightly and tried to steady our breathing and our heartbeats, and regain our equilibrium.

He nuzzled his face into my neck and whispered, "God, Shell, I never knew such intense pleasure. I was sure I had died and gone to heaven!"

"Hmm, me too," I whispered back. We lay there in each other's arms, stroking and caressing, while we spoke softly to each other.

Suddenly Clive sat up abruptly with an agonized look on his face. "Oh my God!"

"Clive, what is it?" His expression made me afraid, and when he didn't answer, but just stood up and stared at the table, I finally understood. After all our careful planning and sensible precautions, we had forgotten to use the condom!

We stared at each other in consternation. Clive was absolutely broken up, more so than me. If I became pregnant he would never forgive himself.

"Christ, Shell, I'm really sorry." He thumped his forehead with the heel of his hand. "What an idiot I am. How could I have forgotten something so important? Your Mum will never forgive me, after I assured her that I would take such good care of you. And your Dad – well, I don't even want to think about what his reaction will be."

He was beginning to panic. He looked at me with such expectations of doom written on his face that I wanted to comfort him. "Ease up, Clive. It's not the end of the world. They might never need to know 'cause I might not be pregnant. In fact, I'm sure I'm not. I should be in my safe period."

"Safe period?" He looked at me bemusedly and then he realized where I was headed. "Oh!" He pounced on the ray of hope. "When was your last menses?"

Anybody other than Clive would have said 'period', he had to say menses. "I'm due one in a few days."

He didn't look relieved. "That doesn't mean you can't be pregnant."

"It's highly unlikely; there's only a small window of opportunity for conceiving each month. I'm absolutely certain I'm not pregnant."

He still did not seem convinced. I tried again to reassure him. "Relax, Clive. Here, have some grape juice." I topped up his glass and handed it to him. The candle was burning down and had begun to flicker. I blew it out and turned on the light. I moved around quite unselfconsciously in my naked body. It just felt so natural to be naked with Clive that I didn't even realize that I was, until I saw him looking intently at my body.

My skin tingled. I could tell that he wanted me again. I picked up the condom and placed it on the bed, and then I stood behind him and wrapped my arms around his body, while I pressed myself against him. "Love me again," I whispered against his ear.

He turned around to face me, bent down and picked me up bodily, and deposited me on the bed. He lay down beside me and we kissed deeply. Our hands and lips caressed and explored each other's bodies until the sensations again became almost too intense to bear. This time we had taken our time and slowly built up the excitement until we were again ready for the ultimate.

Then he took the condom and ripped it open. I watched him impatiently as he squeezed it meticulously before rolling it onto his erect organ. I could see that having to break stride to put on a condom could be a real kill-joy, and I was glad that in a few weeks from now, when the Pill started working, we could dispense with them completely. I conveniently forgot for the moment that in a few weeks I would be back in school and Clive would be back at university in Durham.

This time our lovemaking was much slower; several times we approached the brink of orgasm and retreated, only to approach it again. Finally we could no longer contain ourselves and when the release came it left us again completely out of breath and trembling.

Afterwards we must have both dozed because I was jerked awake by the ringing of the telephone. Clive roused himself and grabbed his robe, leaving the room. I looked at the clock and saw that it was nine-forty-five. I couldn't believe it. Where had the last three and a half hours gone?

I got up and went into the bathroom. I decided to have a bath before going home so I turned the taps on to fill the bath. As I came out of the bathroom Clive returned from answering the phone.

"That was Yvonne. She got my number from your Mum. There's some problem with Stephanie; they're at St. Thomas' hospital."

My heart dropped. That probably meant that Winston had beaten Steph again. What was the matter with him? And with her, to stay with him.

Clive and I shared the bath. If I hadn't been in such a hurry to get to the hospital, it would have been a wonderful experience, but as it was, I rushed in, had a quick wash down, and rushed out. Clive cleaned the bath for me; it was a pleasant surprise – Daddy and Delroy never cleaned the bath, and I understood from other people that the men in their families didn't either.

I borrowed Clive's phone to call Mavis and tell her that I was going to the hospital. She was expecting that but she told me not to stay long as it was already after ten. When Clive and I arrived at the Accident and Emergency unit Yvonne was waiting for us.

"What's the low-down, Eve?" I greeted her. "How bad is it?"

"Don't know yet, she's in with the doctor. She '*fell*' down the concrete stairwell of her block of flats." Yvonne stressed the word 'fell' to show her scepticism.

Stephanie, although only sixteen, had defied her mother, who was a single parent, and moved out of their council house at Clapham and into a flat at Stockwell with Winston.

"God! How I would love to get my hands on that Winston and give him some of his own medicine!" I looked around the waiting room. "Is he even here? How did you find out?"

Yvonne sighed and looked around for a vacant seat. There were none; the unit was busy tonight and there were a lot of people waiting to be seen by the medical staff. We leaned up against a wall and Clive went off to get us some coffee.

"Of course he's not here." Yvonne sounded weary. "The next door neighbour is my Mum's friend, and she knows that Steph and I are friends; she doesn't know Steph's mother so she called me after she called the ambulance."

"Did she say what happened? Where's the baby? Have you called Steph's Mum?"

Yvonne answered the last question first. "She's on her way. Should be here any minute. The baby's with Mrs

McCalla, my Mum's friend, but I expect Social Services will take him into care if Steph's Mum doesn't take him."

I thought of that gorgeous little boy and my heart went out to him. He would probably be shunted from foster home to foster home; Social Services wouldn't let her keep him if they considered her to be living in a dangerous situation, and they would definitely be investigating the circumstances of her 'fall.' In fact, they would probably put *her* into care as well, because she was, under the law, still a minor.

I was about to ask Yvonne again what Mrs McCalla had told her when Steph's Mum came in. At the same time the nurse came out of the cubicle where Steph was being treated and approached us. Miss Griffiths was just in time to hear the nurse tell us that they would be admitting Steph.

I didn't know Stephanie's Mum that well. She was not in my parents' circle of friends and I had only seen her in passing on a couple of occasions. From things Steph had said, I surmised that she was not particularly maternal, and was more interested in partying and having a good time, than in Steph or her siblings. They had been left pretty much to raise themselves, with Steph playing the role of mother to her younger brothers and sisters.

Miss Griffiths was quite young, no more than thirty two or three. She had had Stephanie at a young age herself and had not been pleased at being made a grandmother so young. She was heavily made up with blue eye-shadow, false eyelashes, rouged cheeks and bright red lips. Her fingernails were almost an inch long, and painted the same shade as her lips.

She wore a weave-on hairstyle and an extremely tight pair of hot-pants, with a bolero type top, and three or four inch stiletto heels.

She didn't greet us; having heard the nurse say that

Sweet Home, Jamaica

Steph would be admitted, without enquiring as to the condition of her child, or the whereabouts of her grandson, she began to berate Steph.

"If dat gyal did listen to mi, dis 'ouldn't happen! A try tell har fi learn from my mistake. Dat bwoy Winston stay just like har faada!"

Her voice was strident in tone. People were staring at us. I was outraged. Never one to hold my tongue, I lay into her.

"Miss Griffiths, are you interested in the condition of your daughter, or are you going to stand here and curse her all evening?" I was hopping mad. "Steph can't learn from *your* mistakes, she has to learn from her own. Maybe if you had set a better example, this wouldn't have happened to her."

She stared at me in stunned surprise. She opened her mouth to say something, but a burst of applause stopped her in her tracks. We were the centre of attention. I had not realized it, but my voice had risen above normal, and we had a captive audience. Clive had returned with the coffee and he came up to me and said, "Easy, Shell."

Miss Griffiths closed her mouth and turned to the nurse, a black woman, who looked at me with approval, and nodded her head. Then she spoke in a Nigerian accent. "Your daughter has a broken jaw and two broken ribs. She's badly bruised and concussed. A porter will be along shortly to move her to a ward; meantime the doctor would like to have a word with you." She held the curtain of the cubicle aside and ushered Miss Griffiths inside.

I stepped forward to enter, but the nurse stopped me. She spoke kindly. "You should go home, dear, there's nothing you can do. You can come visit her tomorrow."

I was reluctant to leave, but Yvonne and Clive led me out. I was so angry that if I was cut with I knife, I wouldn't bleed. I was angry at Winston, at Miss Griffiths, but most of all, I was angry with Stephanie. How often had Yvonne and Joy and I begged, pleaded and cussed her to get away from that guy.

The police and Social Services would get involved; the hospital would notify them. But at the end of the day, I expected that Steph would stay with Winston until he killed her, not because she wanted to, perhaps, but because she was afraid to leave him.

It was late when we got back to Brixton, but I wanted to go back to Clive's to make love again. I felt that my first experience had been marred by poor Steph's problems, and I wanted to exorcise them from my mind by being washed in Clive's love. When the mini-cab dropped off Yvonne, I whispered to Clive, "Can I can home with you for half an hour?"

He put his arm around my shoulder and kissed the side of my mouth. "It's very late; your parents will be worried. Tomorrow is another day."

"But I need to make love to you again to exorcise the hospital from my brain," I whined.

"Hush, the driver will hear you. Anyway, it's too late.

The cab was already turning into Josephine Avenue. I was bitterly disappointed but I gave in gracefully. Clive paid off the cab and I retrieved the key from under the flower pot and we went in. Mavis was waiting up, as I had expected.

"How's Stephanie? What happened to her?" Mavis was more concerned than Steph's Mum had been.

In the cab on the way from the hospital Yvonne had told us what Mrs McCalla had told her. She said she had heard Steph screaming, but didn't pay much attention because, as she said, 'they were always at it.' But when it went on for what she considered too long, she went and banged on their door. She said Winston opened the door and brushed past her, almost knocking her down. She said she went in and found the baby crying, and Steph lying on the living room floor, moaning. She called an ambulance, and then Yvonne, and took the baby home with her.

I told Mavis what I knew, and after she had commiserated she said she was going up to bed. I didn't want Clive to leave yet, so I said I would make some tea. After Mavis went up, I tackled him again.

"Y'know, we could easily have a quickie before you go home. Everyone's fast asleep except Mum, and I don't expect she'll be back down tonight."

"Good heavens, woman, you've turned into a right sex maniac. Is there no satisfying you?" Clive leered at me. "I can see I'm going to have problems keeping you watered."

"Clear off and guh weh!" I pressed up against him. "Tell mi yu nuh want mi."

He shook his head. "Can't do that."

"Aha!"

Any further comment I had intended to make was cut off by his lips descending on mine. I undid his flies and his manhood sprung forth. He hoisted my skirt and I rapidly stepped out of my panties. As he impaled me on his shaft he said on a gasping breath, "I hope to God this is really your safe period," before he exploded inside me.

CHAPTER NINE

The Campbell Family

The summer ended; the twins had had their twelfth birthday party. Joy, Yvonne and I had gone back to school for our sixth form year. Clive had returned to his studies at Durham, and Steph and her son were living in sheltered protection somewhere in North London.

It was a glorious autumn, that year of 1977. It was Indian summer, the warm sunny weather lingered past September and into the middle of October. The leaves turned wondrous shades of browns and red and orange and gold, before falling gracefully to carpet the road and sidewalks along Josephine Avenue, and the grass and walkways in Brockwell Park

It had been a bumper year for acorns and horse chestnuts – or 'conkers' as they are commonly called – and other seeds, nuts and berries; and hoards of squirrels ran helter-skelter collecting their winter supplies. It was going to be a hard winter; the bumper harvest showed

Sweet Home, Jamaica

that.

Daddy and Mavis had booked their fare to spend Christmas in Jamaica. It would be their first time back home since arriving in England in 1964 and they were full of excitement. I was excited too; Mavis was going to see what information, if any, she could find out about my birth mother.

I felt a surge of affection for Mavis. No-one could ask for a better mother. She and I had become almost like sisters, and I found myself telling her little things about me and Clive that I would normally reserve only for my close friends.

December blew in very cold and windy, and Mavis and Daddy showed off about spending Christmas in beautiful, warm, sunny Jamaica. I wished I were going with them, as did the rest of the family. The twins complained that Samantha was too young to benefit from the experience and that as Delroy and I had both been born in Jamaica they should now have the opportunity to see 'the land of their forefathers.' They had recently watched *Roots* on the TV and had decided that they wanted to research their own roots.

To everyone's surprise, my own included, Delroy suddenly showed an inclination - no, perhaps I should say a sudden strong desire – to go to Jamaica with Daddy and Mavis. He said he could pay his own fare; like me, he had saved regularly for most of his life and could afford it. But Daddy said the twins and I could not be left without protection for six weeks. Delroy gave in gracefully.

I commiserated with him. "Never mind, Del. I'm sure you'll get a chance to go soon."

I actually wouldn't have minded going to Jamaica myself. I had never thought much about Jamaica, the island of my birth, but since I had found out about my mother I had developed an interest in the island. I had bought some books at *W.H. Smiths* and picked up some more information along with my map from the Commonwealth Institute. I had also started to buy *The Weekly Gleaner* every week to keep up with what was happening on the island.

Daddy and Mavis flew out on the seventh of December, one week before my seventeenth birthday. It was a dry clear day, but very cold. Marse Wilfred drove them to Gatwick airport, taking the twins along for the ride even though it was a school day.

Delroy and I settled in as temporary heads of the household, while the twins tried their best to test us to see how far they could go. Daddy had said that if we couldn't make them behave, we were to call Marse Wilfred to give them a whipping. We all knew Marse Wilfred wouldn't lift a finger against them, and the twins laughed Daddy to scorn.

However, I had my own methods of bringing them to heel. I was in charge of the finances; Daddy had given me a portion of money for housekeeping, school, and other essentials. There was also money for our weekly pocket money and a little extra to buy Christmas cards and presents for our friends. Whenever the twins were rude or out of order, Daddy would suspend their pocket money. I now adopted the same practice, and, with Christmas approaching, the twins soon came to heel.

I turned seventeen on the fourteenth and Delroy produced a present from Daddy and Mavis as well as one from himself. I was overwhelmed by my parents' present to me. It was a full set of *Encyclopaedia Britannica;* I knew it must have cost a bomb.

Delroy gave me ten pounds worth of book tokens and the twins gave me some cosmetic jewellery, which I couldn't wear because I was allergic to anything that was not gold.

Sweet Home, Jamaica

School broke up for Christmas and Clive came down from Durham. I had been making sure to take the Pill religiously so we would no longer have to worry about condoms or safe periods. I would have to be creative in order to get to spend quality time with Clive, given my charge over the twins. Mrs Brennan next door proved to be a godsend; she had ten children of her own, two more hardly made a difference, and luckily for me, the twins loved going there.

Christmas came, and we all went to Clive's house for Christmas dinner. I had helped Miss Myrtle with the preparations, including the baking and icing of the cake. None of us were particularly fond of turkey, so roast chicken and stuffing was the order of the day.

Dad and Mavis had phoned on a couple of previous occasions, and they phoned again on Christmas day. There were no phones up in the country where they were staying, and they had to drive down into the town of Old Harbour every time they wanted to make a phone call. Invariably they had to wait in a queue to use the town's single call box.

They said they were having a grand time visiting with relatives and old friends. Both of Daddy's parents were still alive, but Mavis' father had been dead since shortly before she had left for England. Mavis said she had not had time to make any enquires yet regarding my birth mother, but that as soon as the Christmas festivities were over she would make it a priority.

They returned from Jamaica in the middle of January, full of plans to buy a plot of land to build a house. Daddy already had a house on a piece of land which he had bought shortly after my birth, but it was a small board structure which now housed one of my uncles and his family. Daddy decided to let them keep it.

But the vacation had whetted their appetite for the

land of their birth, and they started planning in earnest; they didn;t want to wait till they retired to go home; they would go as soon as it was financially viable.

Hardly known for my patience, I gave Mavis no time to re-adjust and settle back into her routine before I pounced on her to learn what, if anything, she had learned about the whereabouts of my birth mother.

"Did you find out anything about Miss Campbell, Mum?" I asked her eagerly.

"Good God, Michelle, mek mi come off-a di plane good nuh?"

They had only been home for a few hours but I thought she could have at least given me a yes or no. I thought about telling her so, but then I re-considered; it was best not to 'get her back up.'

Two days later, when she still had not mentioned it, I decided to throw caution to the winds and broach the subject again. It was Saturday evening and we were in the kitchen. Everyone else was off about their business; the twins and Samantha were next door, Daddy was at the pub and Delroy was moping in his room because Joy was unable escape her parents to go out with him.

I was seasoning up (marinating) a leg of lamb for Sunday dinner, to give us a break from chicken, and Mavis was grating a coconut for the rice and peas. She had been in an upbeat mood since her return and was still full of excitement at the prospect of building her and Daddy's dream house in Jamaica. I was happy for them and tried to share in her happy excitement, but I was impatient to know if she had found out anything about my mother.

She was telling me that they had made an offer on a piece of land a few miles outside of Old Harbour.

"Is a big piece a land; ten acres. Wi can buil' wi house, and have nuff space to plant out fruit trees and do likkle farming." She laughed happily. "Yu faada fancy himself as a genkleman farmer."

I laughed with her and said, "And I suppose you fancy yourself as a gentleman farmer's wife?"

"But of course; how yu mean!"

We worked happily alongside each other. Mavis had finished grating, and was juicing the coconut. I washed some red peas and put them to soak in a pot. The preparations for Sunday dinner finished with, I made two cups of cocoa and we adjourned to the living room. It was my time now, and I wasted none of it.

"So Mum, *pleeease* put me out of my misery." I didn't have to elaborate; she knew exactly what I meant.

"Okay, yu been very patient." She took a sip of her cocoa and placed the cup on the coffee table. I was tense with anticipation. I was certain that she had some information; otherwise she would have just told me that there was nothing to tell.

I watched her intently. She smiled at me, and I was sure. She *had* found out something. Her next words dashed my hopes.

"Well, nuhbaddy seem to know which part shi deh now; shi was teaching in a school at Bois Content, then she move to Town in1965, and from there-suh, nuhbaddy know which way she turn."

"Oh." I was bitterly disappointed. Then I had a thought. "What about her parents, my biological grandparents; they must know something? Did you talk to them? Who did you ask?"

Mavis took another sip of her cocoa. Mine had been totally forgotten about and was sitting on the coffee table growing cold.

"Well," she said, "after mi ask around in di distrikt and hear that shi left Country, A went to si har madda. Yu faada was against di idea, but A finally convince him."

Mavis had learned from one of Daddy's brothers that

Claudette Beckford-Brady

Delisia had never forgiven her parents for taking away her baby. She had finished her schooling and gotten a teaching position at Ludford Mount School at Bois Content. She had continued living at her parents' home, barely on speaking terms with them, until her father had demanded that she either treated them with respect, or leave.

She left. She didn't go far. She rented a small board house at a place called Breeze Mill. She kept herself to herself, had no men friends and few female ones, and stayed there until she went to Town (Kingston) in1965. From there, she had disappeared into thin air.

Two months after Delisia left Country, her father had fallen from an ackee tree and broken his neck. No one, not even his wife, could understand why a sixty-five year old man would climb an ackee tree when he had sons to do that for him. There were whispers of broken hearts, regrets and suicide.

Delisia had not attended the funeral. From the day she left and went to Town she had never returned to the country.

When Mavis could get no further information, she went to see Delisia's mother at Gravel Hill, which was just a stone's throw from Joe Ground. Mavis felt the woman had a right to at least know that her grandchild was alive and well and wanting to connect with her family.

As it turned out, Mrs Campbell already knew that they were in the area; all the local communities were closely knit and everyone knew everyone else. Nobody's business was private.

Mrs Campbell had greeted Mavis very cordially and they had had a good talk. She said that over the years she had asked Daddy's family about my progress from time to time, but she had asked them not to mention it to Daddy in case it was a sore point. My heart warmed to this unknown grandmother of mine. I had not been 'out of sight, out of mind' for her. She cared about me.

She was extremely pleased and excited to know that I was interested in finding my biological family, and wanted to know all about me. Actually, my thoughts had not really gone beyond my mother to an extended family, but now I realized that I wanted to know them all.

Mavis had not learned anything new about Delisia's whereabouts. Mrs Campbell said that from the day Delisia moved out of their house, she had not seen or heard from her. She said that she had gone to the school where Delisia worked on several occasions, but her daughter had refused to see her.

When her husband died, Mrs Campbell had sent to Kingston to try to locate her daughter to let her know that her father had died. They had discovered that she was teaching at a school in Trench Town; she was found, but when she was informed of her father's death and impending funeral, she said that her father had died the day they took her baby away.

I was a little disturbed at this image of my mother as an unforgiving, heartless person who, despite the death of her father, was not prepared to unbend even a little. At the time of her father's death five years had elapsed since I had been taken from her; surely that had been enough time for some little measure of forgiveness to creep in?

I had intended never to forgive Mavis and my father when I learned that Mavis was not my mother, but try as I might, I could never really stay vexed for long. Granted, losing a child obviously has a much greater impact than merely finding out that your father's wife is not your mother, but still, her father had died, for heaven sakes.

Her father had died and that had had absolutely no impact on her whatever. Yes, she had been distraught and devastated by the wrenching away of her child; any normal woman would have been, but surely, if she had loved her parents at all, surely she could have offered her mother a little comfort, even of a temporary nature?

She could have gone away again afterwards if she still felt so inclined, but I was willing to bet that if she had gone back to 'Country' on her father's death, she and her mother would have reconciled.

My heart filled with love and pity for this unknown woman who was my grandmother, and at the same time I felt anger towards my biological mother. I held no resentment toward my grandmother for the part she had played in separating me from my natural mother; in fact, I felt almost certain, without knowing why, that the whole thing had probably been the brainchild of my grandfather. I was sure my grandmother had been forced to go along. I just could not imagine a mother forcing another mother to give up her child.

In any event, whatever the role she had played, I thought she had suffered enough. She had lost her daughter and grand-daughter, and then her husband. Enough was enough. Time now to try and make things right again.

But Mavis' information had left me no closer to finding my mother. She had dropped off the face of the earth. Still, I had learned plenty about my biological family.

I had eight uncles and numerous cousins. My mother was the only girl, and the youngest child, and had been her father's favourite, until she had gotten pregnant and disappointed him so.

Six of my uncles were abroad; four in the USA, one in Canada, and one was actually living right here in England, in Birmingham. The other two uncles still lived in Jamaica and worked the fifty or so acres of coffee, chocolate (cocoa) and ground provisions that the family owned.

I couldn't understand how my mother could have cut off her entire family - even her brothers who had had no part in taking her child - for so long. The more I thought about it the more convinced I became that something had happened to her. Perhaps she had died and no one had known who to notify.

I did not want her to be dead, but the thought that she might be alive and well somewhere without letting her family know was most disturbing to me. That depicted a cold, unfeeling personality; an unforgiving nature.

If that was how my mother was, I had not taken after her in that respect. No, the impression I was beginning to get of my mother was not to my liking; not how I imagined her to be in my fantasies.

Mavis got up and left the room, saying she would "soon come back." I sat in silence, my cold cup of cocoa totally forgotten, and mulled over everything I had learned from Mavis.

The last anyone had heard of my mother, she had been teaching at a place called Trench Town in downtown Kingston. I would try to find it on my map later, but in the meantime I wondered if I wrote to the Jamaican Ministry of Education, would they have any information about Miss Campbell's whereabouts; that is if she was still teaching in Jamaica. It was a chance; a starting point at least. I would try it.

Mavis returned with a large brown envelope in her hand. She handed it to me without saying anything. I looked at it, and then looked at her questioningly. She smiled, waiting for me to open the envelope. I turned it over in my hands and examined it thoroughly. It was a plain envelope with no writing or anything on it. And it was sealed.

I shook it, and finally, Mavis, who seemed rather anxious for me to open it, said, "Yu know Shell, is *inside* di envelope yu suppose to look, not on di outside."

I opened the envelope very carefully. I peered inside,

and then removed the contents. There were a number of photographs and a smaller envelope, also sealed. I knew without being told that these were photographs of my biological family. I assumed the smaller envelope contained a letter from Mrs Campbell, my maternal grandmother.

"Mum! You had these all along and you took two days to show me?"

"Well, dem wasn't going to run weh, yu know." She sat down beside me. "Patience is a great t'ing, Michelle."

"A virtue, Mum," I said, absent-mindedly, but automatically.

"Okay; a virtue. Anyway, meet yu other family."

She took the photos from me and looked at the back of one of them. "Right, dis is yu Uncle Kenneth."

I took the picture from her and looked first at the back. In a beautiful scroll was written the words *Kenneth Campbell*. I finally turned the picture over, and looked at my mother's brother, my biological uncle, for the first time.

He was a dark skinned man with smiling eyes, somewhere in his late forties or early fifties. I liked the look of him. To my surprise and consternation, tears welled up in my eyes and I felt a rush of love for the unknown man. I quickly blinked away the tears and sneaked a surreptitious glance at Mavis to see if she had noticed my emotion. If she had she gave no indication of it. I prided myself on not being a 'cry-cry' emotional female, and too often in recent years I had found myself contravening my own edict not to be a 'crying sort of a person.'

Mavis handed me another picture. "Yu Uncle Clement." One by one I looked at my eight uncles. They seemed to range in age from the mid thirties to the late forties or early fifties. My mother was the youngest child and she would be thirty-four now.

Sweet Home, Jamaica

All of my uncles bore a striking resemblance to each other. When I looked at the last picture I got a surprise. Uncle Cornell, who Mavis said was the youngest, was a bearded, dreadlocked Rasta man.

I wondered curiously why all my uncles' names began with a K or a C. It was something I would have to ask them about when I met them, for it now went without saying that I would link up with them. I wanted to meet them all in person and get to know them.

There was a faded black and white wedding photo of my grandparents and a recent colour one of my grandmother by herself. And then Mavis handed me another photo.

I took it and looked at it. My own face looked back at me in black and white; but no, it wasn't me. My mother, Delisia; it had to be.

This photo must have been taken before 1965 when she left 'Country.' She looked to be around my age in the photograph, and she was smiling, so I assumed it was taken before I was born. I couldn't imagine her smiling so happily if I had recently been taken from her.

I looked at the face that so resembled mine. *Where are you, Mamma?* I asked the question silently in my mind, while staring intently at the photograph, perhaps subconsciously willing it to give me an answer. But of course it couldn't.

Mavis brought me out of my reverie by handing me the smaller sealed envelope. I opened it carefully and took out the letter which I had correctly assumed it contained. It was written in the same beautiful scroll as the names on the back of the photographs, and I knew it was my grandmother's writing.

"*My Dear Michelle,* she wrote,
I was so excited when I learned from your mother – of

course I consider Miss Mavis to be your mother – that you wanted to know about your other family. I am so grateful for Miss Mavis' generosity in being willing to share you with us, and thank you, for wanting to know us.

I was rather surprised at the grammatical correctness of the letter. The sentence composition was in standard Queen's English, punctuation was in place and she paragraphed. That told me that she was an educated woman. I don't know why it should have surprised me, but it did.

I smiled ruefully to myself as I thought of what Clive would say when I told him how surprised I had been to discover that my grandmother was educated. He would say, *"That's your snobbery and patronizing attitude coming to the fore again, Michelle Freeman."*

I read on.

"My dear, not a day has gone by that I have not wondered about you. I know how you look; your father's mother is gracious enough to show me photographs when she receives them, but I would love to know what kind of personality you possess. I hear that you are very bright in school, and that does not surprise me; Delisia and all your uncles are extremely bright people, and I myself taught school for many years.

"My dear child, a letter cannot suffice to say all the things I want to say to you. I hope that sometime in the not too distant future, with God's help, we will find a way to meet and learn all about each other.

In the meantime, your mother's brother, your Uncle Keith, lives in Birmingham. I have written to him about you and I'm sure he will make arrangements to meet you very soon.

Sweet Home, Jamaica

Well my dear, I am waiting impatiently to hear from you. Write me soon and make your old grandmother happy. Much love and affection to you, my granddaughter.

Miriam Campbell.

Miriam. I had always liked the sound of that name. I imagined anyone with that name would have a tranquil personality. I looked at the photo of my grandmother again. Yes, the name suited the face.

"Well, what yu t'ink?" Mavis' voice brought me out of my reflections. "Uh? What? Oh, I think they look like a wonderful, well-knit family. I think I would like to get to know them, but I wonder what Daddy will think."

Mavis sighed. "Yu know, A kyaan't understand why yu faada suh dead set gainst di idea of yu knowing yu madda family dem. Well *I* think yu have a right, if yu want to, and yu nearly a adult now, suh A wouldn't worry too much bout Daddy. Suh long's yu nuh cut wi out-a yu life."

"Of course not! You all mean *everything* to me. Finding additional members of my other family isn't going to change that." I hugged Mavis. "Thanks for everything, Mum. You're a super champion and I love you."

Mavis hugged me back and replied, "Love yu too, Shellie."

Although I had already returned to school, Clive was not due to return to Durham till the end of the month, and later that evening I showed him the photos and the letter from my Grandma. When I told him how surprised I had been at the well-written letter he responded, as I knew he would, that I was too snobbish and patronizing, and he must have thought I'd lost my mind when I doubled up laughing.

"Wait, what happen to you? I said something

amusing?" He looked at me in perplexed surprise. I gasped for breath and said, "I knew you were going to say *exactly* that. I could have said it with you."

"What yu saying; I'm getting predictable in my old age?" He put on a comical face, bent his body into a caricature of an old man and quoted what I recognized to be a verse from an *Enid Blyton* book, except that he changed the gardener into a lawyer.

"A poor old lawyer said, 'Ah me
My days is almost done,
I have rheumatics in my knee
And now it's hard to run.
I've got a measle in my foot
And chilblains on my nose,
And bless me if I haven't got
Pneumonia in my toes."

I laughed delightedly and joined in the second verse with him.

"All my hair has fallen out,
My teeth have fallen in,
I'm really getting rather stout
Although I'm much too thin..."

By this time we were both laughing so hard we couldn't continue. I'd had no idea that Clive had read any of Enid Blyton's books, let alone memorize verses from them. When I could catch my breath I gasped, "Well, you are a dark horse! I didn't know you had read *Enid Blyton*."

"Oh? And why should that be so surprising?" Clive glared at me in mock belligerence.

"Well, because I just can't imagine you reading *The Famous Five* or *The Secret Seven*."

Clive snorted condescendingly. "Well let me tell you

something, Miss Know-all who has read everything, I too have read extensively with no respect for gender or genre; I read anything and everything from *Wind in the Willows* to *Shakespeare.* So there!"

His tone of voice made me expect to see him stick his tongue out and that set me off laughing again. Clive glared at me and said, "Are you laughing at me, young lady? Right, you've had it," and with that he began to tickle me mercilessly.

Now, if there is one thing I hate more than anything else, it is to be tickled. But as much as I hated it I could not stop myself from laughing helplessly when it was being administered. And, as I knew it would, our horseplay turned into intimacy and we wound up making mad passionate love.

Afterwards I lay in Clive's arms and we talked about my other family. Clive had been against my trying to find my biological mother because he had thought I would end up hurt and disappointed, but now that he had seen the photos of my family and read the letter, he was more at ease with the idea. I told him that I was intending to write to the Ministry of Education in Jamaica to see if I could get any information from them regarding my mother.

*

A few weeks later I was in my room doing an English assignment when the telephone rang. A short while later Mavis called up to me to pick up the extension in her bedroom. I did so, expecting it to be either Clive or Joy.

"Hello?"

"Hello," said a deep West Midland accent. "Is this Michelle Freeman?"

I had never heard the voice before. I wasn't sure I wanted to admit to being Michelle Freeman before I knew who I was talking to. I guessed it must be okay if Mavis had sanctioned the call, but still...

"Aahm, who is this?" I asked the voice at the other end of the line.

"My name is Keith Campbell and I understand....."

"Uncle Keith! Yes, this is Michelle." In my sudden excitement I rudely interrupted him. "Oh this is great! Grandma said you would contact me."

It had been very easy for me to slip into using the term "grandma" and now I found it just as easy to say "Uncle Keith" to this unknown man.

The deep voice held amusement when it replied, "Well, is nice to speak to mi niece at last. How yu do, mi niece?"

"I'm very well, thank you, Uncle Keith. Gosh, it's really great to hear from you. I can't wait to meet you!"

"Well, Michelle, my wife and children all feel the same way. I told them I would come and get yu when school break up for half-term but them pestering me to drive down to London one weekend, so we plan to come next week."

I was almost speechless with excitement and anticipation, almost, but not quite. "Oh Uncle, that's fantastic! I wish it were tomorrow!"

His accent was a curious mixture of Jamaican and West Midland and although his speech was interspersed with patois it was evident that he spoke English well. We spoke for nearly an hour, at the end of which time I had learned plenty about him and his immediate family, and a little more about my mother.

Uncle Keith was the seventh son, following behind Clifton and coming before Cornell. He was nearly thirty-nine years old, and had been in England since he was nineteen, three years before I was even born. Although he had had no part in the decision-making and implementation of taking me from my mother, he too had been totally cut off by Delisia. Prior to my birth they had written to each other on a regular basis; Delisia had told him when she got pregnant and how happy she was about it.

He said he had been disappointed that she had 'fallen' before completing her education, but hadn't thought it such a big deal, young girls got pregnant every day; but their father had been furious. Delisia had written to her brother imploring him to intercede with their father on her behalf so that she could keep her baby. Uncle Keith had written back saying that she knew full well that when Pappa made up his mind about anything there was no changing it. He had never heard from her again.

And yet he had tried to intercede on her behalf, but as he had known before trying, he got nowhere with his father. He had written several letters to Delisia before she left Country, but had never received a reply, and he, like all the others, had absolutely no idea where in the world their baby sister was.

He said he still worried about her constantly, and prayed every day that she would come home and be reconciled with her family. I told him of my idea to write to the Jamaican Ministry of Education to see if I could get any information.

Uncle Keith sounded doubtful. "Their systems at Home are not as structured as ours, Michelle, and even if they do have pertinent information I doubt they would just divulge it to a third party. I suspect your letter would end up in somebody's 'pending' tray with not even the courtesy of an acknowledgement."

"But it's worth a try, don't you think, Uncle Keith?"

"Well, if we are going to search for her in earnest, it's best to leave no stone unturned. Do your thing, Niece, you find yu Mamma."

I was encouraged by Uncle Keith's words, and his tacit indication that he too was now a part of the search. We went on to speak of himself and his immediate family.

He had been in England for twenty years with regular visits home every couple of years. He was a Civil Engineer by profession and told me he had worked on many of the roadways and bridges in the country. I was most impressed, and needless to say, proud.

He was married to Vilma; had been for eighteen years, and they had four children between the ages of four and sixteen. Vilma was a nursing Sister at Birmingham General Hospital. Of my cousins there was one boy and three girls. I couldn't wait for next week-end so I could finally meet them.

After the call ended I realised that I had forgotten to ask Uncle Keith why all their names had the K sound. Still, it wasn't important; I could find that out anytime. I went downstairs to fill Mavis in. She already knew about the planned visit; Uncle Keith had cleared it with her before speaking to me. Daddy was not home and I was worried about what his reaction would be, but Mavis assured me everything would be fine.

Yu mek yu faada sound like a unreasonable somebaddy. Him accept seh yu want to know yu madda people dem now, so him naa guh cause nuh problem. Yu leave Daddy to mi."

I was happy to concur.

I thought it would take forever to get to the day of the planned visit, but as it turned out the events of the next few days put it completely out of my mind.

CHAPTER TEN

Dark Days

Monday morning; 6th of February, 1978. It began as an ordinary Monday morning. I got up, made breakfast and got the twins off to school, and left Samantha next door at the Brennans'. As I left the house to go to school myself, a light powdery snow was falling. I rather hoped it would get heavier and settle; it had been a long time since I had enjoyed the pristine whiteness of newly fallen snow.

This was my penultimate year at school; next year I would enter the Upper Sixth and conclude my final A Level exams. My first class was English Literature. Miss Williams was doing a credible enactment of a scene from Shakespeare's *Macbeth* where the three witches were chanting incantations over their bubbling cauldron. She played the part of all three witches, changing her voice and posture with each character.

She had the class roaring with laughter, when the door opened and Mrs Walsh, the Headmistress, entered. She spoke quietly to Miss Williams and I saw them both look my way. I felt a sudden shiver of apprehension.

Miss Williams came to my desk and said quietly, "Michelle, would you go with Mrs Walsh, please."

I wanted to ask her what was wrong, but my throat had closed up. I had a terrible premonition of impending doom. I got up and walked towards the front of the class where the Head was waiting for me. I could feel the eyes of the entire class on me, their curiosity palpable. Mrs Walsh placed her hand on my shoulder, gently, I thought, and said, "Come with me, please, Michelle."

I felt terrified. Something was terribly wrong. I could sense it in every nuance of both teachers' body language. I began to speculate wildly in my mind, now almost panic-stricken. *Something has happened to somebody in my family.* Why else would I be called out of an important A Level class?

I followed the Head along the corridor and through the assembly hall to her office. She had not said anything further to me during the walk, and I was too terrified to question her.

We arrived at her office. The door was open and both Daddy and Mavis were there. It was immediately apparent to me that Mavis had been crying, and I had never seen Daddy looking so sombre. My panic increased.

I was vaguely aware that Mrs Walsh had not followed me into the office, but had closed the door upon my entry. Mavis, who had been leaning against Daddy, rushed over to me, hugged me, and burst into a fresh fit of weeping.

To describe how I felt would be a mammoth task. I wanted to know what was wrong, yet I was afraid to know. I had never seen Mavis cry like this before and I somehow knew that some-one had died.

But who? My mind jumped frantically to my siblings and then to Clive and his parents. Un-acceptable!

Sweet Home, Jamaica

Idiotically my mind jumped to a line from a TV show called *Lost in Space* where the robot always says, *"...does not compute..."* when something was illogical or didn't make sense. This definitely did not compute. No one belonging to me could possibly be dead; these things only happened to other people.

Daddy eased Mavis away from me and said, in the gentlest voice I have ever heard him use, "Sit down a minute, Shell."

My heart lurched. I remained where I was, rooted to the spot. I couldn't sit down if I wanted to, and I didn't. "What is it, Daddy?" My voice came out in a hoarse whisper. I tried to look into Daddy's eyes to see if I could read anything. He avoided my gaze. I turned to Mavis, who had obviously made a great effort to pull herself together. She too avoided my gaze, but spoke to Daddy.

"George, maybe wi should wait till wi get har home to tell har."

"Tell me what?" Of a sudden I was deadly calm. Still terrified to hear the news, but strangely calm. I repeated the question as neither of them seemed inclined to respond. "Tell me *what*, Mum?"

Daddy steered me to a chair and pushed me down onto it. I closed my eyes, held my breath, and waited. I already knew that some-one had died; the only question was who?

"Dere was a' accident." He paused, and I waited, breath still held. He continued. "It's Clive; he was hit down by a car..." He paused again. He didn't need to continue. I knew the worst. My teachers' attitude, Mavis' tears and Daddy's sombre kindness all added up to one thing.

Clive was dead.

I exhaled slowly, my eyes still tightly shut. I felt calm inside. Dry-eyed. A few moments of silence, and then I felt Mavis's hand on my shoulder. "Shell?"

"Yes Mum?" My voice sounded normal to me.
"Did yu hear what yu faada just seh?"
"Yes, Mum."

My eyes were shut tight, but I could feel my parents exchange glances. There were another few moments of silence, as if they were both at a loss as to what to do next. They were saved by a gentle knock on the door.

I heard the door open and the clatter of tea-cups on a tray. I heard the tray being placed on the desk. Every sound was magnified. I heard Mrs Walsh say, sotto voice, "How is she?" and my father reply, "It don't hit har yet." I heard tea being poured and then someone was trying to hand me a cup.

I opened my eyes, pushed the cup away, sloshing tea into the saucer, and stood up. "I want to go home." I spoke in a normal tone of voice, and headed for the door. Taken completely by surprise, I was halfway through the assembly hall before anyone caught up with me.

"Michelle, wait nuh. Drink some tea first." It was Mavis.

Tea. The quintessential English panacea for all ills. *'Have a cuppa; you'll feel better.'*

"No thanks, Mum. I just want to go home."

"Ahright. But wi have to wait far a taxi, snow falling heavy outside."

"I'll go get my coat."

Mavis followed me to the cloakroom where I put on my coat, scarf and gloves. I glanced out of the window. The light snow which had been falling on my way to school had turned into large thick flakes which were coming down very fast. This looked like 'settling' snow. I remembered my wish of the morning; that the snow would settle. It was being granted.

When we arrived back at the Head's office my school bag had somehow made its way from my classroom to wait for me. Mrs Walsh didn't call a cab, but drove us home herself.

It was a short drive; I didn't live far from the school, and the trip was made in complete silence. When we arrived home I asked Mavis to fetch Samantha from next door. I spoke in my normal voice with no hint of tears or sadness. Mavis looked hard at me, as if trying to gauge my state of mind. She and Daddy exchanged glances, but nobody said anything, and then she went out, to return a few minutes later with Samantha in tow.

Samantha was growing fast and would be having her fourth birthday in March, just about five weeks away. She was a lively, gregarious child who loved being surrounded by others, and was in her element when let loose among Mrs Brennan's brood of ten. Normally it was a struggle to get her to come home, but today, for some reason – could it be possible that a child so young could pick up on vibrations? – For some reason, today she came without protest.

Delroy was at work and the twins were still at school. Daddy and Mavis seemed bemused by my total lack of emotion. I could feel them watching me as I went up the stairs to my room, carrying Samantha piggy-back style. I turned my back to the bed and released my hold on her. She let go from holding on around my neck and dropped down onto the bed, screaming with delight. She loved being bounced around on the bed, which was nice and springy.

I played with her, bounced her around, and tickled her until she screamed with laughter. Then I hugged and kissed her until she started to squirm. She wriggled out of my grasp and said, "Yu queezing mi, Shellie."

"Oh, sorry Sam-Sam. Didn't mean to. Shall I tell you a story?"

"Yeaaah! Tell the one about Bwedda Wabbit and the

Taw Baby."

I sat her on my knee and started to tell her the story. I had left my room door open and I was vaguely aware that Daddy and Mavis were standing in the passage watching me. Mavis said something to Daddy and he turned and went away, while she came on into the room.

Samantha said, "Sit down, Mummy; Shell's telling me a stowy." She had lost her baby lisp, but she still could not wrap her tongue around the letter R and invariably substituted W in its place. Rachel and Rebecca were "Wachel and Webecca."

Mavis sat down on the bed beside us and listened to the story with Samantha. I pretended she wasn't there. Mavis had a way of observing and scrutinizing people that was quite disconcerting at times, and sometimes she would make deep and profound statements that were worthy of a practicing psychologist. All the while I was telling the story, I was absolutely aware that she was studying me closely.

I came to the end of the story and Sammie clapped her hands happily and said, "Now the one with Bwedda 'Nancy an' di cooking pot."

Before I could reply Mavis stood up and said to Samantha, "Go downstairs, Sammie. Daddy got somet'ing special fah yu."

"Ooh, what, Mummy?" She slid off my lap and turned towards Mavis.

"Gwaan downstairs and si," Mavis replied. "And tek time pon di stairs!"

Samantha left the room and I ignored Mavis and took a book out of my school satchel. Mavis gently took the book from me and said, "Shell, look at me." I reluctantly met her gaze. "Shell," she continued, "A don't sure if yu did hear and understand what yu faada seh to yu in Miss Walsh office?"

Sweet Home, Jamaica

I held her gaze. "Yes, Mum, I did."

She was silent for a moment, and then she said, "How yu feel?"

"Okay," I replied. Mavis sighed deeply. "Shell, yu cannot feel okay. Tell mi what yu t'ink yu faada said, mek mi si if yu have it right."

"Daddy said that Clive was dead." I said it in an emotionless voice.

Mavis sat back down on the bed. I averted my gaze and looked out of the window. She took my hands in hers and said in her gentlest voice, "Myrtle and Wilfred on dem way to Durham. They get di call just after yu leave fah school dis morning." She paused. When I made no reply she went on. "A kyar skid out a control pon di icy road and lick him down while him was waiting to cross di road."

Why was she telling me these things? I didn't want to know. I stared out of the window and said nothing. Mavis shook me. "Michelle, are yu hearing mi?"

"Yes Mum."

"Well, seh somet'ing, fah heaven sakes." She sounded exasperated but I knew she was not angry. She was worried because I was not reacting in the way she would have expected me to on receiving such devastating news.

I said, "I just need to be alone for a while."

"Dat's di last t'ing yu need. People need dem family round dem at a time like dis. Delroy coming home from work at lunch time, and di twins' dem teacher bringing dem home now."

My heart sank. I could tolerate Samantha; even craved her company, but I couldn't face anyone else just now. I looked out of the window at the swirling snow flakes and I hated them. I would never enjoy snow again, not as long as I lived. I looked back at Mavis who was watching me.

"Mum, *please*. I really don't want to see anyone right now. I missed my English Lit. class today; I need to do

Claudette Beckford-Brady

some reading to catch up."

Mavis looked at me for a long moment, and then she shook her head, kissed my cheek and went out, shutting the door behind her. She probably thought I might find some comfort in my books. I knew she was worried, but I couldn't help it.

I picked up the book that Mavis had taken from me and opened it up to *Macbeth*. Maybe if I concentrated hard and didn't give myself time to think I might avoid the reality of the situation. I read the entire play and wrote a synopsis; then I answered a list of twenty questions relating to Shakespeare in general, and his other works.

I had just put away Shakespeare and taken out *Pride and Prejudice* by Jane Austin, when there was a knock on my door. I ignored it and opened my book. I heard the door open, but did not look up. I felt the bed sink as someone sat down beside me. I stared at the page without seeing the words; waiting for who-ever it was to say their piece and leave.

"Hi-ya, Shell." It was Delroy.

"Hi, Del." I replied.

"God, Shell, I just can't believe it! It seems impossible, doesn't it?"

I made no reply but continued staring at the page. As Mavis had done, Delroy took the book from me and turned me to face him. "Shell, you've got to snap out of this. You've got the parents really worried. Cry, scream, even swear if you want to, but don't withdraw into yourself. Let us help you through this."

I really loved my brother, but I just wanted him gone. I was not yet ready to acknowledge the fact that I would never see Clive again, and I was beginning to resent the fact that everyone wanted me to shout from the rooftops that he was dead. My mind was not ready to absorb the fact and I was not going to force it. The quickest way to get rid of Del was to play along with him.

"Honestly, Del, I'm fine. I just want to take some time to reflect. If I need you, I'll call, okay?"

He seemed rather doubtful, but he got up and went towards the door. "Promise, Shell?"

"I promise." I closed the door behind him.

I picked up the book that Delroy had taken from me and opened it. I tried to read, but stray thoughts were starting to creep into my mind. I knew what I had been told, but I knew that Clive couldn't really be dead. Why would they tell me something like that? If Clive were dead, wouldn't I feel it in the depths of my soul, loving him the way I did?

It was all a mistake, of course. When Miss Myrtle and Marse Wilfred got to Durham they would find that it had all been a ghastly mistake. Any minute now the phone would ring, and everything would get back to normal.

But what if it *wasn't* a mistake? What if Clive was really dead? No; that didn't bear thinking about. Wait for the phone to ring. Any minute now.

The minutes turned into an hour. Mavis came up with sandwiches and lemonade and insisted that I force some down me. It was easier to give in than to fight her. And still the phone did not ring.

Mavis tried to draw me out in conversation but I would not be drawn. Finally she said, "Yu want mi send Samantha up?" I shook my head. Not even Sammie could help me now. Only a ringing telephone.

The day turned into afternoon and then evening. The snow continued to fall. I closed the curtains and turned on the light. I took off my school uniform which I was still wearing, and put on a pair of pajamas, all the while listening for the telephone to ring.

Delroy brought up my dinner and stayed to make sure I ate at least a part of it. I managed to force down a few mouthfuls of the rice and peas and chicken that was the left-overs from Sunday dinner. After Delroy had gone back downstairs I roused myself sufficiently to go and brush my teeth, but decided to forgo a bath, just for tonight.

I returned to my room, and my waiting. And still the phone did not ring. I - somehow - finally fell asleep still waiting for the ring that would tell me that it had all been a horrible mistake.

I slept fitfully and woke with a start on several occasions. The night seemed like it would never end, but of course, it finally did. I did not dream.

Tuesday morning dawned gloomy and grey. I woke up with a dark cloud of despair hanging over me. When I dragged myself out of the bed and opened the curtains it was still dark outside; all I could see was my own reflection in the window glass. My clock-radio switched itself on and I listened to the BBC news.

Practically the whole country was under a blanket of snow, and schools and businesses were closed; only essential services were working and people were being advised to stay indoors, unless it was a matter of life and death.

I turned off the radio and went into the bathroom. I didn't want to hear any more about snow and death. The two would forever be linked together in my mind. I bathed and brushed my teeth, got dressed and went downstairs.

Mavis and Daddy were around the dining room table drinking tea. They were startled at my entry, obviously surprised. I told them both good morning and was startled at the sound of my own voice. It sounded hoarse and gravelly, as if I had been crying, which I hadn't.

"Shell! Yu nevah have to get up. A was gwine bring yu some tea, but A nevah expect yu fi wake suh soon." Mavis jumped up and came to hug me. "How yu feel dis maaning?"

Sweet Home, Jamaica

I extricated myself from the hug and said, "Did Miss Myrtle phone last night? Was it a mistake?"

Daddy and Mavis looked at each other again. They had been doing a lot of that lately. Daddy too had gotten up from around the table and had stood by while Mavis hugged me. Now he came forward and said, "Sit down, Shell. Mavis, bring har some tea."

I sat down. Then he turned back to me and said, "Wilfred phone last night. Dem have to stay up dere fi a few days to sort out everything and pack up Clive t'ings." He pause, then went on, "Dem si him. Him doan't mash up bad; hardly a mark pon him body; is internal injuries kill him."

I really didn't want or need to hear that. Details made it too real and I wasn't ready to accept it as fact yet. I turned to go out of the dining room and Daddy grabbed my hand. "Where yu going, Shell?"

"Up to my room."

At that moment Mavis came out of the kitchen with a cup of tea and two slices of toast on a plate, and overheard my words. She said, "Wait, Shell. Sit down wid Daddy and mi likkle, nuh."

I really didn't want to. I needed to go to my room and think about what I had just heard. But I didn't have the strength to fight Mavis and Daddy over it. I sat down and Daddy and Mavis did too. I sipped half-heartedly at the tea and nibbled at the toast, my eyes cast down. I could feel them both watching me.

Then Mavis said, "Shell, what yu need is to have a good cry and get some of di grief out of yu system. Wi know how much yu did love Clive, and yu gwine miss him bad, but yu young, and yu wi' find love again."

She meant well, but she had said the wrong thing. I sprang up from my chair, knocking over the tea in the process, and faced them.

Claudette Beckford-Brady

"I will NEVER love anyone else! I will love Clive till the day I die and he will never be dead to me!" and with that I ran out of the dining room and up the stairs to my room. I slammed the door and collapsed onto my bed.

And then the tears came. And came... and came. In floods, and torrents, and great wracking sobs that tore my chest raw, and left me struggling for breath. Vaguely I was aware that the door had opened and there were people in my room. Someone was holding me and some-one else was shooing out the twins who had started bawling as well, whether in sympathy with me or in genuine grief for Clive, whom they had liked.

The snow which had eased up during the night was now falling heavily again, although I was not aware of this till much later. The damned snow, which had caused the death of my man.

The next few days passed in a blurred surreal world of whispers and people tiptoeing in and out of my room. Miss Myrtle and Marse Wilfred returned from Durham and a fresh round of crying commenced. Eventually, however, I, who was not a crying sort of a person, was all cried out.

Once the crying had stopped I set out to get on with my life. I became stoic and insisted on returning to school. I absolutely refused to attend the funeral; I told them that as far as I was concerned Clive was still alive in my heart and I refused to bury him, either literally or figuratively.

The snow had stopped falling after a couple of days and things were beginning to return to normal. The once pristine white snow was now a muddy, slushy, dirty grey, and it was melting fast. Within a few more days, all traces of it were totally gone; school had re-opened and I was back in class.

The day of the funeral was a school day. I went to school despite pleas and entreaties from everyone, except, surprisingly, Clive's parents. They sided with me and told

Sweet Home, Jamaica

me that everyone had their own way of dealing with their grief, and if mine was to remember Clive as he was, instead of watching him being placed in a hole in the ground, well, they could understand. Miss Myrtle said I didn't need to attend his funeral to prove to anyone that I had loved him; they all knew how much I had.

Half term came and went and it was strange not having Clive around for the holidays, but gradually, day by day things began to look not so bleak. I missed him terribly, and I found a certain amount of comfort by going to his house and spending time in his room, where we had made such passionate love. I cried a lot on the occasions spent in his room, and sometimes his mum joined me and we would hold each other and cry.

I started spending more and more time at his house, mostly weekends at first, but gradually increasing until I actually lived there, visiting my own home only intermittently. Miss Myrtle had changed from a happy-go-lucky, jovial woman into a quiet shadow of herself and seemed to find great comfort in having me around her. It was Mavis who suggested that I should move in with them. I was happy to agree. Clive had been their only child, and I would do my best to become a beloved daughter to them.

If Clive's death had turned his mother into a pale shadow of herself, it did something amazingly strange to Marse Wilfred. He started drinking heavily and to our distress and dismay, started fooling around with other women. And to make matters worse, when he was found out he was unrepentant, claiming that he could die at any moment and he wanted to enjoy some of the good life before he did.

Miss Myrtle seemed indifferent to his drinking and philandering, just drifting along from home to work and back again. I did most of the work around the house, and tried to make her life as comfortable as possible.

Claudette Beckford-Brady

Mavis and Daddy tried to reason with Marse Wilfred but to no avail. He continued on his downward spiral.

Clive's death had changed me too. I was now much quieter; not quite as feisty and outspoken as I had been. I was kinder too; less cutting and sarcastic in my dealings with people and more willing to concede in an argument, even when I knew that I was right.

Once I had gotten over the initial shock and grief of Clive's death, I had decided that what Clive would want was for me to make a success of my life and be happy. I set out to achieve the first part by being completely single-minded about my studies, which was not difficult for me. The second part would take a while longer.

The planned meeting with my maternal uncle and his family had not taken place. The snow and Clive's death had thrown everyone out of sync and now I was in the middle of mock A Level exams. It would be summer before the anticipated event could take place.

Meanwhile my friends Joy and Yvonne had been having their own dramas during the time of my bereavement. Yvonne had discovered Mikey's infidelity and had gotten into a fight with the white girl. I told her that it was beneath her dignity and she was belittling herself. I told her to follow my example; concentrate on her studies and forget about men for the moment. Within a week she was sporting a new boyfriend.

Joy, on the other hand, had just about had enough of her parents. She had been a virtual prisoner in her home, only being allowed to go to school and church. She had started playing truant from school in order to spend time with my brother Delroy, who had flexible working conditions and could organize his workload so as to give him some free time during the day.

Joy was just waiting until she was eighteen so she could legally leave home. She and Delroy planned to get a flat together as soon as they could. But that could not happen for over a year. I would be eighteen in December of this year, but Joy would not reach her majority till the following May.

I tried to encourage her not to cut classes as we were so close to finishing school, but she said she had enough O Levels to get a 'decent enough' job. It was no use my appealing to Delroy; anything Joy wanted, Joy got, and if she said this was how it was to be, then Delroy just went along with her.

I wrapped up my exams by the middle of June and was out of school for summer. I would be going on to Upper Sixth in September and finishing next June, after which I would attend the University of London for a three year degree course. But for the next couple of months I was a free agent. I felt confident of my exam results and knew I would get good grades. In the meantime I decided to improve myself by taking evening classes in Computer Studies, and Creative writing at Brixton College.

I had already started work on what I called 'my bestseller'; banging out chapters on the portable typewriter I had received as a reward for good exam results. I still worked at *Boots* Chemist five days a week, and volunteered at the library one half day. Between all this and taking care of the household chores at Mummy Myrtle's I found I was stretched pretty thin. However, I like being too busy during the days to think about Clive, but at night I indulged myself and re-lived our time together.

The pain of his death was not so intense anymore. I still missed him terribly, of course, but I could think about him without crying now. Mummy Myrtle too seemed to be perking up a bit and returning to her old self. Mavis said that I should take credit for that because I kept Clive alive for her, by talking about him with her, and that sometimes that's the best way for a person to grieve; by talking about their loved one.

Daddy Wilfred continued on his drinking and whoring binge until one evening I came home to hear him and Mummy Myrtle having a real rip-roaring quarrel. She was telling him that if he didn't shape up he would have to ship out. I was about to go quietly upstairs and leave them to it, when I heard a resounding slap and a crash of broken glass. I heard Mummy Myrtle cry out and I dropped my bag and ran into the living room to see what was going on.

Mummy Myrtle was on the floor amongst broken glass from the china cabinet; there was blood but I couldn't see where it was coming from. I cried out and ran to examine her to see where the injury was. She sat up and started brushing herself off. I told her to keep still because she was inadvertently brushing at the broken pieces of glass with her hands and lacerating them.

I removed all the broken glass from her person and sat her in a chair. The blood was a false alarm; she had received a few minor lacerations which she had caused herself by brushing at the glass. She had fallen into the cabinet and broken it but had escaped any serious cuts.

She was crying. After I had made sure there were no serious injuries I turned my attention to Daddy Wilfred, who seemed to be stunned by what had happened. He just stood there in the centre of the living room as if lost, muttering, "God, Myrkle. Mi sarry. Laad God, mi sarry."

I looked at him scornfully and in disgust. I knew Daddy had never hit Mavis and wouldn't dream of it. If they had an argument he would quicker walk out and stay out for a few hours, but he never stayed out all night as Daddy Wilfred had taken to doing. And if Daddy was unfaithful to Mavis it was a well kept secret; no humiliating her in the community as Daddy Wilfred was doing to Mummy Myrtle.

I thought of Clive. He wouldn't be able to fathom this if he were alive. He had never known his parents to be anything but loving. *I* had never known them to be anything but loving, that is until Clive's death. But then, if he were alive, this situation would not be. This was a direct result of his death.

But that did not excuse Daddy Wilfred. I looked at him and said in the coldest voice I had, "Clive would be *so ashamed* if he were here to see this. He would expect you to comfort and cherish his mother in a time like this; instead you've taken to abusing her. *I'm* ashamed of you."

To my surprise and great consternation, Daddy Wilfred suddenly collapsed into a chair and started sobbing. Loud wracking sobs that sounded almost like an animal in pain. I was shocked and frightened. I had never seen a grown man cry before. I was at a total loss.

Meanwhile Mummy Myrtle was still sitting in the settee crying quietly to herself and holding her jaw where I assumed the slap which I heard had landed. I quickly picked up the phone and called Mavis. I asked her if Daddy was there, could she and him come over quickly. She must have heard something in my voice – I don't know – fear, panic – something – for in less than five minutes she and Daddy were on the doorstep.

They could stay outside and hear Daddy Wilfred's wracking sobs and when they came in I gave them a brief and speedy summary of what had transpired. I directed them into the living room; Mavis gasped and ran over to Mummy Myrtle. Daddy stood as if at a loss as to what he was supposed to do; finally he went and put his hand on Daddy Wilfred's shoulder.

Mavis and I got Mummy Myrtle out of the living room and upstairs. I steered them into Clive's room, which was actually now my room, and left them, telling Mavis I was going to make some tea. Before I went into the kitchen I sneaked a look into the living room. Daddy Wilf had stopped crying. He seemed to have sobered up somewhat, and he was talking to Daddy in a quiet voice.

I made a pot of tea and placed four cups on a tray with milk and sugar. I knocked on the open living room door and entered. The talking stopped. Without saying a word I poured two cups of tea, added milk and sugar and went out. I added another tea bag to the pot, topped it up with boiling water and took it upstairs, placing it on what used to be Clive's homework table.

Mavis had cleaned up Mummy Myrtle who seemed to be feeling a little better. She gave me a watery smile when I handed her the cup of tea, and said, "A don't know what wi would do widout yu, Shellie. Yu such a good girl; nuh true Mavis?" and Mavis replied, "Yu know weh yu-a seh, Myrkle; dem nuh come better dan Shellie."

I was touched, and slightly embarrassed. I decided to make light of it. "Thank you both, but Mum, remember what a holy terror I was a few years ago? Especially the time you told me I couldn't go on the school trip to Stratford, and you blurted out the fact that you were not my birth mother?"

Mavis laughed. "Yes, back den yu really was a – weh yu call it – holy terror? A wha dat?" and we all laughed; me a little hysterically.

I had deliberately steered the conversation into lighter waters because I did not want to face the reality of what had just happened. But it was there hovering in the background, and suddenly Mummy Myrtle said, "Yu know seh is di first time in twenty two 'ears of marriage dat Wilfred evah put him han' pon mi?"

I bridled indignantly, and before Mavis could say anything, I said, "Well it better be the last, or next time I'll phone the police and let them lock him up! You just let me know if he *EVER* hits you again, Mummy Myrtle!"

At that moment there was a knock on the room door; I thought it was Daddy but when I opened the door Daddy

Wilfred was standing there, looking fifteen years older, and rather embarrassed. I had no sympathy for him. I stared at him coldly and he refused to meet my eyes. I wanted to bawl him out, but he was Clive's father, after all, and therefore a little restraint was called for.

I went out into the hallway, pulling up the door behind me. "Daddy Wilf, I can't believe you actually *hit* Mummy Myrtle. You've turned into an alcoholic and you need treatment. Clive must be turning in his grave to know what level you have descended to...." I was interrupted by a hand on my shoulder. It was Mummy Myrtle. "Shell, leave it."

Daddy Wilf was standing with his head bowed. He did not attempt to defend himself. I knew he was sorry and ashamed; I could see it in his body language; but I was not yet ready to forgive him. He had committed the unforgivable in my opinion; he had hit a woman, and to make matters worse, that woman was his wife. This could be the beginning of a long slippery slope, and I was not about to just stand by and watch them slide.

Mummy Myrtle took Daddy Wilf's hand and started leading him towards their own room. He followed her meekly. I knew she had forgiven him already; I heard it in her voice when she told us that it was the fist time he had ever hit her. I did not think she should forgive him so easily and I started to protest, but Mavis shushed me and pulled me back into the room.

Shellie, leave it. Is none of our business. Is a married couple dat."

"But Mum, suppose he hits her again? You know that once a man start to hit you, him nuh have nuh stop fi stop," I said, quoting my friend Yvonne who had told Stephanie the same thing about her then boyfriend, Winston.

But Mavis insisted that we all go home and give the

Richards time to themselves to sort out their differences. I reluctantly complied.

As it turned out, that incident was the catalyst that returned Daddy Wilf to his normal self. It appeared he had so shocked himself by what he had done that he was spurred to change. And he did it all himself with no help from Alcoholics Anonymous. The philandering also stopped and he and Mummy Myrtle returned to being the loving couple they had always been.

A few years later Daddy Wilf confided to me that it was more my dressing him down and telling him how ashamed Clive would be that had spurred him on to change.

Whatever it was, I was relieved, because my life was getting rather crowded and I didn't want to have to be worrying about Mummy Myrtle being alone and vulnerable.

August came and it was now six months since Clive had died. We all still missed him very much, but life was returning to normal and I was now ready to pick up the pieces and restart the process of bonding with my maternal family. Mavis had apprised them of the tragedy which had taken place in my life and I had received letters of condolences from Grandma Miriam and all the uncles. Uncle Keith had phoned on several occasions, but I had not spoken to him myself.

So now, with everything being rosy again, so to speak, I made time to connect with Uncle Keith and his family. And so I planned a trip to Birmingham to begin the process of linking up with my maternal relatives.

CHAPTER ELEVEN

Meet the Keith Campbells

New Street Station, Birmingham. Hustling; bustling; noisy. I stepped off the train and scanned the platform. Uncle Keith was meeting me; we shouldn't have any problems recognising each other, we both had photographs.

I saw him straight away and he saw me at the same time. I waved and we started walking toward each other. I was excited. I was meeting unknown members of my family for the first time, and the feeling was hard to describe.

Uncle Keith did not stand on any ceremonies. When he reached me he took the week-end case from my hand, placed it on the ground and hugged me to him tightly. When he finally released me I looked into his face and saw that there were tears. I was shocked and surprised.

He held my face with his two hands and said in an emotional voice, "If I didn't know better, I would swear that you were my baby sister. You look exactly like yu mother when she was your age."

I felt all choked up myself. I had been full of excited anticipation and a little nervousness; what would Uncle Keith and his family be like? Would they like me, or would they find me too superior and patronising. I didn't think I was, but Clive had always accused me of being that way. I would have to be very careful how I portrayed myself to them.

In the event I need not have worried. When we got to the house, all the family were waiting to greet me, and it was as if we had known each other all our lives. I was hugged and kissed by everyone and called "Cousin Shellie."

Everyone wanted to talk at the same time and it was a veritable cacophony in that house in the suburbs of Birmingham. Finally, Uncle Keith bellowed for everyone to shut up, and calm returned to the household. Uncle Keith then proceeded to give me a welcome speech.

"Shellie, I don't know if yu can imagine how surprised and pleased I was when Mamma write and tell mi 'bout yu. And now, to see yu in person, looking suh much like yu mother, well..." The emotion seemed too much for him and he trailed off and hugged me again. Then he continued.

On behalf of my wife and children, I take great pleasure in welcoming yu into the bosom of yu family. Welcome home, child; welcome home."

There were cheers and hand clapping. I felt that an acknowledgement was called for.

"Thank you, Uncle Keith, and thank you all. This means so much to me. The moment I found out that Daddy's wife was not my mother, I resolved to find her." I paused, but continued quickly before anyone could say anything. "Don't get me wrong; I love Mavis; she's the best mother anyone could ask for, but I still want to find my birth mother."

Sweet Home, Jamaica

Uncle Keith replied, "Yes, Miss Mavis is a remarkable woman. Mamma told me how she seek her out in order to share you with us. Another woman might not be so generous."

I felt very proud of Mavis in that moment. I went on to tell my new-found relatives about how I had discovered that Mavis was not my mother. I hastened to assure them that our animosity toward each other was all in the distant past and that we were now as close as a mother and daughter could be. The family curled up laughing when I related the lengths I had gone to in order to get to go to Stratford-upon-Avon with my class.

The ice was well and truly broken and I fit right into the Campbell family straight away. I felt as if I had known them all my life, and found that we were all very much alike in many ways. Uncle Keith couldn't stop exclaiming over how like my mother I was; both in looks and mannerisms, he said, and he added that from what he had learned about me so far, I was just as feisty and opinionated as Delisia. I did not take his statement as a criticism; I knew it was not meant as such.

I had arrived with the intention of spending perhaps four or five days, but the time went so fast that I had to extend my stay. I had taken a week's leave from my holiday job at *Boots* and I phoned them up and asked for another week. They had no problem with that.

Aunt Vilma and my sixteen year old cousin, Veronica, took me to the Bull Ring Shopping Centre to buy a few pieces of clothing, since I had only brought sufficient for a shorter stay. I had plenty of money of my own, but Aunt Vilma said that Uncle Keith had given her money for the purchases, and would not allow me to spend any of my own. In the short time I had been amongst them, I had learned not to argue; I rarely won, which was a novel experience for me.

Claudette Beckford-Brady

Aunt Vilma was rather plump and had a bossy streak. But she was also very jovial and found something to laugh at in almost every situation. She and Uncle Keith obviously had a happy and loving relationship; you could see it in the way they related to each other. He was always touching her; slapping her rump or tweaking her ear. Aunt Vilma told me that the secret for success in any marriage is to let the man *think* that "is him run t'ings," while you quietly pulled his strings.

My cousin, Veronica was sixteen, and the eldest of four. She was slightly shorter than I was, about five feet six inches tall, and a little on the chubby side. She had long black hair which revealed the Indian part of our genes; Mavis had told me that my mother "had Indian in her."

I was sharing a room with Veronica. She, like her mother, was a happy person, and she and I hit it off immediately. We filled each other in on our lives so far; I learned that she had completed O Levels this last school year and was heading for A Levels next year. She was planning to go into medicine; paediatrics or gynaecology; she couldn't decide which just yet. Like me, she was an avid reader and we had lively conversations and discussions on a vast range of subjects.

It took her three days to reach the subject of Clive. She was a sensitive girl, and was hesitant about approaching the subject, but as soon as she realised that I was not against talking about him, she was full of questions.

We were lying in bed one night, after having spent a fun day at the beach at Weston-Super-Mare. She had confided to me that she had a crush on a boy, and was lamenting that he didn't seem to notice that she existed.

She had never had a boyfriend, and was sure it was because she was too fat, but, try as she might, she could not shed the pounds. She swore she didn't eat much, and in fact from what I had seen, she really only picked at her food. I consoled her and told her that when she found the right guy he would love her for her personality and not care about her size.

We lay in silence for a while, and I was just floating off into a doze when she whispered, "Shell?"

"Hm?" I replied drowsily.

"Does it still hurt terribly to think of Clive?"

It so happened I had been thinking of Clive just before dozing off. It didn't hurt as badly anymore. The memories now were sweet and tender; although I still missed him, it just didn't hurt as much as it used to. I said as much to Veronica. "Not so much, anymore. It gets a little better day by day."

She was silent for a while, and I thought she had dozed off, when she spoke, again in a whisper. "Could you tell me about him, Shell? That is if it doesn't distress you."

"It doesn't. What do you want to know?"

"Everything. How you met, what he was like – everything you want to tell me."

We talked till late into the night. I told her everything about me and Clive. I held nothing back. It felt good to talk about him to someone who had not known him. It helped me to re-live our time together. When I told her about being allowed to go on the Pill, she got up and turned on the light.

Looking me in the face she said disbelievingly, "Your mother let you go on the Pill at sixteen?" When I nodded she said, "Wow! I should be so lucky! I wouldn't dare approach Mum with anything so presumptuous. Gosh, Shell, I wish I were you!"

Veronica was still a virgin; had never even been kissed by a boy, and she was all agog to know all the intimate details of mine and Clive's relationship. I was not shy to tell her; I told her about trying to rush Clive into having sex with me and how he had reacted. I told her how I had run off in tears and how we had finally made love the next day. She looked at me with new respect after that night.

When I told her about the accident and his death, Veronica cried. And *I* comforted *her*. That night we bonded closer together, and we were to remain firm friends, and not just cousins, for the rest of our lives.

My cousin Joseph was fourteen; two years younger than Veronica. He was a bespectacled young man who nearly always had his head in a book, but when he was ready he was a bundle of fun. He beat me at Scrabble; something nobody had done in a very long time, and earned my great respect.

The two younger girls, Jennifer and Elaine, were eight and four respectively. The whole family took me into their bosoms and I blended and became one with them.

A few days after my arrival, Uncle Keith had called me into what he referred to as his 'study.' This was the room where he kept all his work related stuff; his drawings and calculations and his engineering paraphernalia. He had told me that he was one of the engineers who had worked on the famous 'Spaghetti Junction,' a criss-cross of road networks, bridges and fly-overs which connected the West Midlands to all other parts of the country.

He promised that he would take me on a tour of the Junction before I went back to London. But for now he wanted to talk to me about the search for my mother.

During the time of my bereavement, he had taken it upon himself to write to the Ministry of Education in Jamaica, seeking any information he could get regarding my mother, his sister. As he had expected, no response was forthcoming, but he had asked a friend in Kingston to visit the school in Trench Town where Delisia was last known to teach. The friend had learned that Delisia had left that post to take up another at Excelsior Girls' School.

The lead was followed and it was established that

Sweet Home, Jamaica

Delisia had taught there until 1972, when she apparently acquired a visa, and went off to the United States. That was just six years ago. The news was encouraging. At least we knew that she was alive and well up to that time. Now we would have to invent creative ways to expand our search.

I was pleased that Uncle Keith had taken an active role in the search for Delisia. I felt encouraged; that it was only a matter of time before she was located and persuaded to re-connect with her family.

I asked him if he had any ideas as to how to proceed from here. He said we could try placing advertisements in the UK and North American Press or on community radio in areas with large Jamaican populations, such as Miami and New York. I asked him if that wouldn't cost an awful lot of money and he replied that no amount was too much to spend if it meant finding his little sister.

I suggested that if Delisia did not want to be found she could just blithely ignore all appeals. Uncle Keith said that it was possible someone other than Delisia, who knew her and her whereabouts, would see or hear the ads and contact us. He even said he was willing to put up a reward, and the rest of my uncles were all willing to pitch in wherever needed.

I spent a wonderful two weeks with my family, and when it was time to return to London we all parted with sadness. But we were only a phone call away, and Uncle Keith said they were planning to visit Jamaica at Christmas and they would be pleased if I could find the time to come with them; he would pay my way.

I was excited and said that I would love to go with them, but that I could buy my own ticket. Uncle Keith got dictatorial and told me that he would buy my ticket and no arguments. I meekly accepted.

I returned to London full of happy excitement about my

Claudette Beckford-Brady

planned trip to Jamaica at Christmas. It would mean missing the first two weeks of term in January, but I was confident I would not fall behind in my work.

I was still living at Mummy Myrtle and Daddy Wilfred's house. Things were rosy again between my two 'in-laws' and I did my best to fill the void left by Clive's death, and I believe I was successful in doing so. In any event we were all very happy, and I was being spoiled rotten by them.

All that they had intended to spend on Clive was now being spent on me. I got two lots of pocket money every week; one from my own parents, and one from Clive's. I had tried to protest to Daddy Wilf that I did not need it, but he insisted, and so I accepted it gracefully and put it away in my savings account each week.

I returned to school in September and buckled down to concentrate on my lessons. During the half-term holidays I set about shopping for clothes to take with me to Jamaica at Christmas. Joy was unable to come shopping with me, because whenever she got the opportunity to elude her parents the time was invariably spent with Delroy. However, Yvonne and I made the trek into the West End and I bought up lots of skimpy little summer outfits which I got at end of season sale prices.

Joy had opted not to go on to Upper Sixth. She left school and got a job as an Administrative Assistant at Lambeth Town Hall, which she said didn't pay too badly, and she was just counting the months till next May when she would turn eighteen and could legally leave home.

Yvonne and I lamented the fact that our two friends, Joy and Stephanie with whom we had been sparring since we were little more than toddlers, had taken different paths in life.

We weren't really too worried about Joy; we knew she would be okay. For one thing she was still going out with my brother and they were 'going steady,' and for another

Sweet Home, Jamaica

she had a good steady job with prospects for promotion.

Stephanie, however, still gave us cause for concern. She had been living in sheltered accommodation in Tottenham, North London, and had subsequently been placed with a foster family, along with her son, till she was eighteen and could apply for a Council flat. Yvonne and I had visited her there, and had discovered, to our dismay, that Steph had not only taken up with another Rasta, but was actually pregnant again.

However, this Rasta was totally different from Winston. He was quiet and humble and obviously highly intelligent. He was an Executive Officer in the Civil Service and I was patronizingly surprised that a Rasta should hold such a high-ranking position in Government Service.

At first I found it difficult to understand how an intelligent, educated person could be a Rasta, worship a man named Haile Selassie, and smoke marijuana, but after conversing with Benji, I have to say I can understand how some people could be convinced of the ideology.

Benji did not even try to convince. He spoke simply and in a 'matter of fact' way, as if there was no room for doubt, and he backed up his arguments with quotes from the Bible which were quite convincing. However, me being a person without a single religious bone in my body, I declined to be converted. And I was most definitely not on board with the smoking of the weed.

But after the visit Yvonne and I agreed that Steph appeared to be happy, and there were no signs of abuse. And her son, Nkrumah, who was fifteen months old, seemed happy enough, and called Benji 'Dada.'

Nkrumah had been given the nickname of 'Little Lion' which invariably had been shortened to just 'Lion.' I was sort of relieved for him; Lion was bad enough, but not nearly as bad as Nkrumah. I had also established that Steph and Benji had no intention of letting him grow dreadlocks until he was old enough to decide for himself if he wanted to.

This made my respect for Benji grow, because if it had been left up to Steph and Lion's biological father, Winston, I'm sure they would have 'locksed' the little boy.

December came and I geared up for my trip to Jamaica. All my preparations had been made for some time; there was only a little last minute packing to do. We were leaving on the eighteenth, four days after my eighteenth birthday. Remembering that Delroy had shown an interest in going to Jamaica last year when Daddy and Mavis were going, I invited him to come with me, but he declined, saying this was a time for me and my other family.

The whole family were excited for me; pleased that I had connected with my birth family. At first Daddy had been a little reticent but I had made sure to pay him special attention and not let him think that I was abandoning my nuclear family, and he had gradually come round to accept the idea.

My eighteenth birthday dawned cold, but clear. A crisp frost had fallen the night before but the sun was out and making sparkling diamonds on the grass and plants. As I stood at the window in Clive's room, which was now my room, and looked out on the back garden, I sadly contemplated that this day would have marked our fourth anniversary; we had started going out on my fourteenth birthday.

But I was not allowed to be sad or downhearted. Both Mummy Myrtle and Mavis had taken the day off from work, and preparations were in full swing for my birthday party later that evening. My two sets of parents had collaborated in planning the party despite my protests that I didn't want one. I was told not to be ridiculous; how can one not *want* an eighteenth birthday party.

Only my brother Delroy and my best friend Joy

understood why I wasn't particular about having a party. The parents were not aware that today was more than just my birthday. Or so I thought, until Mavis took me one side and spoke to me.

"Shell, I remember seh is on yu birt'day yu did meet Clive, suh it stand to reason dat yu would feel a likkle low to-deh. But yu know seh Clive wouldn't want yu to be sad, and to-deh yu become a' adult. Is a time fah celebration, suh remember Clive, but not wid sadness."

I don't know why it should, but it always surprised me when Mavis made sage remarks. That superior attitude again, Clive would say. But Mavis' words did help to lift the gloom and I began to get into the spirit of things.

The cake was made and decorated with pink roses and the number eighteen written in blue icing. Curry goat was cooking in a big pot, chicken and fish were being fried, and drinks were outside keeping cold.

Around three o'clock the doorbell rang and when I went to see who was there I got the surprise of my life. There on the doorstep was the entire Campbell family, all grinning and thrusting presents at me.

I'd had no idea they were coming. I had not expected to see them until Monday at the airport; we had already agreed that we would meet there. Now here they all were, and I was extremely happy to see them. After hugs and kisses I managed to find out that Mavis and Mummy Myrtle had arranged for them to come to the party, and to stay in London until Monday when we would be flying out.

Accommodations would be a little cramped but it would only be for a few days. There was a spare room at Mummy Myrtle' which was allocated to Uncle Keith and Aunt Vilma. Veronica would share my room, while the two younger girls would use my old room at home. Delroy said he would sleep on the settee and let Joseph use his room.

No member of my nuclear family had yet met any of my

maternal family in person; Mavis alone had spoken to Uncle Keith on the phone, but the way everyone just fit in and blended together, you would have thought we had all known each other for years.

The twins and Samantha adopted Jennifer and Elaine and carted them off on some pursuit or other, probably to introduce them to the ten Brennan kids from next door. As the only boy, I thought Joseph might feel isolated, but he was never so happy as when his head was stuck in a book, so I turned him loose on my bookcase - and my collection was extensive - and left him to browse happily.

I was a bit apprehensive about Daddy meeting the Campbells, but as it turned out everything went well. Daddy and Uncle Keith had actually known each other as boys, and greeted each other easily. Uncle Keith was lavish in his praise of Daddy and Mavis and said I was a great credit to them. He congratulated them on being open-minded enough to help facilitate the search for Delisia and to connect me with my maternal family.

And to help matters along, it turned out that Uncle Keith was a champion domino player, and Daddy ever loved a challenge.

It was a wonderful eighteenth birthday party. All my friends were there; I had personally begged Joy's mum to let her come celebrate with me. It took a lot of persuasion, but she finally agreed, as long as Joy was home by 10.30pm. We had to be satisfied with that. Yvonne and her new boyfriend and several of my friends from school were there, as were Steph and Benji.

To my surprise, Uncle Keith and Benji found a lot to talk about, and later Uncle Keith remarked that Benji was a most intelligent young man. I replied that it was only a pity he had to be a Rasta, and Uncle Keith said sternly, "Don't judge or condemn, Shellie. The Rastafarian religion, when practiced properly has a lot going for it. Your Uncle Cornell

Sweet Home, Jamaica

is a Rasta, and one of the best people I know."

I had the photos of all the uncles and I remembered that Uncle Cornell was a Rasta. I had never thought of Rastafarianism as being a religion, but I respected Uncle Keith and if he said it was, then it was. I apologised to him and was about to slink away when he said, "I used to have locks too, yu know. Is when I was coming to England I cut them off."

I looked at him with my mouth open. He laughed and said, "Close yu mouth, Shellie, fly might pitch een deh."

I was actually quite speechless. I couldn't quite see Uncle Keith with dreadlocks. A sudden thought occurred to me. "Did you use to smoke weed, Uncle Keith? Does Uncle Cornell smoke?"

Uncle Keith looked around him theatrically and said, in a stage whisper with his hand partially covering his mouth, "Don't tell anyone, but I still have a puff now and then. And yes, yu Uncle Cornell burn him herbs."

It was the first time I had heard marijuana referred to as 'herbs'. My conversation with Uncle Keith, and my previous discussions with Benji gave me pause for thought, and I determined to look further into the Rastafarian religion to see what merits it held.

But that would be for another time. Right now I was in the middle of celebrating my coming of age. The candles had been blown out, the cake cut, toasts made and now it was being demanded that I start to open the scores of presents I had been inundated with.

While the music thumped and the guests danced, my best friends and I, together with my cousin Veronica, tore through wrapping paper and ended up with a pile of assorted gifts; a hairdryer, curling tongs, a nightdress case, books and records, perfumes and bath oils, gift tokens and various other things useful to a young woman.

I was bemused when, amongst the gifts, there was

nothing from my parents or my surrogate parents, and nothing from Uncle Keith and Aunt Vilma. I was a little hurt at first, but then it dawned on me that they must have something special to give me. It was inconceivable that they would fail to give me anything on my most important birthday.

I was right. When all the guests had gone and the clearing up completed – it didn't take long, there were many hands to make light work – we all congregated in the living room. The younger children had gone to bed but the twins, who were now thirteen, had been allowed to stay. We had to sit on the floor because the furniture had been moved out to accommodate the dancing, and had not yet been put back.

Daddy cleared his throat and demanded everyone's attention. He puffed himself up, assumed an air of self-importance, and launched into a slightly inebriated speech.

"Mi dear dahta, A tek great pleasure, at dis great psychological moment, an' on dis great suspicious occasion..."

The entire roomful of people collapsed with laughter, even Mavis, who I was not sure had realised what Daddy had said. Daddy too appeared not to realise what he had said, because he just stood there saying bemusedly, "Is wha?"

When I could catch my breath, I gasped, with tears streaming down my face, "*Aus*picious occasion, Daddy; auspicious."

"Da's what A said. An' oonu nuh have nuh mannahs." He turned his attention from me to the other occupants of the room, some of whom were still in fits of laughter. "A trying to give mi dahta a birt'day speech and oonu deh intrupt mi!" He slurred the word 'interrupt.'

Daddy never actually got rip roaring drunk, but he often got what we referred to as 'cherry.' This was one of those times; he had had *just* a little too much, and it could make him a little belligerent, but not out of control. Mavis quickly rushed to smooth his ruffled feathers, and I tried, with a little difficulty, because I was still laughing myself, to quieten the room.

Eventually calm was restored and Daddy resumed, mid sentence, which threatened to set me off laughing again.

"....this auspicious occasion of yu eighteen birt'day. A remembah di day yu baan like it was yessiday, an' a kyaant believe yu tun big ooman a'ready." He paused, took a sip of the beer he was holding in his hand, and continued. "Yu madda and mi..." He reached for Mavis' hand, "yu madda and mi," he repeated, "wi proud a yu. An' wi waan to gi' yu a good start in life, suh we waant yu fi tek dis likkle gif' and work pon it mek it grow fi yu."

He handed me an envelope which he had been holding. Amongst cheers and handclaps I opened the envelope. Inside was a certificate of deposit for a thousand pounds.

I was speechless for a moment. A thousand pounds seemed like a lot of money. How could the parents spare that amount to give to me? Delroy had not been given anything like that on his eighteenth birthday, or since, I was sure of it. I glanced guiltily at him, but he smiled at me, oblivious to what I held and what I was thinking.

They were all waiting for an acknowledgement from me. I found a smile somewhere and pasted it onto my face. I injected great delight into my voice and exclaimed, "Oh, thanks, Dad, Mum. This is overwhelming; I wasn't expecting anything like this!" I hugged and kissed them both.

The pleasure on my parents' faces was my reward. Even though inside I was not quite comfortable with the gift, I knew they took great pleasure in giving it to me and I could not disappoint them by being less than enthusiastic. Meanwhile the twins were clamouring to know what I had got, so I handed them the Certificate which they examined and passed around.

Then it was Daddy Wilf and Mummy Myrtle's turn. They took centre stage and Daddy Wilf began his speech. "Shellie, yu is a angel send down from Heaven by God, to give me and Myrkle comfort. From di day mi son Clive bring yu into wi life, yu bring us nutting but joy and pleasure, an' A don't shame fi seh dat when A need dressing down or pulling up, yu don't 'fraid fi dweet."

He paused, and I knew we were all thinking of the time he had gone on an alcoholic and whoring binge, shortly after Clive's death. He continued, "Yu is more dan a dahta to wi, Shell, an' now dat wi one-son gone, yu is all wi have lef'. Wi love yu like yu-a fi wi own, an' Myrkle an' mi tek great pleasure fi gi' yu dis pon di occasion a yu eighteen birt'day."

More cheers and handclapping, as I was handed another envelope. I opened it and looked at some unfamiliar documents. On closer inspection I realised, to my great shock, surprise, and delight that they were documents for a car, and they had my name on them. And something else was still inside the envelope; I shook it out, and it was a car key.

Once again I was speechless. And a little emotional. Daddy Wilf's references to Clive made me realise just how much I still missed him. My cousin Veronica, whom I had noticed was very empathetic, squeezed my hand, and I knew she was silently offering me comfort. The twins were pressing me to see what the envelope contained. I ignored them and went to embrace my surrogate parents.

I couldn't speak to thank them, but our embrace said everything, and after the emotions were put away, and I had shown everyone the contents of the envelope, Uncle Keith said to me, "Can yu drive, Shell?"

"No, Uncle Keith, but I'm sure gonna learn now!"

"Well, perhaps this will help yu," and he handed me yet another envelope.

So many envelopes in one night. What could this one contain, I wondered. I opened the envelope and inside was a receipt for twenty driving lessons, to be taken at my convenience, with a reputable local driving school. It was obvious there had been some collaboration with the selection of my gifts. Uncle Keith was speaking to me again.

I don't think it should take yu more than twenty lessons, but if yu need more, it can be arranged."

The most I could do was hug him and Aunt Vilma. But they weren't even finished with me. I was handed yet another envelope, this time by Aunt Vilma. This one contained a cheque for five hundred pounds.

To say that I was overwhelmed by all these generous gifts would be to understate how I really felt. Uncle Keith had already bought me an airline ticket to Jamaica, and would be financing my entire stay, and yet they still wanted to give me more. Wilfred and Myrtle had bought me a brand new Mini which must have set them back several thousand pounds, and my parents had not only given me a great party but also a large sum of cash. Surely I was the luckiest girl in South London.

It had been a most marvellous eighteenth birthday; the only blot being the fact that Clive was not there to celebrate with me. And, in another few days, I would be embarking on a new adventure; flying off to Jamaica to see the land of my birth, and to meet my maternal grandmother and all my uncles and cousins.

Later that night as I tried to find elusive sleep – I guess I was still riding high on excitement – I thought of how happy and pleased Clive would have been to know that I had connected so well with my maternal family. He had always been worried that I might suffer hurt and rejection if and when I found my mother. It was still a possibility, but the fact that I had connected so well with the rest of the Campbells boded well for me, and after all, they were in the same position as I was; they too wanted to find Delisia, and they too would be risking rejection if she was found.

I finally found sleep.

The next day, Saturday, Daddy Wilf took me to the car showroom in Balham where my Mini was being kept until my return from Jamaica. I sat in my car and savoured the 'new car smell' and wished I could take her out for a test drive, but of course I couldn't drive.

The car dealer said he would keep it till the end of January but after that we would have to remove it from his premises. I thought he was being quite generous in storing it for me free of cost for so long, and Daddy Wilf hastened to assure him that we would comply with his wishes. I walked on Cloud Nine for the rest of the day and kept referring to 'my car' until everyone got fed up with me.

To make amends, I took all my cousins and the twins and Samantha into the West End to see the Christmas lights. Yvonne came with us, but once again, Joy was unable to escape her parents.

Sunday dinner was a festive occasion. Since I would be away for Christmas, we had a Christmas dinner of sorts; roast chicken with stuffing, and mince pies and custard to follow. It was a very informal meal; we could not all fit around the dining table, so we piled up our plates and jammed anywhere we could find space.

The following morning I would embark on the journey to meet the rest of my maternal family and to see the land where I was born.

CHAPTER TWELVE

A Jamaican Vacation

It was to be my first plane ride; at least to my memory. I had ridden on an aeroplane when I was coming to England, but I had been only three years old, and had no memory of it. My cousins had all been to Jamaica on previous occasions and were veteran travellers; even Elaine who was only four had already travelled; this was her second trip to Jamaica.

I was looking forward to it; the plane ride I mean. Veronica said she loved it up there and Uncle Keith said it was only because she had never experienced turbulence.

Getting us all to the airport had been no simple feat. Seven travellers and their luggage, plus seven people to see them off. Daddy did not have a car, although he was always 'going to' buy one. Mavis, the twins and Samantha travelled in Daddy Wilf's car, while Daddy and I squeezed into Uncle Keith's van with the family and luggage. Daddy would drive Uncle Keith's van back from the airport and keep it till our return.

I had suggested that we use my car but Daddy said no one should drive it before me, and in any case if he drove my car, who would drive Uncle Keith's van back from the airport.

We made it to Gatwick Airport without incident; we had been apprehensive that the police might stop us and say that the van was overloaded. We checked-in our luggage and said our farewells.

It was an emotional leave-taking. I would be away for six weeks – the longest ever separation from my family. I had been on school trips to Europe that lasted three or four days; I once spent a week in the South of France, but six weeks suddenly seemed a very long time to be away from my family.

I hugged the twins and Samantha, Daddy Wilf and Mummy Myrtle. Then it was Daddy's turn. He suddenly seemed to me to be very sad. I had seen him happy and jovial; I had seen him very angry. The only time I had seen him looking this way was when Clive had died. I hugged him and said, "Don't look so sad, Daddy; I'll be back in no time at all."

He held me for a long time. Before he released me, he said, "Don't leave out yu other family dem, Shellie. Yu mus' guh look fi mine and Mavis people dem to', y'hear?"

"Of course, Daddy. That goes without saying. I love you."

Mavis hugged me tightly, and whispered, "Good luck wid yu family, Shell. I hope dey all turn out to be as nice as Keith and his family. Seh hello to Miss Miriam fah me."

"Thanks, Mum; I will."

As I looked back to wave one last time, I saw that both Mavis and Mummy Myrtle were wiping their eyes with a hanky. I blinked quickly a few times to clear my own eyes and my cousin Veronica took my hand and held it. I gave her a watery smile and thought once more how absolutely empathetic she was, always picking up on my vibes and offering silent support.

I got a window seat. I was really excited; not at all apprehensive about being thousands of feet up in the air, with no-one to catch me if I dropped. As the plane took off and climbed, I watched the fields, roads and houses get smaller and smaller until I could no longer see them. In a very short while we were up among the clouds, and then above them.

It was a most exhilarating feeling. Uncle Keith and Joseph, who both accepted flying as a necessary evil, said that the females in the family were aliens since we all liked being in space so much. The ten hour flight was comfortable; not so much as a hint of turbulence.

When we landed at Kingston and I stepped off the plane and onto the tarmac, I was immediately enveloped in a blanket of heat. When I remarked on it, Aunt Vilma said it was comparatively cool. "Yu should come in July or August, and then yu wi' really know what heat is," she laughed.

We cleared customs smoothly, although not as fast as I would have liked, and when we came out to the waiting area I immediately saw Uncle Kingsley. I had studied all the photographs which had been sent to me by my grandmother and knew all of my uncles faces well.

"There's Uncle Kingsley," I said excitedly and ran ahead of the 'Red Caps' who were pushing our luggage. I was in front of the rest of the family, and reached him first. He did not seem like a stranger.

"Hi Uncle Kingsley," I greeted him, and his face broke into a big grin as he grabbed me and hugged me. "Michelle! At last! How yu do, Chile?" He didn't give me a chance to reply, but continued, as he held me at arms length and looked at me, "God! What a way yu favour yu madda, aahm, A mean Delisia."

By this time the rest of the family had caught up and the porters were wanting to know in which direction to turn with our luggage. Uncle Keith was saying, "Let's get this stuff into the van, Kingsley; wi can deal with the greetings later."

Uncle Kingsley directed the porters where to offload the luggage and he went off to get the van. Uncle Keith tipped the 'Red Caps' and in a short while Uncle Kingsley returned with the van. The luggage was stowed and we all bundled ourselves into the van, and we were on our way.

It was starting to get dark as we drove out of the airport. I was bitterly disappointed because I had wanted to see the Palisadoes Strip which is a narrow peninsular of land, approximately ten miles long, which is flanked by water on both sides, giving the impression that one is in the middle of the sea. The spit of land forms a natural breakwater which protects the Kingston Harbour, one of the world's finest natural harbours, and the seventh largest in the world.

The airport is located on the widest part of the peninsular, which is about a mile wide, while at the end of the strip is what is left of the town of Port Royal, after the main part of the town was destroyed by a major earthquake in 1692 and broke off into the sea.

I had read about it when exploring the history of Jamaica, and I had wanted to get out of the vehicle and stand on the strip of land. However, that opportunity would have to come at some other time, Uncle Kingsley said.

He explained that it would not be wise to stop at this time; people were sometimes robbed on their way from the airport, not to mention the politically charged atmosphere of the present time, with gangs of Party-

Sweet Home, Jamaica

affiliated thugs and gunmen currently holding sway in Kingston.

We drove through what Uncle Keith said was downtown Kingston, along Spanish Town Road and on into Spanish Town proper. From Spanish Town we picked up the Old Harbour Road and when we got into the town of Old Harbour we turned right at the clock and proceeded up Darlington Drive and along the Colbeck main road. All the while Uncle Keith was giving me the guided tour, although it was now very dark and I could not really appreciate what he was showing me.

Once we left the town of Old Harbour the street lights became few and far between. Nevertheless Uncle Keith was extremely pleased with the few there were; the last time they had been in Jamaica there had been no lighting at all in this area. Uncle Kingsley told him that 'light' – meaning electricity – had reached Country just this past year.

In between the few light posts, though, it was pitch black on the country road leading to Gravel Hill where my grandma lived, a darkness that was broken only by the van's headlights and some lighted windows as we passed through the various small districts. Despite the arrival of the electricity, most of the houses along the route seemed to still be lighted by means of kerosene oil lamps; the occasional house was, however, lit by electricity.

Uncle Keith and Uncle Kingsley identified some of the places as we passed through, and I almost died laughing at some of the place names. We passed a place called Planters, one called Kirrout, and another called Ooman Pan. I sought elaboration from the Uncles.

"Is that translated to be Woman's *pan* that people carry things in, or *pond* which holds water? And what is the derivation of the name?"

Neither one knew, and I thought that was disgusting,

Claudette Beckford-Brady

and told them so. "You have interesting sounding place names and have no idea how they came by those names? Weren't you even curious enough to try to find out? I think that show a distinct lack of interest in your own area. I bet you that by the end of the week I will know everything about this area."

They were amused at my incredulity. Uncle Keith said, laughingly, "Not everyone has your appetite for knowledge, Shellie, but if it helps any, the proper name for Kirrout is Crawl Pen."

"No, that's no help, Uncle. It makes for more confusion. If the place is named Crawl Pen, why is it called Kirrout? There must be a story there somewhere."

"Well if there is, I don't know it. You, Kingsley?"

Uncle Kingsley answered in the negative. "Sarry, kyaan't help. But yu know, Michelle, if yu start investigating place names yu might jus' as well write a book pon di subject. Yu have place like *Wait-a-bit,* and *Gi-me-mi-bit* and such di-like.

I went on to learn that the road we were travelling on marked the border between St. Catherine and Clarendon. The houses on the left hand side of the road were in Clarendon while the ones on the right were in St. Catherine.

It was around eight-thirty when Uncle Kingsley said, "Well, here we are, Michelle; Home, Sweet Home."

The van turned off the road and went down a fairly steep incline before pulling up in the yard in front of a large single-story house. The house and yard were brightly lit and I noticed with a measure of relief that there was electric lighting on the premises.

The place was abuzz with excitement. I saw a rather stately-looking elderly lady silhouetted in the doorway of the house and a group of around a dozen persons standing or lounging in the yard. As the van came to a halt all the persons converged on it and the door was pulled open. A cacophonous serenade ensued until finally, above the din, a voice bawled out, "Satta! Everybaddy tan tuddy!"

The noise miraculously died down. It was amazing. Even the dogs which had been adding their rendition to the welcoming serenade were silent. The crowd of people around the van fell back, and a tall, bearded, dreadlocked man, whom I knew from his photos to be Uncle Cornell, stood in front of the open van door.

"Greetings, Belov`ed. Give t'anks to di Most High fi oonu safe arrival."

Uncle Cornell was softly spoken now, and it was difficult to equate him with the voice which had commanded such immediate obedience. But I was to discover that he was the dominant male in the Jamaican branch of the family, despite being the youngest, and he ran things with a firm hand of discipline, but which was yet tempered with fairness and understanding.

Uncle Cornell was a tall man, slightly taller than Uncle Keith. He was of slim build, but wiry and strong. His dreadlocks reached down to his waist when worn loose, but more often than not they were wound around his head, or stuffed under a large knitted hat. He was the youngest son, and the only one of my uncles who had never been abroad. He had declared that if and when he decided to leave "…this little Rock name Jamaica," it would be to go to "Madda Africa" and nowhere else. He, together with Uncle Kingsley and their sons, worked the land which supported the family.

Uncle Keith stepped out of the van and the two brothers embraced. "Greetings and Love, little brother," said Uncle Keith. "Give thanks, indeed."

The rest of us had trooped out of the van and greetings and hugs and backslaps were being exchanged. I was included in this, and was hugged and kissed by people I did not know, until my hand was taken by Uncle Cornell and I was led away to the veranda where Grandma Miriam was waiting to greet me.

Grandma Miriam was beautiful. I was surprised at how petite she was; her photos had not indicated this. She was of slim build and looked much younger than her seventy-two years. Her long hair, which was still mainly black, was drawn up in a bun on top of her head, and the few strands of grey at the front gave her a distinguished look.

Uncle Cornell led me to the veranda where Grandma was waiting. Her face broke into a radiant smile as we approached. "Mamma," he introduced, "behold yu long lost grandchild."

Grandma Miriam and I looked into each others' eyes for the first time in our lives and the emotion was overwhelming. She opened her arms and I stepped into them. No words were immediately necessary. As her arms closed around me, I leant into her and hugged her tightly.

We stood like that for a few moments holding tightly to each other, and when she finally released me she stood back, and I could see that, like myself, there were tears in her eyes, but they were tears of joy; we were both smiling. When she started to speak I realised that we had an attentive audience of people hanging on to our every word.

"Michelle, my dear, A can hardly find words. You are yu mother all over again. Same size, same features, everything. A feel like seh Delisia has come home."

Before I could respond to my grandma's words, I heard someone say, "A only hope shi nuh facety like Delisia used to be," and Uncle Cornell reply, "Hush yu mout' and gwaan a yu yaad," and further added before anyone else could say anything, "as a matter a fack, everybaddy gwaan home. Give Mamma some time wid Michelle; oonu wi' si har tomaara."

Sweet Home, Jamaica

There were no arguments. In a very short time the yard was empty, leaving only Uncles Kingsley and Cornell's families.

We sat on the veranda and Uncle Kingsley's wife brought out fried fish and bammy - a kind of flat round cake made from cassava flour, which can be steamed or fried - which we washed down with home-made lemonade, made with fresh limes from one of the lime trees in the yard.

Grandma couldn't get enough of me; she sat beside me and kept on touching me, as if to make sure I was really there. She was full of beaming smiles now, and reminiscences about Delisia, my mother. I don't remember if she had greeted Uncle Keith's family or not, but I was beginning to get worried that they might resent the attention Grandma was lavishing on me.

My three younger cousins, Joseph, Jennifer and Elaine had gone to bed, as had Aunt Vilma; we were all still on British time and it was somewhere around three of four in the morning in England. My eldest cousin, Veronica, was sitting on the veranda with Grandma and me, and the three brothers, Keith, Kingsley and Cornell.

I should have been tired - we had been travelling for the best part of eighteen hours - but I wasn't. I looked at the people gathered on the veranda and felt a sense of well-being and kinship. These were my people; my blood kin. I belonged.

I suddenly had an overwhelming longing for my natural mother. I wanted to hold and hug her as I had my grandma. It was the first time I had felt this depth of feeling for my natural mother. My quest to find her had previously been based mainly, I think, on curiosity, and pique and peevishness, because I had been denied the chance to know her, but now I really wanted to find her for love's sake.

Claudette Beckford-Brady

Naturally the talk on the veranda was mostly about my mother. After asking about Mavis and the rest of my other family back in England, Grandma had jumped onto the subject of Delisia and could not come off. I didn't mind. I sat there and listened to tales and anecdotes from my mother's childhood.

I learned that she was opinionated and stubborn, always wanting her own way. At times she could be vengeful and unforgiving. She had been thoroughly spoiled, being the baby of the family and the only girl.

Grandma said that Delisia should not be held solely to blame for the way she had turned out; the entire family had to take some responsibility for the part they had played in shaping her personality; after all, it was they who had spoiled her by giving her everything she desired, until she had come to accept it as her God-given right to have everything her own way.

I loved Grandma for saying that; I had been uneasy about those negative traits in my mother's personality, which I had noticed without ever seeing her. Now they could be mitigated to some extent, and I was sure that once we found her and she fell back into the loving arms of her family, we could all help in trying to expunge those traits from her personality.

I learned that she was extremely gifted and excelled in all subjects. She had made her parents so proud when she had told them that she wanted to attend the University of the West Indies to study law. She would be the first and only person from the district to go to the University, and that was made even more special because she was female. Grandpa had said he was so proud that if he had to sell everything he had to send her there, he would gladly do so.

But then my mother had gotten involved with my father while she was still in high school, and had fallen pregnant with me. Grandpa had been livid. At first Delisia

Sweet Home, Jamaica

had refused to tell him the name of the baby-father, but eventually he had wrung it from her. He had sent Marse Bysam, the local police officer, for my father and given Daddy an ultimatum.

Take the child when it was born, and do what he wanted with it, but stay away from his daughter now and forever, or else....

My father had agreed to take the child. He was already living with Mavis and had one child; my brother Delroy. Delisia had begged and pleaded in vain; had written to all her brothers abroad begging them to intercede with their father on her behalf, but to no avail. I had been taken from her and handed over to my father. Delisia had never forgiven her family. She had left the district, cut ties with her entire family, and disappeared from the face of the earth.

Grandma said she had been willing to take me and raise me herself, but her husband would have none of it, and his word was law. "But," Grandma said, "in retrospect it is just as well that you were raised by your father and his wife. If you had been raised here, history might have repeated itself and you would have been even more spoiled than your mother had been. As it is, you are a credit to your parents."

I felt proud for Daddy and Mavis that my grandma should hold them in such high esteem.

I could have talked all night, but finally Uncle Keith said we had six weeks to catch up, and it had been an extremely long day. So we all retired to our respective sleeping quarters and turned in.

When I woke the next day the sun was high in the sky. I was annoyed because I had wanted to experience my first Jamaican morning; Daddy and Mavis had often talked about drinking dew water from coco leaves, and watching the sun come up over the hills and I had wanted to experience this. I lamented the fact to Grandma, who I found out in the yard under a pimento tree, shelling gungu peas.

"Never mind. Yu will have plenty of Jamaican mornings to experience." She got up and took my hand. "Come eat some breakfast."

I declined the breakfast, telling Grandma that I did not usually eat so soon after waking; it always took a couple of hours for my appetite to kick in; however I was partial to a long cold glass of juice or lemonade.

Grandma said that Uncle Keith, Aunt Vilma and Joseph were up, and had eaten breakfast and gone "a-bush" with Uncles Kingsley and Cornell. I was bitterly disappointed that I had slept so late; I too had wanted to go to the bush with them. Grandma consoled me and said there would be plenty of other opportunities.

My morning thirst quenched, Grandma set a large wash-pan behind a curtain and poured hot water into it. "Come bathe, Michelle." She added cold water to dilute and left me to get on with it.

I had discovered last night that there was no bathroom attached to the house. We had used a flashlight to walk the short distance to the pit-latrine, and chamber pots (or chimmies) were provided under the beds.

Although the house now had electricity, which it hadn't the last time Uncle Keith et al had been here, there was no plumbing. A large concrete catchment tank supplied the yard with water, which was occasionally supplemented in times of extreme drought with spring water from the property.

I went to get my bathroom bag, bathed and cleaned my teeth. I dressed in a pair of shorts and a tee shirt, and combed my hair before going back out into the yard.

The yard was a large flat dirt area between two steep slopes. The main road ran above the yard at the top of one slope and below was another steep slope where corn and gungu and sorrel were planted. I marvelled at how they were able to cultivate such steep hillsides.

It was a very large yard and full of all types of trees, none of which I was familiar with, outside of books, but which were easily identifiable by their foliage or their fruit. Tall coconut and majestic breadfruit and ackee trees towered over the outer edges of the yard, while smaller citrus – orange, tangerine, lime, grapefruit – stood at various intervals. There were mango trees, sweetsop trees and many others that I did not know, even from books.

There were two other smaller houses situated across the yard from the main house. I discovered that these belonged to Uncles Kingsley and Cornell and their respective families. I noticed how all the houses had neatly cultivated flower borders around them, and many potted, as well as free growing plants were situated around the yard. Each house also had its own outside kitchen and pit latrine.

Grandma put her gungu peas aside, washed the gungu grime from her hands, and took me on a conducted tour of the yard, pointing out certain trees to me.

"Every tree in the yard," she told me, "represent one member of the family, either living or passed on. Each time a child is born, their navel string (umbilical cord) and a tree is planted."

She showed me the eight coconut trees which represented my uncles and various other trees for some of my cousins. Then she took me a little distance away behind the house and showed me two pimento trees. "These two trees are you and your mother."

I looked at her in surprise. "I have a tree here, Grandma?"

"But of course. A planted it and yu navel string mi-self. Don't forget, yu were here for a full four weeks before yu went to yu father."

I looked at the two trees with affection. These trees represented me and my mother. A piece of both of us were buried here, in this ground. For the first time in my life I felt like a Jamaican person; in England I was British. But that obviously was not so, I was Jamaican; I had been born right here on this island, and my umbilical cord was buried right here on this very spot where I was standing.

My parents had applied for British citizenship for themselves, Delroy and I; the twins and Samantha qualified automatically by virtue of being born there. Here, I did not have to apply to become a citizen; I had an inalienable right by virtue of *my* being born here. I was a Jamaican.

The discovery filled me with a deep sense of contentment, a sense of having come home at long last. There had been occasions in England when white kids at school had called me various unpleasant racist names and told me to go back to where I came from. I would take umbrage and tell them that I was just as British as they, but now? Now I had discovered that I did not want to be British; I had discovered that I was a Jamaican, and there was no better feeling in the entire world!

I held a crushed pimento leaf to my nose as Grandma showed me to do; I was well pleased. It had a fresh pungent smell which I loved.

Pimento, or allspice, as it is commonly referred to on world markets, is Jamaica's only indigenous spice. It is called allspice because it is purported that the pimento berries has the combined flavours of clove, cinnamon, nutmeg, and pepper. I read in one book that Jamaican pimento is regarded as being the best in the world and has a virtual monopoly on world markets. I was glad they had chosen pimento for my navel string tree.

I asked Grandma where her tree was and she said she didn't have one here as she had not been born into the

Sweet Home, Jamaica

family, but married into it. Her navel string was buried in Bartons, a district across the valley from Gravel Hill, where she had come from to marry Grandpa Campbell.

Back in the main yard, she showed me my late grandfather's tree, which was a guinep tree situated in a corner of the flat area known as the 'babbeque' which was used for drying crops.

Afterwards I helped Grandma to shell more gungu peas. I had never seen green gungu before; the only type we got in England was the dry packaged ones. I loved the fresh smell of the peas which Grandma had picked just that morning from a patch below the house, and despite the sticky black gunge which it left on my hands I enjoyed shelling them.

Grandma said that the fifty acre property produced all the fruits and vegetables the family needed, and the only things that were shop-bought were things like flour, salt, rice and cornmeal. They even made their own sugar from the sugar cane grown on the land. When meat was required they sold a cow or a goat to Marse Richard, the butcher, who then gave them back a portion of the meat. The family raised no pigs due to Uncle Cornell's Rastafarian beliefs.

The rest of the morning was spent being properly introduced to Kingsley and Cornell's wives, whom I had met briefly the night before, and to some of my cousins. Uncle Kingsley's wife was named Eula and they had eight children ranging in age from twenty down to three. Their eldest, Lydia, already had two child of her own. One of the boys, Rueben, was my age.

Uncle Cornell wasn't legally married but he and his baby-mother, Bev, had seven, and she was currently six months pregnant. Their eldest was eighteen, and the youngest two.

I did not meet all these cousins on the one occasion.

Claudette Beckford-Brady

Some of them were out working, and there were others who did not live at the yard. Some of the uncles who lived in North America had grown-up children still in Jamaica. Some of them lived nearby, and had been at the house last night, but in the excitement of our arrival and Cornell's banishment of everyone from the yard we had had no opportunity to be introduced. Some of these cousins also had children of their own. In truth, I had a very large extended family.

After meeting who were available to be met, Grandma took me around the back of the house past my navel string tree and we walked up a grassy slope toward a stand of trees on an otherwise barren hilltop. When we got to the top and I looked out I was struck with awe, wonder and surprise.

Spread out before me was a panoramic view of blue hills and green valleys, dotted with trees, houses and patches of cultivation. I saw a gleam of silver far down below which Grandma said was the river. She said I was looking eastward and if I came out here in the early morning I could experience a beautiful sunrise over those hills.

Gravel Hill was located north of Old Harbour. To the west were Clarendon and the parishes beyond; while to the south were Old Harbour Bay and the sea, and of course, to the east lay the parishes of Kingston & St. Andrew, and St. Thomas. Northwards across the central mountain chain which formed the backbone of the island lay the parish of St. Ann.

Grandma explained to me that the road above the house marked the border between St. Catherine and Clarendon. We lived on the St. Catherine side, and funnily enough, some of the extended family lived over in Clarendon, just across the road.

I had read extensively about the island of Jamaica, and

Sweet Home, Jamaica

listened attentively when Daddy and Mavis were talking about it. Though the largest island in the English speaking Caribbean, it is nevertheless very small; a mere four thousand square miles. From west to east it is approximately one hundred and forty six miles long, and fifty one miles from north to south at the widest point.

The terrain is mainly mountainous, with nearly half the island being over a thousand feet above sea level. I asked Grandma if she had any idea of the elevation where we were standing, and she said we were nearly two thousand feet up. Looking to the north and west I could see more hills above us. Far to the east where I couldn't see it, Blue Mountain Peak loomed seven thousand four hundred feet into the air.

Grandma and I returned to the yard to find it full of people. Veronica and the younger girls had finally woken up and Uncle Keith and the others had returned from "bush." In addition several cousins had come over to see "Delisia's girl."

Uncle Cornell was chopping coconuts and handing them round. On seeing me he grabbed back the coconut he had been about to hand to Uncle Keith and said, "Ah, Michelle. Greetings likkle niece; come partake of yu first jelly coconut from off-a yu family land."

I took the coconut from him and looked doubtfully at it. Aunt Vilma, Joseph and the girls all had coconuts to their mouths, their heads tilted back while they drank. I sniffed the nut and was unable to detect any reason why I shouldn't try it. I tentatively put it to my mouth and took a small taste. It was good. I put the nut back to my mouth and started drinking.

I was not good at it. Instead of going into my mouth most of the liquid ran from the nut and spilled onto my tee-shirt. I took the nut from my mouth and said, "Could I get a straw, please?"

There were hoots of laughter from the persons gathered in the yard. I looked round to see the source of the hilarity and discovered that it was me they were laughing at. I stared in perplexity, wondering what I had said to merit such humour. I was soon enlightened.

Uncle Keith said with amusement, "Only old people and babies use straw out here, Shell. And then is bamboo straw they use. If yu really want a straw one of yu cousins can go cut one fah yu."

I politely declined. "That won't be necessary Uncle Keith," I said with dignity. "I am neither old nor a baby," and with that I returned the nut to my mouth and carefully, this time, I commenced to drink, and managed to empty the coconut without spilling any more of the cool sweet liquid.

I met some more of my cousins and spent the next couple of hours getting to know the family.

I had not eaten any breakfast so I was glad when I heard Bev, Uncle Cornell's baby-mother, calling us for lunch. We all sat outside on benches set under the big guinep tree which had been planted by my grandfather's parents at his birth, and under which his navel string was buried. Bowls of green-gungu soup cooked with salt beef and coconut milk was served and I had never tasted anything so good.

Everything in the soup, right down to the cassava-flour dumplings, had been produced on our land. The beef; the gungu; the dried coconut. The breadfruit, yam, coco and dasheen. The pumpkin, carrots, peppers, skellion and thyme. It made the food taste extra special.

After lunch about a dozen of the cousins took me down to show me the river. It was a merry party that made the trek. I was not by nature a shy person and everyone treated me as if they had known me all their lives. We talked and joked and made fun of each other's accents.

Sweet Home, Jamaica

The Jamaican cousins wanted to know how it was that I spoke differently from the Birmingham cousins, who pronounced the word *Birming-gum.*

The terrain was a little tricky to traverse. There was a narrow, well beaten path, but in places the going was very steep. There were overhanging branches that had to be held out of the way and the occasional large rock to climb over or around. I was warned to watch out for "cow itch" which is a type of stinging nettle or poison ivy. "But I don't know what it looks like," I said worriedly.

On the way down we went through slopes of coffee and cocoa trees. My cousins, including my English cousins Veronica and Joseph, identified the different trees to me. Some of them I identified easily by their fruit; the citrus and banana trees for instance. I was shown star-apple, jackfruit, and cashew nut trees as well as tambrin (tamarind), guava, and many more.

I marvelled at the abundant variety of things growing on the land and was told proudly that I hadn't seen anything yet. One of the cousins suggested that we play a naming game of all the trees on the land. We took turns in naming the trees.

"Mango."

"Sweet-sop."

"Soursop."

"Custard Apple."

"Guinep."

"Guava."

"Cashew."

"Jew Plum."

"Panganat."

"Panga*what?*" I asked. I had never heard of that particular tree before. My English cousin Veronica enlightened me. "They mean *pomegranate.* That's what they call it out here."

"Pommy*what?*" some of my Jamaican cousins chorused, and we spent a hilarious few minutes laughing at each others' name for the fruit.

We finally arrived at the river. It was an enchanting place. Large trees grew right down to the water's edge and wild bananas and other broad leafed foliage graced the banks. Beautiful flowers of all different colours covered the river banks, and being a nature lover, I set about examining the flora. To my surprise, the flowers that were growing wild on the river banks were the very same flowers that we paid money for in England and grew in flower pots indoors.

I called my cousin Veronica to come and look. "Look here, Verr. Look at all these Bizzy Lizzies and Coleus growing wild. Imagine them growing wild on our very own land while we pay money for them in England!"

Joyce, one of my cousins, exclaimed incredulously, "Oonu pay money fi wile flowers a Inglan'? But oonu nuh easy!"

While I had been admiring the plants and flowers, most of the cousins had stripped down to their underwear and were splashing in the river. To me, being familiar with large rivers in England such as the Thames in London, this was no more than a stream. It was about ten to twelve feet across and not more than four feet deep. But it was our river, on our land, and I loved it.

Joseph said that if we went downstream about two miles, there was a deep swimming hole; the only thing was it wasn't on our land. "Oh?" I said. "Whose land is it on and can we use it?"

Everyone exchanged glances and some of the younger ones snickered. I waited expectantly for an explanation. Their body language and my writers' mind told me that there was a story here.

Sure enough it was forthcoming. It was a bit garbled

and confused, because everyone had their bit to input, but what I finally gathered was this. The man who owned the land bordering us to the east was named Marse Lijah. The river also ran through his land. When Marse Lijah and our grandfather were boys, they had been best friends and that continued into their late teens.

Grandpa had been 'walking out' with Marse Lijah's sister, Dorette. Then one day Grandpa and Lijah had gone over to Bartons, which is a district in the hills across the valley from us, and they had met Grandma, who had just returned from school in Canada, for the first time. Both of them apparently fell hard for her.

Lijah thought he was clear to court her, since Grandpa already had Dorette, but Grandpa apparently had other ideas. A friendly rivalry developed between them to see who could win Grandma's favours and affection. When it became apparent that she leant heavily in favour of Grandpa, and when they announced their impending marriage, the friendship deteriorated into open enmity.

Both Lijah and Dorette stopped speaking to Grandpa. The open boundary between the two properties had been closed off; not with fences, but with threats of dire consequences should *any* member of the Campbell family be caught on Lijah's land. The swimming hole, which had been a favourite recreational spot, was one of the casualties.

However, forbidden fruits always taste sweeter, and the Campbell boys and Delisia had made good use of the swimming hole throughout their lives. On one occasion Marse Lijah had taken out a summons accusing them of trespass and theft of his bananas, but the Justice of the Peace had thrown it out when told of the feud. He had, however, told the Campbells to stay off Marse Lijah's land, and when Grandpa added his voice to this, the boys had desisted.

Claudette Beckford-Brady

But now, two generations later, Marse Lijah was old, and never came this side of his property. His wife had died, his sister had married and moved to Town and his sons were abroad. Marse Lijah was looked after by one of his daughters, but the property was not being worked and since there was no animosity between the next generation there was no reason for us not to use the swimming hole.

By now it was late afternoon and too late to make the excursion to the hole, but we agreed that we would do it soon. Going back up was much harder than coming down and I was ribbed and called "Farriner" because I was neither as fit nor as agile as my Jamaican cousins, and had to be helped with a shove from behind or a pull from above.

And I discovered that my cousins could *see in the dark!* Dusk had caught us on the climb back from the river, and then suddenly it was dark. And I mean pitch black. The luminous dial on my watch told me it was six forty-five, yet it was as dark as midnight. There was no moon and we were travelling through bush without the luxury of city lights.

I could see nothing; not even my cousins. I held on to the one in front and asked them how they knew where to walk. They laughed and told me they could see in the dark, thereby confirming my suspicion. And I believed them. By the time we returned to the yard I was out of breath and exhausted.

CHAPTER THIRTEEN

I Find my Jamaican-ness

Grandma was livid that the cousins had kept me out till dark, but Uncle Keith said placatingly, "'Low dem nuh, Mamma, dem young, and Michelle want to experience country life to the fullness, nuh true, Shellie?"

My cousin Rueben, who was the same age as me, said, "Mamma nuh want even fly pitch pon yu, Shellie; yu nuh mine sharp yu naa guh have nuh fun a-taal." They all called Grandma "Mamma"; I was the only one who called her Grandma and I decided to leave it that way.

But I did have fun, and lots of it. The next six weeks were spent in explorations and enlightenment. I climbed trees and hills, rode the donkey, swam in the river and made coconut drops and 'blue drawers.' I ate all sorts of unknown fruits, and met some very colourful characters. I was game for almost anything and gained the respect and admiration of my cousins who said, "Y'ahright fi a Farriner, Shell. Yu would-a pass fi Jamaican if yu could-a chat patwa."

I was constantly being teased about the way I spoke. Veronica said she was glad the cousins had someone new to laugh at; perhaps now they would stop teasing her about her Birmingham accent.

Traditionally, on Christmas Eve Grandma would go around the district taking gifts of meat and food kind to some of the less fortunate members of the community. This year she took great pleasure in taking me with her and showing me off as "Delisia's girl."

Christmas was a merry occasion. A large contingent from the local branch of the extended family gathered at the yard from early Christmas morning. Preparations had been going on for a couple of days; a goat and a half dozen chickens had been killed, and a weight of fish cleaned and seasoned.

Uncle Kingsley butchered the goat himself; quite expertly it seemed to me although I had never seen an animal being butchered before. I felt sorry for the poor animal but I was fascinated at the way Uncle Kingsley wielded the knife. He told me that if I didn't have a strong stomach I shouldn't watch because he didn't want any vomiting when he pulled out the entrails. I assured him my stomach was cast-iron strong.

Watching the chickens being killed, however, was not to my liking. The cousins held the chickens captive under a basin, leaving the neck and head exposed. Then using a sharp cutlass they beheaded the chicken, released it from the basin and left it to flutter about the yard until it dropped dead. I told them it was cruel but they tried to convince me that the chicken was already dead and therefore felt nothing; it was only the nerves that kept it fluttering around.

I pitched in wholeheartedly to help with the preparations. I watched my cousins dip each chicken into a pan of hot water and then pluck the feathers. I plucked my first chicken with a sense of pride and accomplishment.

Watching the animals being killed did not detract from my enjoyment of the food. I knew that when I got back to England I would be a good few pounds heavier than when I had left.

It started with breakfast. An enormous amount of ackee and saltfish and fried chicken- back had been cooked up. To go with this there was roast breadfruit, boiled bananas, fried dumplings and plantains. We washed it down with chocolate tea or coffee, according to our preferences. The whole day was filled with eating and drinking and generally socialising. I tasted sorrel for the first time and couldn't get enough of it to drink.

After breakfast three barrels were produced and opened. These had been shipped by the North American Uncles from Canada and the United States. They contained shoes and clothing, household items and toiletries, canned foods and books and toys. There were Christmas cards and letters for individuals, including, I discovered, several for me.

I was touched. The North American branch of the family had never met me, and yet they had accepted me sight unseen. I received cards not only from the uncles and their spouses, but also from some of the cousins. I was definitely accepted as a Campbell.

In the evening after another round of eating and drinking we all gathered on the babbeque for a sing-song and story-telling. We sang Christmas carols and Jamaican folk songs, most of which I did not know. Friends and neighbours dropped by for a "bite to eat and a cup of sorrel" and to "meet Delisia's girl."

Everyone exclaimed at how much I "favoured Delisia" and I had to tell them all about my life in England. Grandma had told some of her friends about our search for

Delisia and they wanted to know what progress was being made. We had to tell them that, to date, none.

Later in the evening we began telling duppy (ghost) stories. The setting was right for it. The 'babbeque' or barbeque was a large round elevated area of hard-packed earth where coffee, chocolate, pimento, ginger, and other crops were spread out to dry. In the evenings it was a social gathering place.

Several large trees grew to one side of the circle, and these created eerie shadows. And because it was moonshine, (full moon) and everyone was outdoors, only one light had been left on in the house, thus making everything spookier.

The large guinep tree towered over the babbeque, and cast its gigantic shadow across a part of the yard. I was sitting on the exposed root of the tree, drinking a cup of sorrel.

At the children's request, Uncle Cornell was telling the story of 'The Man Without'n Head' which I recognised to be a version of sorts of the story of Ichabod Crane and The Headless Horseman in *The Legend of Sleepy Hollow* by Washington Irvin, except that the characters and place names had been Jamaicanized.

".....Marse Ichabod couldn't believe him eye," Uncle Cornell narrated, *"but di man pon di harse nevah have nuh head! Marse Ichabod shut him eye, him shake him head. Den him open back him eye again. Di man pon di harse **still** nevah have nuh head.*

Uncle Cornell was enjoying himself. He threw his whole being into the telling of the story, changing his voice and posture to illustrate the story as he told it. He had the children, and even some of the adults spellbound.

The scene was well set. The moonlight and the

shadows cast by the trees and the house made the place eerie. Intermittently the moon would be obscured for a few moments as the occasional cloud passed, but in the main it was bright moonlight. I sat under the guinep tree with a couple of my Jamaican cousins and Jennifer, Uncle Keith's eight year old daughter, who was slightly frightened by the story.

She cuddled up to me and I held her close, reassuring her that I wouldn't let any ghosts get her. Uncle Cornell continued his dramatization. He was on a roll.

"Di harse was a big, black, ugly brute of a animal, wid eyes burning red like coal-fire and flashing like lightning. Him mane reach down to the grung. Him kick up him two front foot dem into di air and froth just a fly out-a him mout'. One bell weh him have round him neck a sing, "ding-a-ling-a ling" as him-a kick up gwaan.

Marse Ichabod start fi trimble, Marse Ichabod start fi shake. Di hair pon him head raise and stan' up stiff-stiff, and cold sweat bruk out pon him forhead. Him nevah know who him fi fraid-a more; di man without'n head, or di harse. Him fraid suh tell him couldn' move, and him heart dis a guh biff-a-buff, biff-a-buff, eena him chess.

Him si di harse start walk toward him, wid di man without'n head siddung proud pon him bac,k and di bell jus' a sing, "ding-a-ling-a-ling." Den di strangest t'ing happen. Right in front a Marse Ichabod eye, di alta rope turn eena chain, and di harse tun eena one rolling calf!

A collective gasp shivered around the babbeque. I had read about the Rolling Calf. It was a demon of the spirit world; a great big luminous bull calf with eyes like coal, and breathing fire, and a long chain around its neck which trailed behind him and made a terrifying noise.

It was known to disguise itself as an ordinary cow, until

Claudette Beckford-Brady

some unwitting person dared to get too close, at which time it would dramatically turn into the dreaded rolling calf. I had not known that it could disguise itself as a horse, as in Uncle Cornell's story.

Jennifer's fingernails dug into my flesh as she grasped me tightly and buried her face in my side. I cuddled her close and whispered, "It's okay Jen; it's only a story; there's no such thing as a rolling calf." I don't think I convinced her as her grip did not relax. Uncle Cornell was still telling his story.

"Marse Ichabad fahget seh him did too fraid fi move, and him turn tail and tek up him foot eena him han' and start fi run. Him could-a hear di chain a draw pon di grung, and him know seh di rolling calf was afta him. Him start run faster and faster. All of a sudden him hear di rolling calf laugh and......."

Uncle Cornell broke off suddenly in mid sentence. He struck a theatrical listening pose and said urgently, as he peered into the darkness beyond the house, "Hush! Quiat everybaddy! Is what dat?"

We all turned to follow his gaze, and strained our ears to hear what he was listening to. Jennifer whimpered and I tightened my arm around her. Then I heard it; the unmistakable sound of a walking horse, a dragging chain and a jingling bell. Jennifer whimpered again, and said, "I want my Mummy."

I knew within myself that there must be a logical explanation; I did not believe in ghosts, or rolling calves; however, I have to admit that a little shiver ran through me and goose bumps broke out on my skin. I hushed Jennifer and told her not to be afraid; I wasn't going to let anything hurt her. She clung tightly to me, her head still buried firmly in my side.

Sweet Home, Jamaica

I returned my attention to listening and peering into the darkness beyond the house. The sounds were getting closer. Then the thing appeared around the side of the house; a white apparition bouncing through the air as if on horseback, but no horse that was visible. And yet, there was no mistaking the sound of hooves on the hard ground, nor the dragging of the chain and the jingling of the bell...

Pandemonium broke loose. Children screamed and ran to find adults to shelter them. Adults exclaimed and shouted in consternation. The yard dogs that were locked up took their cue from the noise and chaos and added their voices to the din. In the midst of all this I noticed that some of the teen-aged cousins were laughing fit to drop.

It suddenly dawned on me that this was a set-up. The cousins had cooked this up; but how on earth did they get that thing, whatever it was, to float through the air like that? As the thing came nearer, it became apparent, but in the meantime Jennifer was screaming and getting hysterical. I tried my best to get through to her.

"Jen, it's only a trick, Baby; it's not a real ghost. Hush." She either didn't hear or didn't care. She continued to scream and I was relieved to see Uncle Keith appear and pry her from me.

I returned my attention to the thing. It had stopped moving and a group of people were congregated around it. Some of them were in fits of laughter. I moved over to join them, and when I saw the "rolling calf" I laughed till I cried.

The white apparition that I had seen moving through the air turned out to be my cousin Levi, dressed in a white sheet with a black cloth covering his head and shoulders, giving the impression in the darkness that he was headless. He had been riding Marcus, the mule, who had been draped in a long black cloth also making it difficult to see him until he was up close. Marcus was wearing a pair of bells on his alter rope.

Uncle Cornell had been a part of the plot, and when Grandma found out she berated him scathingly. "Cornell, yu suppose to be a big man. A understand these boys playing a trick like this but A didn't expect yu to be a part of it. Yu really should know better. Look how oonu frighten the children them."

Uncle Cornell was unrepentant. He kissed Grandma and said, "Jus' cool nuh, Mamma. Di pickney dem love dese kind-a tings. All who crying now will be boasting later about how dem si rolling calf, and dem will be talking about it fi many a Christmas to come. And all who never deh here a guh claim seh dem did si di man without'n head a ride one invisible horse."

Grandma kissed her teeth and pushed him out of her way. "Move from beside me. Yu fahget that you are a big man now; yu tink yu still a bwoy!"

That Christmas was one of the best I had ever spent.

*

I did not leave out my other family. Daddy's parents lived at Joe Ground, which was only a matter of a mile or so up the road, but which I discovered was in another parish. Gravel Hill was in St. Catherine while a part of Joe Ground was in Clarendon. I spent a week with them and visited often the rest of the time. I met my paternal uncles, aunts and cousins. In truth, I had an extremely large number of relatives.

Mavis' father was dead but her mother still lived at Ginger Ridge, which was some miles distant. Although I was not biologically related to her, I was still considered a grandchild, and welcomed with open arms. I spent five days there getting to know that side of the family.

On my return from Ginger Ridge I decided that it was time to sit down with Grandma Miriam and get the Campbell family history. I had picked up various pieces of information through casual conversations, but I wanted it all together and in a logical manner.

Grandma Miriam and I had become very close. I had taken to rising early so I could spend quality time, one on one, with her. She was always up before sunrise every morning, although she had no reason to be, but she said that the early morning was the best part of the day, when the world was washed brand new by the dew, and all was calm and quiet, except for nature's noises. I loved her turn of phrase and told her so.

"Wow, Grandma! I never knew you were a poet. You should write down beautiful words like those."

She had smiled and said, "I do sometimes. And so did your mother. Seems to be a female family trait."

"Really, Grandma?" I had asked. "I don't suppose any of my mother's stuff is still around?"

Grandma had shaken her head. "I'm afraid not; Delisia cleared out all of her things when she left home."

I was disappointed, but hadn't really expected any other answer. "Well," I said, "may I read some of your writings?"

"Such as they are," she had replied.

I too loved the early morning feeling; the freshness of the air which was sometimes, to my surprise, quite chilly. Some mornings I woke to find that I could not see the neighbouring hills due to fog.

Early one morning Grandma and I had gone up to the hill behind the house to watch the sun come up. It had still been dark when we left the house, but as we made our way up the incline to the top of the rise the dawn was breaking. As we crested the rise the sun came slowly from behind the eastern hills and began to gently spread her glow over the land, giving birth to a brand new day.

And a sparkling day it was. There was no other way to describe it. The sunlight flitted and danced out of the sky, and flirtatiously dallied its way onto the leaves and grasses where so many dew-drop diamonds sparkled in a kaleidoscope of colours, and tinged the mango blossom with an amber glow.

The surrounding trees were alive with birdsong as the feathered creatures flitted here and there in playful jollification. I breathed in the crisp clean air and remarked to Grandma that I could well understand why she loved the early morning. "The only thing is," I added, "it's almost as cold as London."

"January and February are usually the two coldest months up here," Grandma replied. "Remember that we are a couple thousand feet above sea level; we feel the cold up here more than they do down on the low. Usually at this time of year we get cold fronts coming across from North America."

We spent a few moments enjoying the quiet of the morning and looking out over the panorama of the lower hills and valleys, before making our way back down to the house.

On the way back we stopped at the two pimento trees which were mine and Delisia's navel string trees. Grandma said it was the place where she felt closest to Delisia.

Grandma had told me that she had planted my tree and navel string herself. Now as I stood underneath my very own tree and squashed a leaf so as to get the aromatic scent in my nostrils, I said to her, "My birth certificate says I was born at Gravel Hill. Wasn't I born at hospital, Grandma?"

"No, yu were born in the very room yu sleeping in now. I delivered you myself, with Miss Imo helping me." Miss Imo was a neighbour from up the road.

"Who named me, Grandma?"

"Yu mother name you 'Michelle' and I named you 'Delise.' Wi didn't think yu father would begrudge us the pleasure of at least naming yu, since we would be losing you."

Grandma sighed. "It was a trying time. Your grandfather was vexed *gone to bed*! And when Pappa Carlton was vexed everybody was in mortal danger, so the atmosphere around here was stink with fear and resentment. A guess as a writer you would describe your grandfather as a 'tyrant.'" She smiled and continued.

"But I loved him, nevertheless. And he had many redeeming qualities. But there was no consoling yu mother. Shi was determined not to give yu up, even braving the wrath of har father to stand up and tell him that to his face. But it was useless. One night when Delisia was sleeping, yu grandfather took yu away and gave yu to yu father.

"When Delisia wake up and find yu gone, shi was extremely distraught and angry. Shi curse us all, and told us how much shi hated us. Carlton told har to pack har things and leave, but A persuaded him to give har a chance, as it was only har grief at losing har child that was making har act that way.

"But A was jus' wasting mi time; Delisia eventually move away of har own free will anyway, and none of us see or hear anything from har since."

We were both quiet with our own thoughts for a few moments. I imagined myself in my mother's place. I don't see how I would have reacted any differently in the first instance. But I was sure that after a suitable period of time, when I had had time to cool down, I would have forgiven them and taken steps to have a visiting relationship with my child, or if that wasn't possible, then at least keep track of her progress by written correspondence. But I was pretty damned sure that I would not have let her disappear totally without a trace.

Grandma broke into my thoughts by saying wistfully, "A try to stay positive and hopeful, but sometimes I despair wi wi' ever find har. Yu uncles in North America have had no responses to their advertisements, and yu and Keith have had none from the UK. There are so many countries in the world where Jamaicans reside; how does one conduct a world-wide search?" She shook her head sadly.

I hugged her. "Don't despair Grandma; it's early days yet. We only started searching seriously a little while ago. If my Mamma is out there anywhere we *are* going to find her, I'm sure of it." Grandma returned my hug and said, "It's good to have faith, child; yu keep yu faith."

We left the shelter of the pimento trees and slowly walked back down to the house for breakfast. I did not usually eat breakfast, but I had discovered after a few days on the island that I had developed an early morning appetite, which Grandma said was a result of the altitude and the out-door life, so I helped myself to a large plate of liver and green bananas and a cup of coffee.

Grandma and I took our breakfasts outside to the babbeque where we sat under the guinep tree and continued to talk. I wanted to know about Grandma's side of the family who hailed from Bartons district, across the valley from Gravel Hill. I had remarked to Grandma that I hadn't met any of her relatives since I arrived on the island.

Grandma explained that she had been one of only three children, a small family by the standards of the time, and the only one still alive. Her older brother had fought and died in France during the Second World War, and her younger sister had died in childbirth in 1947. She had cousins over at Bartons but they had never been close, and after the death of Grandma's parents they had taken over the house and lands which legally belonged to Grandma.

Grandma had taken them to court and won, but had then decided to let them keep the property anyway, since she had no real need of it. But the rift had never really healed and they had not been on friendly terms, being merely polite and civil, for many years.

I asked Grandma to tell me how she and Grandpa Carlton had met, and she more or less confirmed the story I had been told down at the river, about the rivalry between Grandpa and Marse Lijah from the next door property.

I learned also that Grandpa Carlton had been one of thirteen children, most of whom were now deceased, but there were two of his sisters living in Canada with their respective off-springs and one living just a few chains up the road at Bellas Gate. Grandma referred to them as my 'grand-aunts.' The rest of Grandpa's siblings' off-spring were scattered across the island and around the globe.

As was usually the case, the talk returned to my mother Delisia. I told Grandma about the two letters I had written back in nineteen seventy-five and -six. I remarked on how strange it was that they had never been received, given that the family were well known in the district. I would have thought that some-one working in the post office would have at least mentioned to some-one in the family that there was mail for the missing daughter?

"Where did yu send the letters?" Grandma asked.

"To Gravel Hill PO," I replied.

"There's no post office at Grave Hill. Wi use the one down at Bois, or the one at Bellas Gate," Grandma had replied. "But even if the letters had gone to either of them I'm sure some-one would have mentioned it to somebody in the family. Everybody know the story of Delisia."

We were never to discover what had happened to the letters; Grandma suggested that some person working in the post office had been 'fast and inquisitive' enough to open the letters, and then discard them. But Grandma was so pleased that I had myself instigated the process of making contact with my maternal family that I was glad I had done so despite receiving no response.

Claudette Beckford-Brady

I asked Grandma to tell me everything there was to tell about Delisia. I had already learned that she and I were around the same size and build, and that our features were very similar. Grandma said I had all of Delisia's good qualities and none of her bad ones. I was flattered; everyone else, including Clive, seemed to find negative traits in my personality.

I learned that Delisia had wanted to become a lawyer and was going to be the first from the district to attend the University of the West Indies. Grandpa Carlton had still been willing to send her there after my birth, but she had not given him the chance; she had left home and taken up teaching.

Growing up, she had been a tomboy, as was to be expected with eight brothers. She climbed trees, raided birds' nests, played marbles and had fights with the best of them. But there were times when she retreated to her secret corner to read, write poetry or just to commune with herself.

By the time she was three years old she was reading at the level of a six year old. She read voraciously; she was lucky, she had relatives abroad who sent her lots of books, and a mother who was a teacher and who encouraged her tirelessly.

Despite being thoroughly spoilt and liking her own way, Delisia had many redeeming qualities. She was kind to a fault; to humans and animals alike. One day when she was ten years old, a barefooted Rasta man was passing and begged a cup of water. Delisia brought him into the yard, gave him some food, brought a pan of water and washed his feet, and then gave him Grandpa Carlton's good church shoes.

When Grandpa found out, he had commended her on her generosity to the less fortunate, but suggested that next time she give away a more worn pair of shoes. Delisia had told him that if he thought like that then his generosity was worth nothing. She often gave away her own clothes and shoes to the more needy in the district, many of whom went barefoot as a matter of course.

But her redeeming qualities were spoiled by her bad temper when she did not get her own way, and her tendency to hold a grudge for a very long time. Once you fell out of favour with her you ceased to exist for her. She would look straight through you as if you were not there and if you addressed yourself to her she would totally ignore you. Grandma said she had no idea where that temperament came from because Delisia was the only one in the family who displayed it.

I was glad I had not taken after my biological mother in this respect. I could get very angry, yes, but I could never maintain my anger for long. The longest I had ever held a grudge was against Mavis for not being my mother, but look how well Mavis and I got on now.

But regardless of Delisia's negative traits we were determined to leave no stone unturned in trying to find her and bring about reconciliation with her family.

One week before we were due to return to England Uncle Kingsley packed us into the van and took us for a day trip to the North Coast, to the envy and disgust of the Jamaican cousins; but the van could not accommodate any more passengers.

We travelled by way of the Bog Walk Gorge and across what seemed to me to be a very unsafe structure called the Flat Bridge, which spanned the Rio Cobre River. It was a narrow bridge with no guard rails to stop vehicles from going into the river, which, when in spate was dangerously destructive, washing away houses, people and motor vehicles, and sometimes the bridge too.

The bridge could only accommodate single lane traffic; two vehicles could not pass, but Uncle Kingsley said that sometimes two vehicles would enter the bridge from opposite ends at the same time, and both would refuse to back up, and this sometimes resulted in one vehicle going over.

Legend had it that there was a deep hole just below the bridge, and that many cars had disappeared into it never to be seen again. According to the legend, these vehicles were pulled into the bottomless hole by a mermaid, or the 'River Mumma."

The Gorge itself was an exciting place. The road wound alongside the river between towering hillsides of trees and vegetation on one side, and great big boulders on the other side which seemed to hang precariously, threatening to come down onto the road at any time, and in fact did so from time to time, particularly after heavy rainfall.

Uncle Kingsley, in a whisper, because of Uncle Keith's young daughters, tried to point out to me a rock which apparently resembles the female genitalia, which was called 'Pum-pum Rock.' Try as I might, I could not see the rock, and to this day every time I travel through the Bog Walk Gorge, I look for it. I have never seen it, but everyone swears it's there.

There were roadside vendors selling a variety of fruit from ramshackle stalls. Everything that was on sale grew on our own lands and Uncle Kingsley exclaimed at the prices they were charging for the fruit. "If wi did-a charge dem price deh, wi would-a rich nuh bitch!"

To get to Ocho Rios we had to cross the central mountain chain which ran west to east across the island. We crossed by way of Mount Rosser and Mount Diablo, on a narrow winding roadway with numerous twists and turns. Mount Diablo, in Spanish, means the Devil's Mountain and it lives up to its name, as I understand that numerous accidents took place, where some car drivers, too impatient to stay behind slow moving trucks, rush to overtake, often around blind corners.

We passed a place called Faiths Pen, where more roadside vendors sold roast yam and breadfruit and ackee and saltfish, and other traditional Jamaican cuisine. We did not stop to partake, as we could eat those things every day at home, if we wanted to.

Approaching the town of Ocho Rios we travelled through Fern Gully, a three mile stretch of roadway with a unique feature. The road is part of an old river course, and is bordered on both sides by banks of different variety of ferns and other vegetation, which form a cool dark tunnel. Uncle Keith told us that most of the ferns here grew nowhere else in the world.

Vendors selling wood carvings and other artefacts and clothing waved and shouted at us, imploring us to buy. I wanted to stop and look at the things but Uncle Kingsley said the same things would be on sale at Dunn's River Falls where we planned to spend the day.

Dunn's River Falls is situated a short distance from the centre of the town of Ocho Rios. It was the first waterfall I had ever seen and I was enchanted. The waters thundered down over the rocks, frothing and foaming, with a gurgling, chuckling cheerfulness, before relaxing in tranquil repose and calmly, gently, joining with the waters of the Caribbean Sea.

I climbed the falls to the top, went out in a glass bottomed boat to experience the prolific and colourful marine life, and swam to my heart's content. I bought postcards and tee-shirts with Jamaican themes and motifs for my friends, and various gifts for my family and Clive's parents.

I was sorry when it was time to leave, and resolved that some time soon I would return and book myself into a hotel and spend lots of time exploring Jamaica's beaches and attractions, of which Uncle Keith said there were many.

During that last week I went to Ginger Ridge to say goodbye to Mavis' family and spent the last two days with my paternal family. The end of January arrived and so did our departure date.

There was some concern about our driving through Kinston to get to the airport, as there had been three days of riots and civil unrest during the past weeks. Gasoline prices had been increased and this appeared to be the straw that broke the camel's back. The rioting had left seven people dead and many injured, and armed troops were now patrolling the streets of Kingston.

The Michael Manley led People's National Party (PNP) had announced an increase in the price of petroleum products, and had plans to remove the subsidies on corn, soy and wheat products. The Opposition Jamaica Labour Party, (JLP) led by Edward Seaga, threatened to organise further protests if the subsidies were removed, saying that this would immediately increase the price of bread by twenty percent.

Both parties accused each other of having armed gangs of thugs to do their dirty work, and the tension was running high in the city. But we couldn't stay here; we all had our lives to get back to; I had my A Levels to complete prior to entering university in September and Uncle Keith and his family had their business to look about as well.

Finally the day of our return to England arrived and fond farewells were said. It was with a measure of sadness that I left. The last six weeks had been very fulfilling for me. Not only had I connected with my maternal family, I had found a great friend and treasure in my grandmother and we were to remain very close right up to her death many years later. In addition I had discovered my 'Jamaican-ness' and was pleased that I had.

Grandma said her goodbyes to us at home; she did not

like the airport. Too public for proper farewell, she said. She held me for a very long time and when she released me and spoke, there were tears in her eyes.

"Michelle, my dear, it has been one of the greatest pleasures of my lifetime to meet and know yu. Yu are beautiful inside and out, and A really going to miss yu. Please, please don't take too long to come home. A not young anymore, and A need to spend some more time with yu before I die."

My eyes prickled at the thought of her dying. "Oh, Grandma, rubbish!" I said. "You're fit and strong; you're not nearly ready to die yet. But I promise I will be back soon." And in fact, at that moment I made up my mind that as soon as I had finished university I would return to Jamaica to live and work.

Uncle Cornell had heard me tell Grandma that I planned to come back soon, and he said, "*Forward*, likkle niece; never go back, always forward. I man look with eagerness for di bless`ed day when yu will come forward home again."

With all the goodbyes said, we piled into the van and started for the airport. A score of little cousins ran along behind the van as it climbed the incline up to the road, shouting and waving as they ran. The occupants of the van waved back until we turned onto the road and picked up speed, leaving them all in the rear-view mirror.

CHAPTER FOURTEEN

Down to Brass Tacks

We encountered no problems going through Kingston, and landed at Gatwick in what could almost be described as blizzard conditions. It was sleeting heavily and the north wind gusted icily. Daddy alone came to meet us, driving Uncle Keith's van and bringing all our thick winter coats which we had not wanted to travel with.

It was good to be home. While in Jamaica I had been so busy having a wonderful time that I had not really had time to miss anyone, but now I suddenly realised how much I had in fact missed them all.

Despite being a school and work day, everyone except Delroy was at home when we arrived, including Mummy Myrtle and Daddy Wilfred. Hugs and kisses were exchanged and everyone tried to talk at once, creating a veritable babble of excitement.

After Mavis had fed us all, an invitation was extended to Uncle Keith and family to spend the night in London rather than travel up to Birmingham in the sleet and snow. He declined, however, saying that he would rather take his time and get home today. If they left by three, they could be home by six-thirty, taking it very slowly because of the inclement weather.

When they had gone, I settled down to tell the family all about my holiday and the other branch of my family. Samantha, now almost five years old, climbed onto my lap and snuggled down. She seemed to have grown somewhat in the six weeks I had been away, and had finally lost the residue of her lisp.

"Yu bring present fah mi, Shellie?" she asked.

"Course I did, Sam-Sam. You'll get it soon, okay?"

"Okay, but I'm not Sam-Sam anymore; I'm Sammie. Mummy says I'm not a baby anymore, I'm a big girl now."

"Oh? Okay Sammie. Yu not too big to tickle though, are you?" and I commenced to tickle her mercilessly. She screamed and wriggled vigorously, trying to escape the tickling.

Daddy said, "Suh, Shellie, tell wi everyt'ing bout yu Jamaican experience nuh?"

"Oh, Daddy, it was wonderful! The island itself is so beautiful, and all my relatives, on both sides, are really nice people. I love it so much that I intend to live there. As soon as I'm out of university, I'm going to see if I can't find a job in the media out there."

I told them about my navel string tree, and how Grandma Miriam had complimented them on my upbringing, saying I was a credit to them. I went on to tell them everything about my stay in Jamaica, making sure to tell Daddy lots about his side of the family, so he would know that I had not left them out. He looked a little rough around the edges, as if he had not been sleeping properly. I wondered if anything was worrying him, and hoped he wasn't sickening for something.

Mavis looked young, fresh and happy. I searched her face for signs of worry, which might indicate that all was not well, and could find none. I decided that perhaps Daddy was just working too hard. They had gone ahead and purchased some land in Jamaica and Daddy was taking all the overtime he could get to save enough to start building their dream home.

My brother Delroy came home from work covered in white. The sleet had turned to snow proper and was falling heavily. We hugged and he exclaimed, "God, Shellie, what *did* they feed you on out there. You're as big as a house!"

Mavis and Mummy Myrtle had remarked on my weight gain in much kinder terms. I bridled. "Give over, Delroy Freeman! I've only gained a few pounds and I'll shed those in no time. My clothes are only a *little* tight!"

I wanted to spend some time talking with Delroy but Sammie and the twins kept pestering me about what I had brought for them. They volunteered to help me unpack, their ulterior motives quite undisguised; they wanted their gifts. I reminded them that I didn't really live at home anymore and would be unpacking at Mummy Myrtle's. They were so disappointed that I opened the cases and rummaged for their gifts.

Although I was still living mainly at Clive's parents' house I spent the night at home, sleeping with Sammie in the twins' old room, which had now become Samantha's room. The twins had moved their bunk beds into my old room which was bigger.

Before I went upstairs I phoned Joy. She wasn't home, but I left a message with her Dad to say I was home and could she come for some fried fish, a roast breadfruit and quarter dozen bammies which I had brought for them. I stressed that she needed to come this evening as they had been cooked from yesterday and needed to be eaten as soon as possible, and definitely no later than breakfast

Sweet Home, Jamaica

tomorrow.

It really wasn't as urgent as that; they would keep quite well in the fridge overnight, but I wanted to see Joy. I had missed my best friend as much as I missed my family, and these days we practically had to steal time together. I would be returning to school day after tomorrow, and most of Joy's spare time, when she could steal any, was spent with Delroy.

Her parents were still forcing her to go to church, and she couldn't wait till she was eighteen so she could leave home. Luckily for her, she would be eighteen in May, just four months away. Delroy was already looking for a flat; they were both working and had made up their minds that this was the course they wanted to take. If he found one, he would move in by himself until Joy turned eighteen.

At around seven-thirty Uncle Keith phoned to say they had arrived home safely. It had taken longer than he had hoped because the weather had steadily worsened the further north they travelled and they had run into traffic back-ups. But nevertheless they had finally arrived home, and all was well that ended well.

Joy arrived while I was still talking to Uncle Keith and I wrapped up the conversation, telling him I would call him next week. Joy and I hugged and she said, "Good grief, Shell, you're fat!"

"I won't be for long. But girl, if you had what I had to eat, you'd be fat too. I just couldn't resist the food, and yu know the best part of all? None of it was junk food; all good wholesome food grown on our very own land."

Joy and I spent a pleasant hour catching up on what my friends had been doing in the six weeks I had been away. She told me that Stephanie had decided to return to full time education to take her O and A Levels after her baby was born. I was extremely pleased for Steph and knew that this was Benji's influence.

Claudette Beckford-Brady

Joy also told me that she and Delroy had looked at a nice flat in Stockwell but the rent was too high. They couldn't afford anything too expensive because Delroy was saving to open his own electronic repair shop. And he too was attending college part-time to learn book-keeping.

I suggested that they would achieve their financial goals more quickly if they continued to live at home for the time being, but Joy was adamant about leaving.

I could quite understand her determination to leave, because if Mavis had been anything like Joy's parents, I too would be seeking alternative accommodation. Lucky for me, Mavis was more enlightened.

Joy and Clive's parents left together; Daddy Wilfred was giving her a lift home. I worried about them being out there in the snow, although it was only a very short drive to take Joy home and return to their house on Brixton Water Lane. I had developed a strong dislike for snow since Clive's death last year.

After they had gone Mavis and I sat round the dining table with cups of tea. Daddy and the girls were watching *Crossroads* or *Coronation Street* or some such soap opera on the TV in the living room. Delroy was upstairs in his room doing whatever he was doing.

We sipped our tea and talked. I told Mavis about her family at Ginger Ridge and how glad they were to see me. "Y'know," I said to her, "I don't think they even remembered that I wasn't your biological child until I mentioned the fact that I was staying with Delisia's family."

We chatted about various things, quite comfortable and at ease with each other. Mavis asked me if I had met any interesting young men who tickled my fancy. I laughed. "I had a few of the local yokels try their luck, but I wasn't game."

I gave her a few anecdotes about the Jamaican chatting up techniques and we laughed happily together.

Sweet Home, Jamaica

The next morning I was relieved to see that the snow had abated during the night. The sky had lost that ominous leaden grey which it had worn the day before, and although it was still bitterly cold, an insipid sun was making an attempt at an appearance.

When I got up Delroy, Daddy and Mavis had already left for work and the twins and Samantha were eating breakfast prior to leaving for school. I felt unusually hungry; I had picked up the habit of eating breakfast while I was in Jamaica, so I made some scrambled eggs and toast and ate a large bowl of cornflakes.

The twins looked at me in surprise and Rachel said, "Holy Mackerel, Shell! For some-one who never eats breakfast you're doing well! No wonder you've gotten so fat!"

She said the whole sentence by herself without any input from Rebecca. When they had been younger they had often shared their sentences; now it seemed they had developed independent thought processes.

The twins were now thirteen years old and had matured somewhat. They no longer tried to confuse their teachers by switching classes and identities, and their marks were improving.

It was now time for me to get down to brass tacks and throw myself back into my routine; school and my evening classes at Brixton College during the week, and my Saturday job at *Boots*.

Mummy Myrtle said I was spreading myself too thin, and to tell the truth I agreed with her. She suggested that I should give up the job at the chemist's since I was now getting two lots of pocket money every week. I was reluctant, but eventually agreed.

It was the best thing I could have done. With my new-found time I started banging out short stories and submitting them to various publications. To my surprise, not only were they accepted but I was actually paid quite well. I also entered various literary competitions and won medals and certificates, gift baskets, book tokens, and even a trip for two to France. In a very short time I was earning more from my writing than I had earned from my one day a week at *Boots*.

The money was good, but better than that was the fact that I was now considered a professional writer; I was being paid. My family and friends were proud of me and yes, dammit, I was proud of myself too. I never tired of seeing my name in print. I did not write using my own name, but the people who were important knew it was me. And in the meantime, I continued work on my novel.

The only fly in the ointment was the fact that Clive was not here to help me celebrate my fledgling success as a writer.

February had been the first anniversary of Clive's death, and his parents and I spent some time reminiscing and looking at old photos. We still missed him terribly, but time had dulled the pain somewhat, to the extent that we could talk about him without tears and even laugh at fond memories.

I had not dated anyone since Clive's death. A few guys from school and a couple of Delroy's friends had asked me out, but I had no inclination to date. It was nothing to do with my love for Clive or the way the guys looked; it was just that I had more important things on my mind.

My first two priorities were to complete my studies in the shortest possible time and gain some work experience preliminary to taking up my career in Jamaica, and to achieve more success with my writing.

At the end of the Summer Term, my A Levels finished, I left school for good. I would be starting at the University of London in October to do my degree in Media and Communications. It was a three year course, after which I intended to gain some work experience for a year or two before relocating to Jamaica.

I found myself a summer job working at a local newspaper, the *South London Gazette*, as a Filing Clerk and relief Receptionist. The publication was based in Thornton Heath in Croydon. It wasn't a very glamorous position, and did not pay well, but I was inquisitive and did not confine myself to my duties alone, but insinuated myself into the workings of the paper.

For the next three years, during all my holidays from university, I worked at the paper, moving from department to department until I understood how the whole paper worked. The editor, Mr Howard, took a shine to me and mentored me for the three summers I spent there.

During my time at the paper I submitted various articles which I thought were of interest to the paper's readership, and to my delight not only did Mr Howard accept them for publication, he also paid me for them. I was now a freelance journalist.

In the Spring of 1981, I got the opportunity to do my first piece of real reporting. I had almost completed two years of my degree course and Mr Howard at the *South London Gazette* was facilitating my search for as much practical experience as possible.

Although only April, and not yet full summer, the weather was extremely hot. Tempers in general were short and easily frayed, and this manifested itself in an explosive situation between the mainly black community in Brixton, South London and the police.

The relationship between the police and the ethnic community was not good at the best of times. Unemployment in the general population was running extremely high, but among the young black men it was at a much higher percentage. Many of these young men survived by 'hustling,' which covered a variety of 'careers.'

These included selling drugs, pimping, cheque book and credit card fraud, muggings, extortion, burglary, robbery, and the 'fencing' of stolen property.

There were a lot of derelict houses on Mayall and Railton Roads which had been 'squatted' by these hustlers. The area was commonly referred to as 'The Front Line' or just 'The Line' and was a centre for all kinds of unlawful activities. At nights, 'blues' dances were kept, with sound systems blaring out Roots Rock Reggae music until morning, and disturbing the law-abiding residents of the area, such as my friend Joy's parents.

From time to time the police would do a sweep (or raid) of the area in an attempt to shut down the Front Line, but as soon as they were gone, The Line would return to business.

Accusations of racism and brutality were constantly being levelled against the police; many young black men were being harassed under the 'suss' law, which meant that the police had the power to arrest them on mere 'suspicion' that they may have committed, or had been about to commit, a crime.

Ninety-nine percent of those arrested were young black men. Some, waiting innocently at bus stops, or otherwise minding their business, were picked on and arrested for 'loitering with intent,' and various other obscure crimes. A black man driving a nice car was also 'suspicious.' He had to be a drug dealer or a pimp or both. It was the consensus within the black community that such was the general mind-set of the police.

So, with mutual dislike and mistrust, the unbearable heat, and the general frustration, it would not have taken much of a spark to ignite such a potentially volatile situation. On this particular day in April, a hot sweltering day, a single incident sparked what was to become out and out war between the police and the predominantly black

Sweet Home, Jamaica

community, and which was to become known in history as The Brixton Riots.

On Friday, April 10, two police officers were supposedly trying to help a wounded young black man to hospital. While they waited for the ambulance, the frustrated youths of the area assumed that it was the police officers who had injured the man, and were now preventing him from getting urgent medical attention.

They took it upon themselves to forcibly take the young man from the police and drive him to a hospital themselves. In the meantime, others who had remained on the scene began throwing bricks and rocks at the police.

This precipitated three days of violent rioting; looting and burning of buildings and cars, and running battles with the police.

My editor, Mr Howard, said this was my chance to write a real news report for the paper. On Saturday, the 11th of April, I was sent out with a photographer and a senior reporter, but it was made quite clear that this was *my* assignment.

It was very exciting for me. I imagined I was a war-zone reporter, and indeed it was like entering a war zone. The streets of Brixton were filled with throngs of youths, both black *and white*, in running battles with the police.

All the storefronts on Brixton Road and Atlantic Road had been smashed in and looters were making off with electrical appliances, furniture and anything that could be easily transported, and indeed some that could not. I saw three men struggling up Acre Lane with what looked to be a queen size mattress, and others were fighting with other large appliances such as refrigerators and washing machines. I saw several people with large baby prams and shopping trolleys piled high with TVs, VCRs, radios, blenders, and the like.

I instructed my photographer to start taking pictures,

and we were treated to a stream of obscenities for our trouble.

We negotiated our way through the rioting throngs and made our way down Coldharbour Lane and onto Atlantic Road. I wanted to go up Railton Road, but there was no getting through there. It seemed the main battle was taking place in that particular vicinity.

We retraced or steps and found our way to Effra Road. All along the way cars had been overturned and several had been set on fire. Small skirmishes were taking place here and there between the police and gangs of looters who were trying to escape with their booty. However, we managed to make our way to the top of Effra Road and turned down Morval Road and on to Barnwell Road, approaching Railton Road from that end.

The entire area was flooded with police in riot gear. I felt very superior as I flashed my temporary press card which I had been given only that day, and was allowed to proceed without hindrance.

TV crews from the BBC and ITV, as well as numerous reporters and photographers from the print media were on site. I felt inflated with my own importance. Here I was, among the professionals, and I loved it. My adrenalin was flowing as I spoke into my tape recorder, describing what I was seeing for future transcription into my written article.

At one point my colleagues and I had to run for cover as a crowd of rioters throwing Molotov cocktails came toward us. We sought refuge down a side street and prayed fervently that they would stay on the main. Thankfully, the crowd surged past and we followed in their wake, hungry for something that would make our news report stand out from the rest.

I interviewed as many people as would talk to me, getting their perspectives on what was happening and what, in their opinion was the root cause of the outbreak of violence. Without exception they cited police harassment and brutality, lack of employment opportunity and just general pent up frustration.

Some also cited the Deptford fire. Back in Januarry nine young black men and women had died at a house party in Deptford, South-east London, and the black community was sure that the fire had been started deliberately by racists. This tragic incident was still fresh in the minds of many members of the community.

Eventually, after tear gas and water cannon had been brought into play, the riot was finally quelled. Brixton was in shambles. Buildings and cars had been burned and shops and stores had been looted. Miraculously, only two persons were injured, according to official reports - both police officers - but a total of two hundred and eighty-two people had been arrested, the vast majority of them, black.

When I wrote my piece the editor accepted it with only a few minor changes and when the paper came out with my name - my own name as opposed to the pseudonym I used for my fiction - my head swelled to bursting point. I called all my friends and old schoolmates asking them if they had seen my article in the paper. I sent copies of the paper to Uncle Keith and Grandma Miriam, hi-lighting my article. If Clive were still with us he would have chastised me for showing off.

Mr Howard commissioned me to write several follow-up articles; to investigate cause, interview police and residents and riot participants, assess the current situation, offer potential solutions and give a general overview.

After the situation had been stabilised I went out into the community with my notebook, my tape recorder and my photographer. This time I was not accompanied by a senior reporter.

After the riots a former Judge, Lord Leslie Scarman, was appointed by Margaret Thatcher, the Prime Minister, to investigate and report on the disorders. His report stated that "...*racial disadvantage is a fact of current British life...*" and that "...*urgent action is needed if racism is not to become an endemic, in-eradicable disease... in our society.*"

The report also stated that the police had to share the responsibility for the eruption of violence, and recommended the swift weeding out and dismissal of racist officers,

As far as I was concerned I was now a fully fledged professional investigative journalist. And I was not the only one puffed up by my small success. Daddy was so proud that he invited some of his friends to come and "drink to di success of mi daughter, di newspappa reporta." Never mind that it was only a small newspaper with only South London readership.

Mavis and the rest of the family, including Mummy Myrtle and Daddy Wilf, were just as chuffed. Uncle Keith and family sent me a congratulatory telegram saying, *"GOOD ON YOU SHELL STOP KNEW YOU WOULD EXCELL STOP PROUD TO BE YU FAMILY STOP*

My appetite was now whetted for more opportunities to do active reporting, but I still had another year at university to complete. I had been contemplating whether or not to try out my aptitude for television or radio, but having tasted the print media I decided I liked it sufficiently to stick with it, at least for the time being.

The *South London Gazette* was fine for a holiday job, and indeed I gained invaluable experience working there, but it was only a local paper with limited circulation and it was not where I wanted to be; I wanted to work for a major newspaper for at least a year, so that when I finally went to Jamaica I could claim the experience.

I was astute enough to know that my sojourn at the *South London Gazette* had been extremely cushioned; I had

Sweet Home, Jamaica

been 'adopted' by Mr Howard, the editor, and treated as his protégée. I knew that if I was successful in gaining entry to Fleet Street I would probably have to start out by making tea, filing papers, running errands and just being the general 'dogsbody.' I knew it was an extremely competitive, dog eat dog world, and that I would have to fight for every bit of recognition. But I was up for it and I *would* succeed.

A few weeks after the Brixton Riots, on May 11th, we received news that the great Jamaican reggae artiste, Bob Marley, had died. It came as a shock, because he was only thirty-six years old, and in the prime of his career. He, along with artistes like Jimmy Cliff, Desmond Dekker, and Millie Small had put reggae music on the world stage, and I had most of his recordings. Stephanie and Benji were even more distressed than I at the musical genius' untimely passing.

I returned to university for my final year in the autumn of 1981. At the end of the academic year I should graduate with a degree in Media & Mass Communication. At some point in the future I would return to university to do my Masters, but before that I wanted to be an award-winning journalist.

While I was busy with my studies and my writing, others were also busy getting on with their own lives. The twins were in the Fifth form and would be doing their GCSE exams this year. They had no intention of moving on to further education; their priority was to leave school as quickly as possible and start earning.

They both openly had boyfriends; none of the cloak and dagger business I had indulged in with Clive during the early days of our relationship. They had matured nicely and we were all great friends, Mavis included. Samantha was seven and more academically inclined than the twins, even at her tender age. I had introduced her to books at an early age, and she was an avid reader already.

Meanwhile Delroy and Joy had been living together for over a year. They had found a bed-sit to rent on Acre Lane. It wasn't very large but the rent was reasonable and it was within walking distance of both their jobs, so they had no fares to pay.

Joy's parents had thrown a blue fit when she informed them that she was moving out, and when they discovered that she was going to be living with a *man*, they outright dis-owned her. Delroy went to see them to present his credentials, so to speak, and to let them know that he was a decent, hardworking young man, who would take good care of their daughter.

They cursed and rebuked him in Jesus' name and told him he and Joy would burn in everlasting hell fire. Joy had tried to dissuade him from going to her parents, but dear Delroy had felt it was the right thing to do. And when Joy said, "I told you so," he said he was glad he had made the effort.

Joy herself did not seem much affected by the fact that her parents were not speaking to her. "So much for their forgiving Christian attitudes," she said with no trace of rancour or bitterness. "I'll be fine; I've got Delroy and you Shell and all your family."

Daddy and Mavis had been doubtful about Joy and Delroy moving in together. They did not want any bad feelings with the McKenzies, but Delroy convinced them that no matter what happened he would always be polite and respectful to Joy's parents. "If there is to be any bad feelings," he told our parents, "it will be on their part."

Daddy and Mavis knew that Delroy was a solid, upstanding young man, and after all, both he and Joy were of age. There was nothing anyone could do about it.

Our other friend, Stephanie, continued to live happily with her Rasta-man and her two children in Tottenham,

Sweet Home, Jamaica

North London. Benji accepted Steph's first child as his own, and the child called him 'Daddy.' Steph said that since she and her baby had moved from South London she had not seen Winston, the abuser from whom she had had to flee.

She had also returned to school to do her O and A Levels with a view to doing her degree. I was extremely pleased for her, as was Joy and Yvonne.

Summer, 1982. I graduated from London University armed and equipped with my B.A. Degree. Yvonne also graduated with her Batchelor of Education degree and had already secured a position for September at a school in West Norwood.

I did not commence to seek a job immediately. Between school and university I had just spent a decade in serious study. I had not indulged in all the things that teenagers usually did, such as dating and going to discos or the pictures. I did not know what films were current; in fact the last time I had seen a movie had been with Clive before his death four years ago.

This didn't bother me in the least; I couldn't care less what movies were showing, but I did want to take some time to do the things that I wanted to do before tying myself down to a serious career.

During my final year at university I had not had a lot of time to indulge in my writing, and I wanted to rectify that. I had about eight chapters of my "best-seller" written but I had not touched it in over a year. I had a few short stories that had not yet been offered to any prospective publishers and I set about sending them off and banging out a few more.

My immediate plan was to take six months vacation in Jamaica, suss out my employment prospects down there, - even though I intended to gain my first real work experience in England - and spend as much time as possible on my writing. To this end I purchased a new portable typewriter to take with me. My grandma's place in Jamaica would be an ideal and inspirational place in which to write.

I was in constant touch with my Jamaican family, and had even linked up with the Canadian and American branches. We exchanged letters and photos and the occasional phone call. Over the last few years various cousins had visited England and so I had had the opportunity to meet some of them. Grandma Miriam had also paid a visit to Uncle Keith in Birmingham and spent a week-end with me in London.

Despite our best efforts over the years there had been no sight or sound of my mother, Delisia. We had all but given up the search, although once a year we still placed advertisements in the local and foreign press. But her family and I had found each other and for that we were grateful.

Now I set about making final preparations for my trip. I was full of excitement; there was going to be a family reunion of sorts at Christmas, when a group of the North American uncles and their families would be in Jamaica. Uncle Keith and his family would also be there; they would arrive in mid-December.

Daddy and Mavis were also planning to be in Jamaica for Christmas. They had purchased ten acres of land three miles outside of the town of Old Harbour, in a community named Island Farm, near to Spring Village. Uncle Bertie had already planted out the land with several acres of food and fruit trees and had put the rest into producing cash crops, such as tomatoes, peppers, okra, callaloo and pak choy.

He had also started to build Daddy and Mavis' dream house from plans which one of my Campbell cousins, who was an architect, had drawn up. Uncle Bertie was, according to Daddy, "a Jack of all trades and master of them all."

The twins who had once wanted to go to Jamaica to "research their roots" now showed little interest in going there. They had just left school and were both earning steady salaries working as copy/audio typists with Lambeth Council, but when I suggested that they should go with Daddy and Mavis at Christmas, they declined. Samantha would be travelling with the parents, and Delroy and Joy had other priorities.

In fact, Joy was now pregnant and expecting their first child in January. It hadn't been exactly planned but they were both happy about it. They had moved out of the bedsit on Acre Lane and were now living in a one bedroom flat on Streatham Hill. Delroy had served his apprenticeship as an electronics engineer and was now earning good money. He still had plans to one day own his own business.

Joy herself was still working at Lambeth, although she had moved from the Town Hall to a different position in one of the outer Directorates. She had found her niche in Personnel, and to this end she was attending college on Day Release to obtain accreditation from the Institute of Personnel Management.

Because of her pregnancy, she would have to postpone her certification course and take it up again on her return to work. Her employers had a very good maternity package and she would lose nothing by taking time off to have her baby.

Meanwhile Yvonne, who was teaching Summer School, had fallen in love again. During our school life, and since, she had had a series of boyfriends. Each one had proved to be worse than the last. If it was not infidelity, it was laziness and attempting to live off her.

One poor misguided soul had attempted to get physically violent with her and had quickly learned to rue the day. Yvonne had crowned him with a cut-glass decanter and sent him to the hospital for stitches. He did not press charges, but whenever he saw her after that, he crossed the street.

But now, once again, she was in love. This time I was quite impressed with her friend. He was taking a year off from university and working in the interim to finance his last year. His name was Denzel and he originally came from St. Kitts & Nevis in the eastern Caribbean.

Denzel was a cheerful soul with a laugh that was so contagious that you couldn't help joining in, even if you didn't know what the joke was. I took to him instantly, and Yvonne was so smitten I was frightened for her in case it didn't last. I need not have worried; they were married within a year.

After I had met Denzel I began to reflect on my own solitary state. Joy, Yvonne and Stephanie were all happy in their relationships and some had even started families. I was going to be twenty-two in December and now that I was not busy with my studies I found time to be lonely.

It was over four years since Clive's death and I had not dated at all since his passing. I knew that I wanted to have a husband and family like any normal person. In addition I wanted to have my children while I was still fairly young. Of course I would have to establish myself in my career first before I could start having children. And of course I would have to find the ideal partner. That would be the hard part.

But for now I was too busy to spend much time reflecting. I would be leaving for Jamaica in the middle of July and not returning till January next year. I did a flurry of shopping, buying clothes for myself, and packing a barrel of goodies to be shipped for the cousins.

Daddy Wilfred and Mummy Myrtle had received a substantial insurance settlement for Clive's death, and they told me to see if I could find a piece of land somewhere near Daddy and Mavis. They both hailed from other parishes in the island but had decided to build their retirement home near my family.

The twins, who would be seventeen in a few weeks, had booked a series of driving lessons which they intended to take in a marathon session, starting as soon as they got their provisional licences. They insisted that they would pass their tests long before my return, and that I should leave my car with them. I agreed, since Delroy had bought an old Ford Cortina, and had no need of it, but gave him the keys, with strict instructions that they were not to drive until they had passed their tests.

The day before I was due to leave, Uncle Keith and family arrived from Birmingham. We had a great re-union. Daddy was now quite at ease with my other family and he and Uncle Keith went off to the pub to shoot pool, along with Daddy Wilfred. Aunt Velma, Mavis and Mummy Myrtle relaxed around the dining room table, sipping tea and catching up. The twins had taken Joseph, who was a couple of years older than them, and gone off on their own pursuits, while Samantha, Jennifer, and Elaine were next door at the Brennan's.

Veronica and I left to go to my room at Mummy Myrtles. While she helped me with my last minute packing we filled each other in on our lives since we had last seen each other.

Veronica said she was dating occasionally but did not have time for a steady boyfriend as her studies took up most of her time; she was going to be a doctor. She was twenty years old and had grown into a beautiful young lady, having lost her teenage chubbiness.

She wasn't as tall as I was, but she was slim and very pretty, with long straight hair that showed the Indian in her heritage. She had also gained in confidence, and told me that she had foolishly lost her virginity to a boy she had thought was in love with her, only to find out that she was only another notch on his belt. She seemed remarkably blasé about it, but I read beneath the outer unconcern and saw the deep hurt.

"Oh, Verr, I'm so sorry! The dirty, stinking rat!" I was angry at this unknown weasel who had so hurt my cousin, although she was trying hard to pretend it didn't matter. But it did matter; very much. A precious gift had been stolen under false pretences, and it could never be retrieved.

I thought back on my relationship with Clive. I had never regretted losing my virginity to him and I wished that Veronica could have had the experience I had had. But she would just have to put it behind her and move on. I told her as much. "Well, what's done is done; don't dwell on it. One day you *will* meet the right guy and this will only be a bad memory."

Veronica and I completed my packing and then we went out to buy some fish and chips. We sat out in the back yard to eat them. While we ate we chatted about my trip to Jamaica and Veronica lamented the fact that she was not coming with me.

"Never mind," I commiserated with her. "But think of the fun we're all going to have at Christmas with the North American cousins."

"Hmm, I suppose," she said half-heartedly. "But Christmas is *years* away!"

I laughed. "No, only five months."

Verr poked her tongue out at me. "Ha ha; very funny, Shell."

At this point there was a ring on the doorbell, and I walked around the side entrance to find Joseph on the doorstep.

"Hey Shell, can I get re-acquainted with your bookcase?" he asked.

"Course you can, Joe. But weren't you out with the twins? Where are they?" We walked back around the side to the back yard where Veronica was waiting.

Joseph grimaced. "I'm not into the loud music and the smoking, so I excused myself."

"Smoking!" I ejaculated. "The twins are smoking?"

"Well, I didn't see *them* smoking, but their friends all seem to, and not just cigarettes either."

I was horrified. I would have to have a heart to heart with my sisters, but I was leaving in the morning and I would be gone for six months. I phoned Delroy and told him what Joseph had told me, and asked him to have a talk with the twins. He assured me he would.

We played a game of Scrabble which Joseph won. He was the only person who had ever beaten me at the game.

The next morning I said my goodbyes to every one and embarked on my journey.

CHAPTER FIFTEEN

Return to Gravel Hill

I landed at Kingston in the evening and by the time I cleared Customs and came out to the waiting area it was dark. The first thing I had noticed when I disembarked from the plane was the heat and the mosquitoes, and I was relieved once we were in the van and getting a breeze from the open windows.

I had been picked up by Uncle Cornell and my cousin Rueben in the same old van used four years previously. As we drove through downtown Kingston I noticed that we did not stop at the red lights, but only gave way to an occasional vehicle. Where the road was clear we drove straight through.

At first I had thought that Uncle Cornell was not concentrating, but when I remarked on it I was told that it was risky to stop.

"Gunman can appear out-a nowhere," Rueben explained, "suh is betta to be safe dan sarry, yu nuh seet?"

Sweet Home, Jamaica

"I guess so," I said, suddenly feeling anxious to get out of the town and up to Gravel Hill as quickly as possible.

Of course I was aware of the socio-political climate in the island; as a journalist and writer I kept up to date with world news and events, and I had a special interest in Jamaica, and read the *Weekly Gleaner* and *Caribbean Times* newspapers and any other literature I could obtain about the island.

I knew about the political 'garrison' communities and the party-affiliated gangs of thugs and gunmen. I knew that crime was rife in the city; however, reading about things and being exposed to those same things are rather different. I'd had no idea that I could actually be in real danger.

I recalled that back in January 1979 when I had last been on the island, there had been political unrest, including three days of riots which had left seven persons dead. Uncle Cornell said that the situation was no longer as tense; but that nevertheless, one didn't take unnecessary risks in Town.

As a journalist I would almost certainly be exposed to some dangerous situations; that went with the territory, but I did not expect to be in danger just going about my personal business.

There had been a change of government in the interim; In October of 1980 Edward Seaga's Jamaica Labour Party (JLP) had won the General Elections and was now the ruling party. Their politics were right of centre, and this appeared to find more favour with the major Western governments than had Michael Manley's socialist policies, and more grants and aid had been forthcoming, helping to alleviate the economic situation somewhat.

Goods which had been scarcely accessible under the Manley regime were now readily available, and the general quality of life was improving. The JLP wanted to take credit

Claudette Beckford-Brady

for this, but their critics claimed that it was more due to the generosity of Western governments who were relieved to see Michael Manley go, than to the JLP's economic policies.

I felt relieved and much safer when we had left the city behind. We did not make good time; the road was in a deplorable condition with numerous potholes.

"Why don't they fix the road?" I said. "Can't they see that it needs repairing?"

"May rain mash dem up," Uncle Cornell said. "Most-a di road-dem stay suh and some much worse. Wait till wi reach fi-wi country road and yu wi' tink dis is di freeway."

He was right. After we left Old Harbour and headed up the Colbeck main road we slowed to a crawl. Uncle Cornell had to pick his way very carefully, and sometimes he would misjudge and we would drop into a pothole. The van was old and the springs had lost their bounce, which made for a most uncomfortable ride.

I noticed along the way that more houses seemed to have electricity than when I was here four years ago, although the street lights were still few and far between.

And as all journeys end, so eventually did this one. It was after ten and only a few cousins were at the yard with Grandma Miriam and Uncle Kingsley. After hugs and greetings were exchanged everyone was banished except the two uncles and their wives, and I was given something to eat and told to go straight to bed.

I did not argue; I was tired from the journey and the tension of coming through Kingston, not to mention the bone jarring each time we fell into a pothole. I was going to be here for six whole months; I could afford to sleep a few hours before starting my holiday.

I slept the clock round. My body must have needed the rest, and perhaps the knowledge that I did not have to study or do assignments helped to relax me, as well as the

Sweet Home, Jamaica

fact that I was once again on the Beloved Island. Whatever the reason, I slept soundly and woke refreshed and eager.

I bathed in the bathroom which had been added since my previous visit, and went in search of food; I had a hole the size of China in my belly.

Grandma fed me with roast breadfruit, ackee and saltfish and chocolate tea, and China disappeared. It was past mid-day and the yard was quiet. "The place seems strangely quiet, Grandma; where are all the cousins?" I asked.

"A told them A wanted yu to myself for a while before them claim yu. A really don't know how yu going to spread yuself between them."

I laughed. "I think they are all going to be in for a disappointment. I'm going to be spending most of my time writing, and for that I will need peace and quiet. I'm going to have to find myself a nice quiet corner where I can set my portable typewriter, hopefully in a setting where I can find real inspiration."

Grandma touched my cheek gently with the back of her hand. "A know the perfect place; A-wi' show it to yu in a while. But first, let mi just drink yu in." She couldn't seem to stop touching me. She continued in a soft voice, "It's almost like having Delisia back again, having yu in my life. I'm glad you're here; A miss yu bad."

I kissed her cheek. "Missed you too, Grand-Mamma. And you know, I haven't given up hope of finding Delisia some day."

Grandma shook her head. "No, Chile; A think if wi were going to find har, wi would-a find har by now. Wi been searching for almost five years. Wi contact every Jamaican High Commission abroad, wi place countless advertisements, wi even send out radio message in North America." She sighed sadly and shook her head again, "No; A think wi can safely seh that Delisia is gone from us

Claudette Beckford-Brady

for good."

I hated seeing my grandma so sad. I wanted to comfort her but words seemed hardly adequate. Platitudes were useless, and she was far too intelligent to insult with them. Before I could find a response Grandma continued with a statement that stopped my heart cold.

"Yu know, Michelle, A'm nearly seventy-six years old; A could die anytime. And y'know, if A could just si Delisia one more time, A could die happy tomorrow."

I was horrified. I had never envisaged my grandma's death. The possibility of such an event had just never occurred to me. I could not, would not, countenance it. I could hear the raw panic in my voice when I spoke.

"Grandma, don't you *dare* say things like that. You might be seventy-whatever, but you are not *old*. You *can't* die; I haven't spent nearly enough time with you!"

The inanity of my statement did not register with me. But just the *thought* of Grandma dying left me with a cold feeling. I thought of Clive's death and my panic increased.

She noticed my distress and rushed to reassure me. "Chile, it was just a figure of speech." She smiled. "Don't worry; A don't intend to die until yu become a famous writer, then A can boast to all my friends: 'that's my granddaughter, the famous writer'."

She hugged me and I forced a half-hearted smile. Grandma was not satisfied. "Chuh, come Michelle, man; yu making mi feel bad; A spoil yu holiday before it even start, eeh?" She got up from the root of the guinep tree where we had both been sitting and took up the vessels I had eaten out of. "A just going to rinse out these things and then I'm going to show you something to cheer yu up. Soon come."

She went off towards the kitchen and I got up and surveyed the yard while I was awaiting her return. The hard packed-dirt area, known as the babbeque, which was used for drying coffee, cocoa beans and other crops, was swept clean. Three dogs lazed in the plentiful shade and several dozen chickens scratched and picked for titbits.

Across the yard where Uncles Cornell and Kingsley's houses were located, several little children played, chasing the hens and squealing in delight. A girl of about twelve or thirteen sat in the doorway of one of the houses plaiting another little girl's hair, while yet another teenager swept in front of the houses with a home-made broom. I could hear the faint sound of a radio playing reggae music.

I waved across to them and they waved back. My eyes returned to their inspection of the yard. There had been changes in my absence. The steep bottom-side of the yard which had previously been used for growing corn and gungu peas now boasted a new board house with glass windows instead of the wooden louvre blades which were standard. I wondered how they had managed to erect a building on such a steep hillside.

All of the houses, except Grandma's were made of cedar board and had zinc roofs. They were built on stilts and the underside, or cellar, was a favourite place for the yard fowls to lay their eggs. The houses were mainly painted white, except Uncle Cornell's, which boasted borders of red, gold and green at top and bottom of each white-painted wall.

Each house had its own outside kitchen which was generally made from woven bamboo with a roof thatched with coconut boughs, and the walls sealed with mud. This was known as wattle and daub.

Inside the kitchens cooking was generally done on large stones, fuelled with wood or charcoal, which was produced by burning green wood in a make-shift kiln or 'skiln.' The wood was packed into a hole dug in the ground and covered with dirt and grass. This was then lighted and left to slowly burn until the wood turned into charcoal.

Claudette Beckford-Brady

There were no bathrooms in the houses, except for the new one which had been installed in Grandma's house. Several pit latrines were located a short walk from the houses and for the very young chamber pots or 'chimmeys' were provided. To take a bath, you either used a large wash-pan, or you made an excursion to the river.

The yard looked good. Everywhere was swept clean and all the houses had beautiful, well looked after plants and flowers in pots on the verandas, beside the front steps and in borders alongside. Hanging baskets of orchids and other trailing plants hung from nails in the walls and even from some of the trees in the yard. A hedging of many-hued Crotons created a riotous splash of colour to one side of the yard.

There had been changes made to Grandma's house too. Her house was the only concrete one in the yard and by far the largest; after all, she had raised a family of nine children within its walls. However, I noticed that more rooms had been added and there was now a bathroom with plumbing and a flush toilet. It also had an inside kitchen.

But to me, the nicest thing about the yard was the abundance of trees. I was constantly amazed at the number and variety of food trees on the place, and they gave the yard a lot of shady nooks where one could sit and get comfortable.

There were a variety of orange and mango trees loaded with fruit in various degrees of readiness, and several well-loaded lime trees. The ackee trees boasted yellow and red fruit, some open, some on their way to opening. Plantain and banana trees bowed under the weight of their fruit, and coconuts sat loftily among green boughs. Two majestic breadfruit trees, filled with scores of green globes, lorded it over everything, including the tall coconut trees.

Every single tree belonged to an individual member of

the family whose umbilical cord, or navel-string, had been planted, together with the young tree, at the time of their birth. Some of the navel-string trees were situated further outside the yard; my own and my mother Delisia's were planted some little distance away towards a rise to the east of the yard.

Grandma returned from the kitchen and said, "Yu ready?" I nodded and she took my hand and led me away. She had promised to show me something to cheer me up, and I was curious about our destination, but when I asked her where we were going, she just smiled and said, "Yu wi' si."

We headed towards the path at the back of the house which led to the pimento grove where my navel-string tree was planted. This path also led to the little hill from where Grandma and I loved to watch the sunrise, but it was afternoon so I didn't think we were headed there. I decided we were going to mine and Delisia's navel-string tree for some reason, but what on earth could be there to cheer me up?

As we came around the side of the house and headed toward the path, I noticed that it was no longer a path, but more like a road. A section of bamboo which had separated the path from the main entrance to the yard had been cleared, and a connecting roadway branched off to join with the path which was now a road. I had not noticed this last night when I arrived.

"This is new," I remarked to Grandma. "Why build a road here? It only leads to the pimento grove and our sunrise hilltop, which are both easy walking distance." Grandma only smiled and said, "Yu wi' si soon enough. Patience, Chile."

My curiosity increased as we passed the pimento grove (or pimento walk, to use the vernacular) and continued up towards the hill. Although the original track was now a widened roadway, the going was not made any easier for those on foot, because the road was not paved but only covered with loose dirt and gravel which was not very compact.

As we emerged from among the pimento trees and I glanced upwards, I stopped in my tracks. I looked at Grandma's beaming face which was watching me eagerly to see my reaction.

I was stunned, to say the least. The last time I had been here this had been an empty, windswept hilltop, graced only by a couple of straggly mango trees and some guava shrubs. But not any longer.

I raced up the hill, leaving little avalanches of gravel in my wake, and Grandma to follow at her own pace. When I got to the top I stopped and examined in close detail the new structure which was where empty space used to be.

It was a beautiful neat, compact little house with a roof-top patio, and it was painted a pristine white. It faced eastward and looked out over the panoramic view of hills and valleys stretching out to the mountains. It stood only about forty feet from the edge of the sheer, almost perpendicular hillside which dropped away to the south and east.

"Wow," I said out loud to myself. I had always thought that this would be a superb place to have a house, but had not really thought it possible because of the difficulty in getting building materials up the track, and perhaps it would have been impossible had they not made a road. There was only one route to the hill top and that was through the yard via the path we had used; it was inaccessible on three sides.

To the front of the house, facing east, there was a very steep descent, leading down to the valley floor and the river. Grandma had said that it was possible to get down there if you were a goat or a daring young rascal. The south side of the hill looked out over Old Harbour and the sea. That side also led down into the river valley and was also very steep.

The slopes were covered in vegetation; shrubs and vines as well as gangly tall coconut trees with bent trunks, and various other fruit trees which were mostly inaccessible to all but the daring. Large clumps of bamboo also grew plentifully here. Behind the house the incline of the descent was not so steep, but it led nowhere except to more bush. That side could be cleared and made into a downward sloping garden.

I walked around the house, examining it thoroughly. It was a proper house, constructed with concrete blocks. There was a flight of steps leading up to the roof top, and a wrap-around veranda encircled the whole house. The windows were large, almost taking up one entire wall, and made out of glass. I peered inside. No furniture; this was a brand new un-lived in house.

Grandma was standing looking out toward the distant mountains when I came back round to the front of the house.

"Well," she said, "what yu think?"

"It's beautiful. Whose is it? Can we go inside?"

We stepped onto the veranda and Grandma turned the handle of the front door. The door opened and we stepped inside. I had been about to exclaim about the unlocked door, but then I realised that not only was this place in-accessible to all but the family – anyone coming here would *have* to come through the yard – but there was also nothing to steal except perhaps parts of the house itself or the fixtures and fittings.

We entered what was obviously the living room, and then walked down three steps to a small dining alcove. A door led from here into the kitchen and through to the back veranda.

Claudette Beckford-Brady

We returned to the living room and went to examine the two rooms which led off on one side. They were fair sized rooms with built in closets; obviously bedrooms. There was a fully fitted bathroom containing both tub and shower. I turned on a tap but no water came out. I looked askance at Grandma and she said that a water tank would be built and pipes run from it. There was, however, electricity; a line had been run from the main house.

Grandma had not answered my question. I posed it again, "Grandma, who does this belong to? Did one of the North American uncles build it?"

"No," she said. "As a matter of fact, yu father's brother, Bertie built it."

"He did? How comes?" I was surprised; there were competent builders among the Campbell cousins.

Grandma took my hand and said, "Let's go up top." She still had not answered the question of ownership but I did not press her again; I would soon find out. I followed her up the stairs to the roof. The view from ground level was already spectacular, but standing on top of the house gave me a three hundred and sixty degree expanse of vista.

From up here I could see not only the panorama of hills, valleys and the sea, but looking back in the direction from which Grandma and I had come, I could see the clearing which was the yard. Grandma's house was visible but the other houses on the other side of the yard were obscured by a multiplicity of trees.

I could also see quite clearly the road which ran above the yard, winding its way up to Joe Ground, Bella's Gate and beyond. An old van was struggling up the road, belching black smoke from its tailpipe.

It was pleasant up there on the roof. It was the middle of July, and quite hot, but a cool breeze was fanning the air and we got the full benefit of it up on the roof. I remarked to Grandma that this would be an ideal place for me to set my typewriter, if I could get permission from the owner. Not only was it isolated from the yard and distractions, but it was a beautiful place which I was sure would help to inspire me.

As I made the remark I suddenly remembered two statements which Grandma had made earlier. She had said she knew the ideal place for me to write, and she had also promised to show me something to cheer me up. A smile broke over my face. I asked her again.

"Grandma, who owns this place? This is the third time I'm asking you. Is it a state secret?"

She laughed outright. "No, Shellie; is not a secret. A wanted to tantalise you."

"Well, you've certainly done that, Grandma. Now, will you put me out of my misery?"

She looked around for somewhere to sit, and not finding anything she went and sat on the top step. I sat beside her.

"This place," she said, "was Delisia's favourite place. Ever since shi was a little girl, shi always said that when shi grow up shi would build har house here."

Her voice held sadness and I took her hand. She went on. "It was understood by every-body that this was Delisia's place, and it's only right and fitting that since shi gone, it should belong to you."

I was speechless. Did I hear right? Did Grandma say that this place actually belonged to *me*? I sought clarification. "This piece of hilltop belongs to *me*, Grandma?" I was confused to say the least. If this way my hilltop, why had Uncle Bertie built....? Of course! But who had financed it?

Grandma broke into my thoughts. "All of yu uncles and plenty of your cousins donate money or building material and Bertie and others give dem time. I did plan to finance it myself, but yu work yu way into everybody heart when yu was here, and everybody did want to be a part of yu gift."

I felt the tears prick the back of my eyes. I didn't understand this. What had I done to deserve family such as these? I, who was not a crying sort of a person, was all choked up and the tears, just beyond the surface of my eyes, threatened to spill over. I needed a few moments to pull myself together before I could make a response.

Grandma had stopped talking and was waiting for me to say something. I got up from the step and stood looking out over towards Kingston and the mountains. I blinked my eyes rapidly to drive the stupid tears away, and turned back to Grandma. She too had risen from the step. I stepped up to her and wrapped my arms around her, and rested my chin on top of her head. She hugged me back. There was no need for words.

When we arrived back at the yard there was a welcoming committee of cousins waiting for me. I was hugged and kissed and everyone wanted to talk at once.

"Welcome home, Shellie, wi miss yu."

"Mamma, yu show har di house yet?"

"Wi hear seh yu turn big writer, Shell..."

"T'anks fi di t'ings yu sen' fah mi last 'ear, Shell."

Finally Grandma made herself heard. "Gracious me, oonu give the chile likkle air nuh! Oonu gwine suffocate har!"

This was the most patois I had ever heard Grandma use in one statement and I looked at her in surprise. "Why, Grandma, that was a mouthful of patois! I thought you always spoke proper." I deliberately said 'proper' instead of proper*ly*.

She grinned, showing her shiny white dentures. "Mi gran- and great-gran-pickney dem nuh andastan English."

She left us, and the cousins and I renewed our acquaintances. We lounged under the big guinep tree at the corner of the babbeque which was my grandfather's navel string tree. I thought how great it was that we could tell the age of practically every tree in the yard, once it was known who it belonged to.

I asked about the new board house on the gungu slope and was told that it belonged to Cousin Levi, Uncle Cornell's eldest. He had left home and gone to live and work in Old Harbour, but returned six months later, saying he missed the country. He had brought back with him a girlfriend who was pregnant.

I discovered that many of the cousins no longer lived in the country, but had fanned out to various places. Some were living 'down-a low' which was how the hill folk referred to the town of Old Harbour; others had gone farther a-field; Spanish Town, Kingston. Two were working in the tourist industry on the North Coast, two were attending the University of the West Indies, and still others had migrated to North America.

In fact the exodus from the country did not just apply to members of my family, but appeared to be a general thing amongst the younger people. What there was of family lands could not sustain the expanding families and there was no other form of employment within the rural district. Many of the young people who remained had decided to forego traditional crops and concentrate on marijuana, or ganja as it was commonly called, because it fetched a better price.

However there were still many cousins left in the country and the ones who had gone were soon replaced, as was evidenced by the number of youngsters around the yard.

For the entire afternoon cousins coming to greet me came and went, including cousins from Daddy's side of the family who lived only a short walking-distance away

When Uncles Kingsley and Cornell came in from the

bush the cousins who did not live at the yard were banished and I was told to wash up for dinner. Over the meal I renewed my acquaintance with Bev, Cornell's baby-mother and Eula, Uncle Kingsley's wife. The baby that Bev had been carrying when I was last here was three years old, and very extrovert and chatty, and they also had a one year-old, making a total of nine.

Later in the evening still more cousins arrived to visit and we got to talking about my new house. I was eager to get it furnished; at least with a couple of chairs for the patio and something to rest my typewriter on. I was told that Daniel, one of my cousins who lived 'down-a low' was making me a small desk and chair and it should arrive any time.

When we heard the sound of the vehicle coming into the yard, someone said, "Si Daniel here now," and we all went around to the front of the house. A big man, who was unmistakably a Campbell, jumped out of an almost new pick-up van and greeted me as if he had known me all my life. His accent was distinctly Canadian; even when he spoke patois there was no trace of Jamaican in there.

"Hey, Michelle, what's happening Cuz? How yu like yu house?" He strode through the throng of cousins and came over to give me a peck on the cheek. He did not give me time to respond to his greeting, but strode towards the house saying, "Where's Mamma?" referring to Grandma. As he went he threw back over his shoulder, "Soon come to yu, Shellie."

Daniel was thirty-eight years old and was Uncle Kenneth's eldest son. He had spent twenty years in Canada, but he hated the cold and so had decided to come home. He had Canadian citizenship so he could go back anytime, but he had vowed never to leave Jamaica again.

I liked Daniel. I had not met him the last time I was here because he had still been in Canada at the time. He had a workshop in Old Harbour where he produced furniture to order, and when work was slow he did construction work. He was big; both tall and broad, although not fat.

He was a very lively, outgoing person, and did everything as if it was urgent. The cousins laughed at him and told him that he had no need to move fast to keep warm any longer; he was in a warm country now, but he said that after twenty years of moving fast he no longer knew how to move slowly. He got very impatient with people who dawdled or had lackadaisical attitudes.

While he was in the house with Grandma I took the liberty of looking into the van. A blue tarpaulin-covered shape which I assumed to be the desk and chair was securely tied and I could find no way under the tarp to get a little peak, to my bitter disappointment.

He came out of the house with Grandma in tow and called to me. "Come on Shell; let's get this baby up the hill," and walked briskly to the van. He called to two of my male cousins to come with us to help him get the desk off the van and into the house, and they jumped up onto the back of the van.

I clambered into the back of the pick-up to join them, while he and Grandma got into the front. Several other cousins who tried to accompany us were told to "clear off, nuh, this don't concern you guys," and we drove off in a rattle of loose gravel.

It was dusk, and knowing how quickly dusk turned into night out here, I knew I would not be able to examine the desk thoroughly until tomorrow. It only took five minutes to get up the hill, and that was only because we could not travel very fast on the loose gravel.

They unloaded the desk and then there was a debate about where it should be placed. I directed them to a spot under the window to the right of the sliding glass living room door. I would get good light and have a spectacular view while I worked.

The tarpaulin was taken off and I looked at my desk and chair. They were beautiful. If I had designed the desk myself, I could not have made a better job. It exactly suited my needs. It was quite small, but with enough space for my portable typewriter, with lockable drawers on both sides and a slide-out piece in the middle which contained grooves for stationery and writing implements.

It was painted white and Daniel said it was made from Blue Mahoe, which is Jamaica's National Tree. The matching chair had a soft blue cushiony seat and arm rests. They were perfect.

I could hardly contain my excitement. I hugged Daniel and said, "I can't believe you did this for me and you don't even know me. I just know that this desk is going to help me turn out some magnificent work. Thank you very much."

My thanks sounded awfully inadequate but there was no mistaking my sincere pleasure in the gift. Daniel grinned and replied, "Well I'm glad yu like it Shell; but I hope yu can see through Mamma. She has ulterior motives in giving you these things, y'know; she trying to entice yu to stay and live up here for good."

Grandma shoved him playfully. "Don't be stupid, bwoy. How Shellie gwine turn into a top journalist if shi stuck up here in the bush. Yu don't have any sense a-taal?"

By now it was almost completely dark and the moon had not risen yet. We returned to the yard and Daniel said he was heading on back down to Old Harbour. "Come down let me show you my workshop one day, Shell, and introduce you to my family." I said I most certainly would, and he left.

A few cousins were still out in the yard and they invited me to go down to the river with them in the morning. I was anxious to get up to my hilltop to see my new desk and chair in the light of day, and to start writing, but I felt that I should at least spend some time with them before I started work in earnest. Once I started writing, I would not want to be pestered to do recreational things if my creative juices were flowing.

The next morning I was up at first light. As early as I was, when I came outside there was a group of about nine cousins waiting to start the trek to the river. They told me not to bother with breakfast as we would cook down there.

I had put on my swimsuit under my jeans and tee-shirt, so I threw a towel over my shoulder, jammed an old hat on my head, and we set off. The sky in the east was tinged with pink as we left the yard and made for the orange walk.

It was obvious to me that someone had taken pains to clear the way to the river. I could see where the bush and overhanging vegetation had been cut back, and in places make-shift steps had been cut in the dirt. I knew this must have been for my benefit, and I protested, even though I was kind of relieved.

Our part of the river was not deep enough to sustain real swimming, so we went downstream to the adjoining landowner's property. Officially speaking, we were trespassing, but since no one bothered to eject us, it didn't matter. In fact it was quite unlikely that the owners even knew when we were there.

I swam while some of the others lighted a fire and put on breadfruit and yellow yam to roast. Others searched for river shrimp and other fish, while still others picked jelly coconuts and other fruit and put them upstream in the water to keep cool.

We spent the entire day at the river, and at various times throughout the day other cousins came and went. It was evening when we returned to the yard and I ate again, before falling exhausted into bed.

I couldn't wait for the next morning when I would go up to my hilltop to watch the sun rise, give my desk a thorough examination, and ensconce myself as a writer.

The story continues in Volume Two.

ABOUT THE AUTHOR

CLAUDETTE BECKFORD-BRADY was born in Old Harbour, Jamaica. In 1964 at the age of seven she joined her parents in Gloucester, England. After leaving school in 1973 she held various clerical and administrative positions before moving to London in 1976, where she joined the British civil service. In 1981 she left the civil service and went to London Borough of Lambeth where she progressed to the level of Personnel & Training Officer. She lived in Brixton, South London from 1977 to 1990 when she left the UK to return to Jamaica where she now resides. Over the years Claudette has won a number of awards for her short stories; **SWEET HOME, JAMAICA** is her first full length book and this current edition is published in two volumes, although there is a single volume edition which incorporates both Volume 1 and Volume two in a single cover.

OTHER BOOKS BY CLAUDETTE BECKFORD-BRADY

Sweet Home, Jamaica, Volume Two continues the saga of Michelle Freeman and her extended family as the story moves into the 1980s where Michelle has become a young woman with ambitions of becoming a famous writer and to live in Jamaica, her homeland. It follows the story of her progress and the path her life takes to the fulfilment of her dreams. Join her in her travels to hot sunny climes as she integrates with her birth family and the local community as a resident rather than as a visitor to the island. Her extraordinary family causes tears and laughter, but through it all Michelle learns to build a life for herself in the land of her birth and becomes accepted into the local community. It is not an easy ride as she discovers that her beloved island is not the idyllic paradise she had envisioned it to be. A bittersweet story of the intricacies of human relations over time and distance.

The Missing Years is the sequel to Beckford-Brady's first two-volume novel, **Sweet Home, Jamaica.** It concludes the saga of Michelle Freeman and her extended family.
The initial reunion with her biological mother was not the tear-jerker Michelle had expected so when the families came together for the five-yearly family reunion emotions were running high. Life for Michelle was already full, juggling a career as the co-owner of SmallRock Publications, plus family life, but things were about to be turned on their head. A bungled robbery, a dead youth and a usually devoted husband who has started staying out all night with no explanation... Is Michelle's husband getting too close to Delisia, her erstwhile mother?
A poignant, heart-warming tale of family relationships and conflict resolution, spiced with fast-paced drama.

Return to Fidelity is Beckford-Brady's third novel.

Enid Maynard-Livingstone is disenchanted with her fifteen-year marriage to Basil, who has a predilection toward girls young enough to be his daughters. However, Edith is not about to leave him and give up the comfortable lifestyle she has become accustomed to after having grown up dirt-poor in a rural Jamaican parish. However, when she runs into an old friend the temptation to give Basil a taste of his own medicine and have a fling is overwhelming.

Leroy Duncan has a happy marriage but lately a difference of opinion is threatening the relationship. Having lived in England for years, Leroy now wishes to return to Jamaica, but Evadne his wife has no such desire. She considers the island to be a backwater, lacking in modern amenities, full of criminal elements, and prone to natural disasters such as hurricanes and earthquakes. She fails to see why she should give up her comfortable existence in the UK for a life of uncertainty.

Set in the UK and the Jamaican parishes of St. Catherine and Trelawny this story gives an insightful and sometimes humorous look at the marital conflicts which can arise when couples find they no longer have the same objectives.